YOUR PRESENCE IS
REQUESTED AT SUVANTO

Maile Chapman

JONATHAN CAPE
LONDON

Published by Jonathan Cape

2 4 6 8 10 9 7 5 3 1

Copyright © Maile Chapman 2010

First published by Graywolf Press

First published in Great Britain in 2010 by
Jonathan Cape
Random House, 20 Vauxhall Bridge Road,
London SW1V 2SA

www.rbooks.co.uk

Addresses for companies within The Random House Group Limited can be found at:
www.randomhouse.co.uk/offices.htm

The Random House Group Limited Reg. No. 954009

A CIP catalogue record for this book is available from the British Library

ISBN 9780224090421

The Random House Group Limited makes every effort to ensure that
the papers used in its books are made from trees that have been legally
sourced from well-managed and credibly certified forests.
Our paper procurement policy can be found at:
www.randomhouse.co.uk/paper.htm

Printed and bound in Great Britain by
CPI Mackays, Chatham ME5 8TD

And with these orders suddenly there stood
a gleam of awesome fire in heaven and earth.
The sky was still; the wooded glens were still
in every leaf, and you could hear no cry
of animals. The women had not heard
that roaring clearly, but they stood straight up,
with staring eyes.

   —Euripides, *The Bacchae*

At the most we gaze at it in wonder, a kind of wonder which in
itself is a form of dawning horror, for somehow we know by instinct
that outsize buildings cast the shadow of their own destruction
before them, and are designed from the first with an eye to their
later existence as ruins.

   —**W. G. Sebald,** *Austerlitz*

And always keep a-hold of Nurse
For fear of finding something worse.

   —**Hilaire Belloc,** *Jim*

YOUR PRESENCE IS
REQUESTED AT SUVANTO

Prologue

We cared only for ourselves. We had large windows, and we watched the sky thicken with snow. We pulled open the metal door to the roof and positioned ourselves along the curving promenade, scraping our lounge chairs over the concrete, turning to absorb the winter sunlight through fur-lined hats and soft, generous coats. From the promenade you can see the cornerstone; we discovered this by carefully leaning out over the railing, into the air, looking down to where the building meets the ground. Pictures were taken, and we'd like to see them now, because we were beautiful then. We'd like to be beautiful again, and in memory we will be, and then we'll tell you all about that winter, including the early deaths, some say preventable, some say one, some say three, that happened at Suvanto. We're nearly ready, we're always almost ready and it takes only a little time for the vessels to flush and fill with memory, and then we can open our eyes, lift our heads, sit up in our beds, and turn to meet your gaze. We'll tell you what we remember;

we love the body as you love a warm wet leather glove, pulled on snugly in cold darkness.

Propped and reading in the bed, pages moving behind the windows of the high private rooms, sometimes we're the ones doing that, but mostly we're happy downstairs, turning, moody in the black dress, hairpins in firelight, a winter tango, staring over one another's shoulders for a slow display of emotion in the cold, quiet country. Just for fun, just among these friends. And in retrospect we love the other creatures too, the dark birds and the small *siili,* our little hedgehog, and that bowl of fish near the heating panel in the Solarium. The hedgehog we think we caught in photos. The fish are floating, pulsing like blood cells in the eye, pulsing like piano and especially violin, like a record turning unattended, fires lit and flaring against the windows, bright against the shadows of the blackening birch, the cedars, and the ever-present pines, the backdrop, the audience, it is so hard to catch attention from the pines. And they are thicker now. But we love the pines outside the windows of that room where we pushed back the couches and practiced, harmlessly. We love everything that we did. Including even the burden of hot water in the bowels, the squeeze in the viscera and trace of metal in the mouth, damp heat at the hairline, and the hidden unpleasantness that returns along with blood. We love these memories because pain is a haunting beyond the muscles and repetition serves a purpose. We are happy that we're happy now, and happy that we're safe now, and so we'll repeat this for you: we are safe and happy now, and this is what we wanted.

One

Julia arrives in August, on an afternoon that is warm and damp and thick with the smell of berries and pine hung low in a buzzing blue sky. Mosquitoes are fat and hysterical, moving in from the sunlit empty meadows to float in the shade, rising and hanging at the screened windows. They are hungry like a personal affront; it is some consolation to know they won't survive the coming drop in temperature.

The car hired to bring Julia here is parked and clicking in the circular front driveway. The windshield is roughened with the yellow and black viscera of insects. The driver is quiet and polite. He had no trouble finding the hospital called Suvanto Sairaala, and he has parked at an angle, expecting to pull away again shortly. He is standing beside the car, waiting. But Julia sits in the backseat, anonymous in her dark fur coat, motionless even after the driver opens the doors and the trunk and begins stacking a set of brown leather suitcases and three silver paper hatboxes on the hospital steps.

Sister Tutor is waiting as well, bent and looking in as an encouragement. But Julia doesn't move. Her legs are bare, she wears a summer dress, she looks ready but she is reluctant, with the cool, slow circulation of the elderly. She holds a pair of peeling snakeskin gloves against her lap. She'd been dozing, and now she is disoriented, and doesn't like that this is her destination. The tall curve of the hospital wall oppresses, and so does the wide shadow cast by the canopy over the front steps, with a verse from the *Kalevala,* just visible, inscribed around the frames of the tall glass doors, which in English would be *Though disease has not subdued you / Nor has death thus overcome you / Nor some other fate o'erwhelmed you . . .*

Apparently, she doesn't have any money in her purse to pay the driver.

"Who put her into the car?"

"A man did, ma'am," according to the driver, and this man told the driver to watch the lady, because she might try to get out of the car, and he should prevent her, but that if by some quick opportunity she did get out he was to put her back and bring her all the way to Suvanto as planned. The man hadn't paid the fare ahead of time, saying it would be settled at the other end. But the lady hadn't any money of her own. The driver stands waiting. He would rather not have mentioned the fare. But it was, in fact, a long drive.

Someone (Julia's husband? or who?) has behaved poorly. Sister Tutor thanks the driver, and what she means is, *Let's not embarrass her,* and she tips the driver herself with the little bit of money she keeps in the tiny key pocket of her apron. He declines; he was not asking for a tip.

"For your kindness," she says, insisting, and sends him in to see the secretary for the rest of the fare. And then she climbs into the backseat beside Julia and introduces herself. They are, roughly, of a common age, and a similar size, one fair, one dark, and they sit together quietly, looking through the pines, up the slope in the direction of the doctor villas and the pavilion where the nurses live.

Sister Tutor can hear the whine of one mosquito bouncing in the car with them, excited by their breathing and by the odor of their skin. She can hear the movement of the pine branches shifting overhead, and outside, falling heavily through the air, Sister Tutor believes she can hear the heat of the sun streaming down through everything. She listens, and then she says, "Well, Julia, let's get out now."

She speaks in Finnish, saying the name in the soft way, *Yulia*. She slides along the seat and holds out a hand. Julia's eyes are flat and dark, partially obscured by kohl that gleams and gathers in her deep orbital shadows. She puts her cold hand in Sister Tutor's, and it seems she'll agree to step out now, and follow. Instead she pulls, slightly, as though trying to draw Sister Tutor back into the car with her. Sister Tutor, perhaps misunderstanding, puts out her other hand, offering a double grip, coaxing until Julia finally slides along the seat and puts her feet down on the gravel.

"Come upstairs," says Sister Tutor, and what she means is, *Let's take off that unsuitable coat, black in the heat, brown in the sun, and visibly full of dust.*

Julia won't look at Sister Tutor, only down at her own feet, blinking slowly under heavy mascara. Still, she nearly misses one of the steps, and abruptly puts her hand back in Sister Tutor's hard friendly fingers.

"Finnish or Swedish?" asks Sister Tutor.

Julia shrugs to say, *It doesn't matter.*

They pass the reception desk, where Sister Tutor waves and the receptionist calls for an orderly to carry up the new luggage. Julia is so small that the hem of her coat touches her heels, the peach satin lining falling down on one side and gliding along toward the elevator as if this is already her nightgown showing underneath. Her hand in Sister Tutor's is only the size of a twelve-year-old girl's, but with ten ruby rings stacked between the swollen knuckles, and Sister Tutor squeezes gently, careful of the rings, the old bones, and tries to make her smile, a little, but Julia won't answer, not even with faint movements of her fingers in return. And though she studies the walls, she does not seem curious about the new surroundings, not curious at all.

Sister Tutor takes her up in the elevator, caged at the front and glassed at the rear, and they can look out over the grounds (and per-haps just see the car departing, following the road away). They walk to-gether down the residential hall, built in a curve to open a wider surface on the southern side, to gather sunlight into the rooms. They follow the curve to Room 527. The bed has been fanned, the room recently aired, and the curtains are open. Despite the sunlight it is all as cool as camp-ing. The windows are just above the level of the surrounding pine forest and the horizon is a rough, green, mesmerizing line duplicated by the bed: a folded green blanket, a thin blue duvet, and a small white pillow staring from the head of the bed like a square, featureless face.

Julia does not ask how to find the toilet or how to get a cup of cof-fee or anything else. With the makeup it may be hard to see, but she's gone waxy, lips too dark and harsh in the lipstick as she slips away from Sister Tutor's hand, sinking toward the bed (Sister Tutor guid-ing), her coat exhaling perfume, exhaling perspiration and the sweet-ish odor of tired rayon, and she shifts herself into position with the toes of her small black shoes pointed toward the ceiling. When Sister Tutor undoes the little silver buckles (*how on earth did she get them on by her-self?*), there is a moment of navigating them over the swollen bones, the bunions of well-used feet, but then, of course, there's relief once the shoes are off.

Sister Tutor looks up to ask if there is anything more she can do but Julia has unfolded a white handkerchief and drawn it over her face, where it moves, trembling as it hides her. She's not crying, is she, em-barrassed by the lack of money in her purse? Probably not. Probably she's tired now. Possibly this is even a dismissal. But that dark lipstick will bleed into the cotton in a minute, showing through like a bruise, calling suddenly into mind the lady Sister Tutor had once seen hit by a cab, dragged in her dress and killed in the street. She'd been crossing to the Helsinki Ooppera, and she died in a crumple of torn taffeta on the black ice of the street while someone ran for help and Sister Tutor, much younger then, fell to her knees in the snow to hold the stranger's crushed hand, skinned and ominously slow to bleed, and waited.

But of course Julia is just going down for a nap, still holding her coat around her. And so, thinks Sister Tutor, pulling the blanket over her bare feet, *That's all right. But I'll leave the door open just a crack.*

It is unspoken in the air: What you need, Julia, is nourishment, clean cotton that breathes, and some sunlight every day while it lasts. Some diversion and some exercise and of course a firm routine. And we will give you that. And we will take away those constricting shoes. And get some others from town, we'll recommend which kind: wider, kinder, more comfortable and more suitable for what your life will be here now.

Julia sleeps. But later someone arrives to pull her sleeves, someone with clammy, uncareful fingertips. She moves aside the handkerchief as the coat is tugged away and looks up at a tucked lip, soft as a rabbit's, and a glimpse of healthy white teeth. The woman gathers the coat and then sinks awkwardly down onto one knee beside the bed, her joints cracking, her strong fingers gripping the edge of the mattress for balance. Her fat bun of dark hair, controlled behind a white cap, touches Julia's arm when she leans down to push Julia's shoes under the bed, out of reach.

"I'm Nurse Todd," she says, her hand braced on the edge of the bed as she slowly gets to her feet, moving as one who favors an old ache in the back. She is flushed as she folds the coat over her arm. Julia holds the handkerchief against her face, watching with one eye.

"I'm the charge nurse for your floor. You'll get the orientation when you wake up. You're welcome to come to me with any questions, anytime."

Julia stares up at Nurse Todd's neck, her mouth, her ear, and then up to the gleaming weight of her hair, every part of her head, but won't meet her eyes.

"Nurse Taylor says she's sorry she isn't here, but she'll stop by later to introduce herself."

Julia looks to the apron, the key pocket, and the fit of Nurse Todd's uniform.

"Say something," says Nurse Todd. "Speak when you're spoken to."

Julia says, "I'll wait for the other nurse."

Nurse Todd presses Julia's coat to her hip with an elbow and leans in, reaching to quickly snatch away the handkerchief, heedless of ripping it.

"Don't worry," says Nurse Todd, folding the handkerchief and putting it away on the far nightstand where Julia can almost reach it. "I can look after you."

But there are the teeth again, above, and a faintly cosmetic odor from Nurse Todd's breath when she reaches across. Julia turns her head to avoid it. She's chilled without her coat, and she wants a cardigan, but her bags haven't been unpacked.

"You're cold," says Nurse Todd, who is not unobservant. "There isn't nearly enough fat on you." She touches Julia's upper arm, and she squeezes, gently, to prove this. Julia moves to sit up, but Nurse Todd's grip tightens heavily in response, contracting until her fingers and thumb meet in the damp fabric at the axilla under Julia's arm.

"See what I mean?" she says. "Not enough flesh."

Julia doesn't react, doesn't acknowledge the choking, thudding pulse in the vein and a growing faintness in her fingers. Nurse Todd gives Julia's arm a tiny shake before releasing it. Then she flips the blanket up to Julia's neck, tucking it quickly, in a practiced way, tightly, too tightly, so that Julia can't easily move.

"I'm sending your coat to the coatroom," says Nurse Todd. "I'll be back."

She turns in the doorway. Julia, temporarily immobilized, stares back at her with a look of helpless hatred, and thus Nurse Todd is satisfied.

The Head of Nursing, who in a more traditional, more hierarchical, more Victorian institution would have been called *Matron* in the old-fashioned way, had been fairly direct with Sunny Taylor in the beginning, extremely direct, by the Finnish standards of the day: "What we want from you is competent nursing, and also patience. You might get annoyed because of them. It should be said."

"Right," Sunny had said then, cool in white and blue. She had a pleasing forehead and a perfect hairline, green veins mild at her temples, nice eyebrows and such clear skin, so reassuring, all very much on purpose. With her school pin and enamel nursing emblem worn neatly, tightly at the closure of her collar.

"And common sense, because you'll feel the isolation here. I notice you worked as a private-duty nurse."

"That's right," said Sunny, legs crossed calmly at the ankles, not drawing attention to those years of twenty-four-hour shifts in homes, in bedrooms, those years that others hadn't wanted, bad capricious pay and light sleep taken in armchairs, at bedsides, cash transactions leading into the lives of people who are always unhappy that a nurse is needed. Unhappy with her, because she was proof that someone there was ailing.

But the Head of Nursing is shrewd enough to know that some have their reasons to choose that life. She doesn't make Sunny elaborate on the years of making do with cupboards full of old towels cut into bandages and the sickening smell of a beef and cabbage dinner being prepared down the hall. She can well imagine Sunny, arriving in the clean uniform dress and bleached apron, neat cap tightly tied, entering the private homes to move the blankets, to change the saturated dressings. To reposition sweating limbs, to replace compresses, to readjust supporting pillows, and then to nap in the chair, then to wake stiffly, changing wet dressings again before going home to probably perform the same duties for the family invalid as well, doing something, for someone, every hour, on the hour, all day and every night. It's not uncommon to find oneself at the center of a ring of continuous, totalizing need.

"Your responsibility will be the top floor. The patients there are mostly the wives and daughters of the foreigners who work for Finn-American Timber. And so, only a few are local women. Only a few are Finnish women, you'll notice."

"Right," said Sunny.

"The timber wives are always up-patients. They really don't need much care."

That would be fine, she thought. That would be quite tolerable, because even though in her mind's ear Sunny heard the spoiled advance voices of the timber wives making their frivolous, unnecessary requests—*bring me my applesauce, rub my feet, where's my hairbrush, now hold the mirror steady while I fix myself*—she knew there would never be a repeat of the crushing responsibilities she'd faced in her off hours during the last several years, at home, with her mother. But of course it couldn't possibly be the same as anything at home, that was the point. She had written letters in response to advertisements from hospitals far away, hospitals as far from home as possible. The letters were a slim bridge to a new place, and then very heavy wheels had been set in motion. A long voyage, some parts over land and others by ship, her ticket paid for and picked up at the terminal, a long time in transit to think, after which she was to find the train station in the center of Helsinki. Board the train to Turku. It will be marked. She would be met after the train. She had followed exactly the instructions sent in a letter by the Head. On the reverse of the letter were the same instructions written in Finnish, in case she went astray. If she went astray, she should show this to someone and they would put her right. She carried one small suitcase past the bright golden buildings around the harbor of Helsinki, finding the bus that would take her to the trains. She had pointed to the letter, not daring to try to say it: *Rautatieasema?*

"*Joo, kylla,*" said the driver. Sunny had money she'd exchanged on the boat and she held it out now in the palm of her hand, but the driver held up his own palm and did not take any; she didn't know if this was a good sign or a bad sign.

But that again was the reason she had left home, to know nothing and to be responsible for nothing except the work placed immediately before her. She had not been drawn all this way merely by the temptation of regular hours, the assurance of being paid, of being treated well. Who would choose such a rupture, such a risk, for merely that? No, she'd come looking for the promise of dislocation, and a quiet place in which to be left alone, protected by the order of an institution in which a natural division would be acknowledged, would be expected, a separation between herself and her previous life inserted as neatly as the emblem pinned to the uniform: *My working self will now be only a version of me, one version, and this dress, this face, this detached smile are all that you can claim of me while I look after you.* She had brought no more than she could carry by herself. Everything else boxed and left behind her. Unsentimental. Eyes forward, the only way. Of course she is sorry. Of course she still doesn't know what the point could have been, why anyone should be made to suffer like that, and then to die like that? Her mother was dead now, finally, thank god. But she had died terribly, and Sunny could not scratch the memory out of her mind, her mother's face, more bony and more hard over time and coming to look eventually like a part of the carved wooden headboard behind her where she sat propped against a small hill of rubber-coated pillows. She had spent years and years propped in that bed. And afterward Sunny sent the mattress to the dump and paid a man to burn it there, because after everything she did not want anyone to carry it away and sleep on it.

"The language barrier . . ." Sunny said.

"You shouldn't worry about the language."

"I don't speak Finnish, I mean, I hope that was clear."

"No, how could you. It's a bilingual region." The Head of Nursing glanced to the window, as if to indicate the whole region, everything, the lakes, the water, even out so far as the archipelago of rocky forested islands in the distance, islands leading all the way to Sweden. Her eyeglasses caught the daylight, opaque, slightly opalescent, until she turned back, her eyes again professional, impersonal, small, blue, and level.

"Really, you can't know this, of course, but Swedish has been the dominating language on the coast for generations. Nearly everyone speaks Swedish, or can understand it. But we speak mostly Finnish here. We're switching our record keeping over, for the first time. It was always in Swedish before, everywhere, but times are different, and it should be in Finnish now."

"I'm afraid I don't speak Swedish either."

"It will be the case that everyone on your floor will understand English. They need English-speaking staff. Can you speak German?"

"A little, from school."

"Then it should be true that Swedish will be easier for you. Swedish is easy to learn. Finnish is quite a lot harder. You can study with Sister Tutor if you want to try to learn. But the timber wives and daughters only come to Finland for a few years. They won't speak Finnish."

"I'd like to try to learn." And then—"How do you say the word for nurse? In Finnish?"

"*Sairaanhoitaja:* that's the word for nurse."

Sunny had not tried to repeat it. "And Head Nurse?" she asked.

"*Ylihotaja.*" And Sunny could not repeat that, either, because spoken Finnish seems to take shape high in the mouth, but low in the throat, counterintuitively for native speakers of English.

"It takes some time," said the Head of Nursing. "It's hard to learn the language and it's hard to penetrate this culture. It takes time to make friends in Finland." The Head's voice was deep, not especially sympathetic but not unsympathetic either. "And for those on your floor, it is clearly easier to come here, to the hospital, than to try to adjust. That is something you'll notice, that they are perhaps lonely, not sick, just lonely. They often come from the outlying timber towns, and they don't always wish to go back."

Ah, thought Sunny, *I'm a fool*; she'd thought the Head was speaking to her personally about her new life here, her new role, about settling in, about the possibility of making friends, and not just about the difficulties that those timber wives had encountered and that had sent and kept them here.

No matter; Sunny didn't care whether she fit in with others, because there would be the small private apartment of her own in which to spend the evenings, a bedroom, a sitting room, a washroom, and her days and nights would finally be as different from one another as the bright and dark faces of the moon, for virtually the first time. Cross the stairs, step over the threshold, shut the door. Time would be divided, and privacy respected.

These years later Sunny's list of things to accomplish in the afternoon includes seeing to the new arrival, Mrs. Dey—Julia, that is—who will live now for a time in Room 527, on Sunny's own top floor, between the reassuringly glossed walls where everything is green and blue, the curtains drawing the eyes outward to the pine trees and up to the beginning of the rough stone outcrops beyond the far side of the water. She finds Julia sitting in one of the two chairs by the window, having slept again and woken to find herself alone, arms bloodless and tingling. The unsheeted bed shows signs of her struggle to get up.

Sunny taps the door: "Mrs. Dey?"

Julia turns to Sunny, expressionlessly, so it seems, but Sunny is of course aware of the assessment taking place; on a first meeting the new upper-floor patients customarily look to her face, as dictated by good manners, but they cannot seem to concentrate on anything she says until they have allowed their attention to glide over her appearance—dress, shoes, natural endowments, including prettiness, or lack thereof— believing, somehow, that Sunny does not notice. If they are polite they try to do this without allowing their eyes to move in the sockets, or they wait until she turns aside momentarily. They want to know what age she is: Younger than themselves? Older than themselves? Does she look smart? Clean? Worth listening to? Now, from Julia, Sunny feels undisguised attention, moving from her shoes up, without the pretense of absentness they normally adopt to mask the looking. Sunny will do the same to her, of course. But later, in ways that Julia won't necessarily feel.

"Am I allowed to leave this room?" Julia says.

"Of course you can leave your room. Do you need the toilet?"

"Is that any of your business? I need my cardigan and I want my coat."

Sunny pulls out the second chair and sits down, a gesture intended to be soothing. "You should come and go as you like. And we'll unpack for you. Didn't Nurse Todd send someone in to do that?"

Sunny smiles. Her eyes are blue with a ring of gold pigment, and her hair, blond and early silver, is bobbed and wavy behind a white cap worn low and back to one side, tied with a wide white ribbon. Lovely, traditional, clean, tight. Her posture and that neat bow in the ribbon conspire to say, *I am busy, but I care about you; believe in me, do what I tell you to do, and you will be well, almost certainly.*

"I was asleep," says Julia, "but the big bitch came in and took my coat." Her eyes have swollen during her nap and the bags below them are taut, like sausage links in shiny casings. *Too much sodium, and a rude mouth,* thinks Sunny, making mental notes, and adding appraisingly: *we'll wash your hair as soon as possible.*

They look at the forms together. Sunny can fill them in by rote, not necessarily because she understands all of the Finnish, but she knows enough, has been learning and practicing when she can. Julia looks down at the stack of papers in silence.

"*Sinun etunimi?*" Sunny says, pointing, but Julia says nothing.

"*Mitä sinun etunimi on?*" she says again.

"Dey," says Julia.

"*Ja sukunimi?*" Sunny waits for the rest. "Your full first name?" she says.

"Julia."

"Don't you understand Finnish?"

"English is better," says Julia, and then Sunny is embarrassed, because Julia apparently doesn't have the patience for her grammatical mistakes. Sunny completes the forms without looking up again, and when Julia has signed her name she sweeps the papers together into a file. She opens the wardrobe and takes out a stack of folded mesh laundry bags. With a laundry pen from her apron pocket she prints DEY across the top of each.

"White bag for white laundry," she says in English, "blue for the mixed, and pink for the foul. Your garments will come back with tags sewn in, but I recommend you put your initials on the inside seam of anything you treasure. Some of the ladies on your floor aren't particular about whose underpants they put on." She offers the pen, a loan.

Would Julia like to see the rest of the building?

"I suppose," she says, reaching for a supporting arm, for Sunny, whom she understands is of value as a first ally, a clear and slim authority in blue. More susceptible than Nurse Todd. And less peripheral than Sister Tutor. She holds Sunny's arm tightly, antagonistically. *I don't want to be here, but since I am, I will be your problem.*

At the nursing station Sunny stops for a word with Nurse Todd, and before she speaks the other says, "I'll have a girl in now to unpack for Mrs. Dey."

"Send up something cheerful," says Sunny, and what she means is, *This patient is cranky and unpleasant.* Julia is looking down the hallway, back toward her door, which she may or may not be able to distinguish among the others along that curving yellowish expanse that now seems to hum, a little vertiginously, in her vision.

Julia steps carefully, pushing her feet gently forward in the slippers they've given her, and Sunny thinks, toenails? Calluses? Someone will have to check.

Nurse Todd sends a message down for a welcome bouquet: ferns and wildflowers from the yard, and one small lily from the greenhouse, from a small bunch cut to supplement the usual sprays of happy greenery left in the wards and dining room. The lilies are a project of the Mrs. Doctors. Eventually, they may even try orchids.

One of the girls will make a small but nice arrangement and bring it up to Nurse Todd, and it will sit for a moment on the desk while she writes a small stiff card: *Tervetuloa,* from the Staff of the Orvokki Ward. By the time Julia sees the lily it will have relaxed a little, softening in the air. They've been kept since cutting in the seldom-used walk-in cooler in the clinical wing—in other words, the mortuary. But does anyone need to know this? No, dear, they really don't.

"I hope you'll let me know if you need anything," says Sunny, as they stand, side by side, waiting for the elevator.

The perfunctory phrase, so often repeated, will eventually lose meaning, because, of course, isn't that why we're here? So that Sunny can look after all the details of our daily lives? At the moment Julia wants her coat back. Nurse Todd has had it shaken and hung in the coat area near the front entrance, where they find it looking a little shocked upon the hanger. She wants to wear it indoors and so she shall, though Sunny can hardly find her arm to support in the wide sleeve. Is support really necessary? She lets go, and Julia pinches her hand back into place. Julia does not listen well during the tour. She turns her head only occasionally. Her dark hair is caught up with glinting hairpins hardly disarranged by her enforced, motionless nap on her new narrow bed.

In the entry hall Julia meets the unsmiling receptionist, who shows her the book near the front door that she should always sign when going out and when returning, to keep the staff informed. For her own good. The receptionist tells her this in Finnish and Julia's eyes drift away. The receptionist repeats the instructions in Swedish.

"*Okej,*" says Julia. To Sunny, she says, with great exaggeration, "I understand."

And then she is shown the long hallway of offices in bright pine, the glass doors of the administrators' rooms that she will probably never need to enter.

"Why show me, then," Julia says.

"There are other rooms you might need," says Sunny. "Come this way." Sunny shows her the dining room, long and narrow, the two rows of tables, the windows extending up to the ceiling, where on this day in August the top panels have been cranked open with a long metal mechanism to keep the fresh air moving. The windows look out over a clearing behind the hospital and the room is filled with natural light. Julia stares up at the ceiling, painted a bright, slick red as a spur to appetite.

"You can sit wherever you like at mealtimes," says Sunny. "We don't have any fixed arrangement. We have a flexible social plan. We think it's better if the patients who are well enough to come down can all mix together. And if you don't feel well some day you can let one of us know by turning the small red tag outside your door, and you'll get your meals in your room."

Julia lingers at the edge, reluctant to step out among the chairs, empty evidence of so many other people all around, unseen now in other parts of the building.

"A cafeteria," she says finally. "How depressing."

"It's not a cafeteria. And everyone here is very friendly."

"I'm sure," says Julia. "Can't you afford tablecloths?"

"There are tablecloths for dinner. It's pleasant."

"I don't believe you," says Julia.

"You'll see, tonight," says Sunny, "at dinner."

Sunny resists the urge to say anything sharper, an urge flicking in her head like a nerve; the tablecloths are in no way her responsibility. But of course Sunny will practice patience instead. Of course she will, because Julia is infirm, after all, and correspondingly grumpy. Sunny is under no personal obligation to like her, and whether she does or not shouldn't matter, because personal feelings are routinely set aside, for the greater good. Isn't that obvious?

Across the hall Sunny quietly opens a wooden door and looks inside to see if the chapel is occupied, hesitating in the doorway. Julia looks over her arm, sees the cross hanging empty on the far wall, lit by the greenish daylight from the uncurtained windows on the shady side of the building.

"No thanks," she says, loudly, then hides her face behind the collar of her fur like an imaginary countess. And she does not look at Sunny, but shuffles ahead, awkward in the slippers, away and down the hall.

They see the Green Room, filled with pots of fleshy foreign leaves as moist and supple as the inner fold of an elbow, and they visit the Solarium, which Julia admires for the windows, but the Radiant Room doesn't look as cozy when the hearth of Finnish granite is cold and empty, and she is unimpressed.

"Never mind," says Sunny. "Just wait until it snows. You'll be glad to sit there."

Sunny knows that Julia will need to be prodded into the schedule, and this is normal. Sunny finds her for dinner that first evening seated in the chair in her room, looking out the window. She's reapplied her makeup, and she's wearing a black skirt and blouse with a fawn-colored ribbon at the neckline. Some might say it is a little too formal, perhaps a lot too formal; these are not prosperous times for most. Sunny takes her downstairs and helps her choose a place to sit, under the red ceiling with neighbors in plainer knit dresses. She introduces Julia around. She finds out about the meal. Julia will accept the roast, the rutabaga, the buttermilk, the heavy plain cake. She looks up, as if hoping to be contradicted, but now she has had her allotment of attention for the day. Sunny will leave her with the others and retire for the evening.

Sunny says, "Enjoy your dinner, ladies."

Oh yes! We love dinner.

And then Julia exhales, and sits back in her chair, looking down at the tablecloth and waiting for the inevitable tiresome conversation to begin. And it does.

There is a small problem, though. When Julia turns to stare at those seated at the other tables a blossom of blood appears above the ribbon of her neckline. And not until it grows, and another appears on her throat—a spot of blood sliding greasily in the wrinkle of her skin—does Mrs. Numminen, on her left, feel compelled to look away discreetly; they've spoken a little, mostly about the mosquitoes. Julia touches her throat and finds blood on her fingertips. She takes out her handkerchief, with its blot of dark lipstick, and Mrs. Numminen looks away again, assuming that Julia is bringing up blood, somehow.

"What is this, now," says Sunny, when Julia appears alone upstairs, wandering past the nurses' station just as Sunny herself was to step away through the door at the end of the corridor toward her own private rooms. She pulls Julia closer to the light.

"It's broken glass," she says. "Little shards. How did it happen?"

The answer is that Julia had been pressed to hurry that morning, pressed to leave her apartment without any help. She'd packed her bags by dropping cosmetics and medicines in among her clothes, including the ones she wore to dinner . . .

"I brought everything," she says.

It is nearly time for Sunny's own dinner but instead she strips Julia, privately of course and with the door closed, and removes the glass splinters with the aid of a strong lamp, her magnifiers, a pair of tweezers, and a cotton ball dipped in disinfectant.

"Raise your arms," she says, and she can be terribly kind, now that there is work to do.

There is a line of soft gray hair under Julia's arms and another faint trace down the center of her back. And there are scars along her arms, a history of dark injections at intervals on her loose, cool skin.

Sunny steps out, has a word, and a ward maid turns on the taps and fills one of the four deep freestanding tubs in the shared bathroom down the corridor. Sunny brings a dressing gown, and Julia slips it on over her half-slip and sturdy black brassiere. She is wearing her own terrible shoes, worn to dinner, fished out from under the bed with a brass-handled cane unpacked from her suitcase. She follows Sunny slowly down the hall, easily enough, until Sunny opens the door to steam and tile, the communal bathroom, warm and damp with a high, tiny window.

"No," says Julia.

"I'm afraid you need a bath," says Sunny.

"None of your business," says Julia.

It really does not matter what Julia thinks, now that Sunny has seen the glass, now that there are specific problems that will be simple to fix. Sunny might not get away in time for her own dinner, but that's fine, that's also normal. She puts a little friendly pressure on Julia's shoulders and tries to lead her into the room, even propelling her from behind, but Julia grips the door frame, sliding her fingers into the gap between the hinges, her rings clicking and catching.

Sunny pauses, because there is only one thing to do, which is to use force, and although she's obviously physically able to overpower Julia, why should she have to? She stops and rests her hands on Julia's tense, thin arms, knowing this struggle is more about resistance in general than about avoiding the bath itself. The look Julia gives Sunny over her shoulder seems to confirm this. And, despite herself, Sunny momentarily thinks of pushing the door shut, crushing those little fingers against the frame. Breaking all of them, surely. Instead, she says, "It's better if you don't make this a difficult process."

She pries Julia's fingers from the door frame, not difficult because Julia is not strong. But Julia kicks, in a way that could be accidental but that Sunny knows is not, hard on the shin and ankle, and her shoe leaves a dark streak on the white cotton where Sunny will have a bruise in the morning. This is quite enough: she shifts Julia's arm sharply behind her back and returns her to 527, the dressing gown falling open along the way. Nurse Todd comes to grasp and lift Julia's feet, ready with two canvas straps under one arm; she does the bulk of the lifting as they get Julia onto the bed and turn her over. Nurse Todd sits firmly on Julia's legs, using her own warm weight. Sunny shakes her head at the straps, even though there is a grim satisfaction in having done this much. She tucks her hair back in place.

"Next time," says Nurse Todd.

"Don't kick," says Sunny. "Don't kick anyone. Do you understand?"

"She'll snap my knees," says Julia, her voice muffled against the bedding.

"Say you won't kick again."

"I won't kick again."

Nurse Todd slides off the bed and stands, slowly winding the unused straps, waiting for Julia to turn over. "Say good-bye to your shoes," she says, pulling them from Julia's feet and taking them with her back out to the nurses' station.

Sunny says, gently, "You need a bath. I'm going to help you, whether you like it or not. The longer we wait, the colder the water will be."

"I won't let you touch me."

Sunny folds her arms across her chest, with a faint smile, thinking, *That's enough, you dirty, ungrateful thing. I'll give you a sedative and another fifteen minutes of my day, but no more than that.*

"I can't let you touch me."

"That's nonsense."

"I won't expose you," says Julia.

"Expose me to what?" says Sunny.

A deep flush pools in the hollows of Julia's cheeks, and her tongue seems to throb in her half-opened mouth. "You're too pure," she says. "I don't want to hurt you." She hides her wrinkled face in her hands, in what may be a moment of purest melodrama; Julia is either crafty or ashamed, and Sunny, surprisingly, can't quite determine which.

Two

Notes are always taken, and in the bright pine administrative offices our detailed records will be kept forever. Remember, too, that sensitive information can be filed separately, in certain instances, for reasons of privacy and confidentiality. We'll swear to it: you can trust Sunny. We've confided in Sunny, we've unfolded tightly hidden specifics and individual secrets, and nothing we've said in confidence has ever flown back into our faces with the bite and scratch we'd feared in other life. She doesn't care. A recitation is in our own best interests. Sunny explains this, still not sure of Julia's anxiousness. Sunny leans forward, and says, "Don't you want to feel better?"

Julia can see the flecks of pigment in Sunny's eyes, and can smell clean things, bleach and cider vinegar, from the collar of her dress, an odor of sincerity. She watches Sunny's mouth when Sunny speaks to her. Is she a little deaf? She mostly doesn't seem to be.

"If you want to feel better, you'll have to tell me what's wrong."

It's clear to Sunny that although Julia is ashamed, or feigning shame, she is nonetheless a bit more animated than previously. From this, Sunny knows she will be persuaded to speak. Of course she'll be persuaded to speak about herself; an initial reluctance is common, but almost always short-lived.

"You won't understand," says Julia.

"Whatever the problem is, Júlia, I've seen it before."

Sunny sits and waits, giving Julia the illusion that tendering her private information will be her own decision, whenever she's ready. And Julia also sits and waits, watching Sunny, this time without breaking eye contact. To meet the gaze of another for too long can signal only one of two intentions, the two oldest intentions in human nature, either a threat of violence, or of lust. And since neither of those intentions, and no combination of the two, can possibly apply here, they reach an impasse. But suddenly Julia smiles, and on that first evening at Suvanto she decides to explain why she is so furiously against being helped into the tall stainless steel bathtub.

In the beginning, Julia says, she felt bruised. And yes, of course, she's a married woman and she knows that it's not uncommon to feel bruised down there after sex, especially, she says, after sex that is not entirely genial. Because sometimes it can be that way, in a marriage. Because relations are complicated. She and her husband had worked together, as host and hostess in the cafés and ballrooms, and sometimes they were paid to work until late at night, and sometimes she was tired, and sometimes her muscles were quite sore, especially if she'd been obliged to stand waiting very long or to teach the steps to too many strangers over a stretch of too many hours; she'd wondered if that was why her body hurt. But this was different. And then she felt deep sadness as well, and then her bones and joints began to ache.

At first Mr. Dey wanted to distract her with dinner at a favorite restaurant near the harbor, where the captains of Swedish vessels often sat over plates of good Finnish game. But Julia did not want the ordeal of dressing herself, or of leaving the apartment. He said that going out would help her to feel better, and maybe if the bruised feeling had not gotten progressively worse it might have. But then very soon her clothing hurt her, and then every step hurt her, and sitting in a room full of other people was out of the question. She held herself stiffly, tried not to move at all. Her back ached, low and constant, and then suddenly, surprisingly, there was a drenching fever. She couldn't hold a pen, a fork, because her hands were damp and clumsy.

She took aspirin and went to bed and woke repeatedly in the dark with her nightgown heavy and hot, soaked through, and twice in the first night she had to change into a fresh one, burning when she took it off and freezing when dressed again. In the morning her glands were swollen, not only in her throat but also in her groin, pressing from within, and also those under her arms. She could feel them with her fingers, slightly smaller than quails' eggs, tender and insistent.

Mr. Dey suggested that she had the flu. The flesh between her legs began to swell, which she would never describe too accurately. She says now to Sunny that she couldn't bear to look. But goes on to describe herself in ugly, technical detail, flesh the color of blood, weeping and hot, sticking painfully to the fabric of her underclothes, making her wish, in a diffuse way, that she was dead.

Julia pauses here, leaning forward on her elbows, fingers interlaced, looking up at Sunny from under her lashes. "Don't write that," she says. "It's just an expression."

"I understand," says Sunny. "Go on."

There were tight, cramping pains, hot and cold down the back of her thighs when she stood, and then also when she sat, and she wanted only to be at home, in bed, wanted to fall asleep and to remain asleep for as long as it would take to make this problem go away.

She wanted to know how long, how long would it last, and she asked the doctor, discreet and known to Mr. Dey, the two of them as sympathetically unmoved as if she'd come down with a bad cold. But he hadn't been able to say. Another week, she hoped, surely it couldn't take longer than that? Another two weeks?

Another six weeks, or six months, maybe a year . . . possibly never. But the intensity will pass.

On her back in the bed she'd moved her legs apart to try to find some relief and thought of pictures of plague from plates in Mr. Dey's books of engravings, terrible images, and the way the glands can swell, preventing the victims from closing their limbs. Evidence of pollution, like grates backing up under a flood of poison. She hated his books. She hated him, everything about him.

Mr. Dey brought tea with a little brandy, and water and aspirin and cold compresses (after which she heard him washing his hands in the next room), and he brought magazines, and newspapers folded open to the puzzle pages, leaving a pen on the bedside table. But she still couldn't hold the pen. And Julia cried often then (and never since, she says), her eyes filling constantly with scalding tears so that her eyelids twitched with fatigue and swelled like steamed shrimps full of dark capillaries, and when Mr. Dey brought a fresh cold towel she laid it across her face, where it grew warm from grief. The fever persisted. She trembled in her dressing gown, trembled under the blankets. He sat on the edge of the bed with his legs crossed at the knee, fully dressed in a suit and tie as usual. He held her hand with one of his but let it go to methodically prepare and roll a cigarette, which he lit and then handed to her.

"Listen," he said, "listen to me, sweetheart. Crying will only prolong your discomfort, believe me."

She'd nodded, without looking up. He'd waited to go on until she met his eye.

"This is not the worst thing," he said, and his manner was patient, yet unconsoling, and not entirely impressed with the seriousness of what was happening.

Again, she'd nodded.

But shame had fallen like a shutter and she could not forget anything because of the pain, firstly, but also because of the changing horror she encountered through her fingertips and in the little handheld mirror she consulted when he went out. He could not be expected to help with the topical treatments, and while she was applying them she could feel that the flesh of her sex had become stiff and hard as ruined leather, spotted with sharp wounds like tiny chips of broken glass.

She said to Mr. Dey, "And how do you know so much about it?"

"You heard the doctor yourself. This will come and go for a few years, and it will stay dormant longer if you take good care and don't worry so much. You know I love you, anyway."

And seemingly she did know this. But under the circumstances she wanted to push, and push, and push, and so she said, "Who else have you seen through this?"

He took the cigarette back from her, and said, infuriatingly, "You heard the doctor. Maybe you already had this when we met, or maybe you did get it from me, but we'll never know, because I don't seem to be sick, do I? You could have got it from your mother when you were a baby. Your mother could have gotten it from your father. Or maybe you had a wet nurse, and maybe you got it from her. There's no way to know how long it's been here, and there will never be any way to know."

"I don't believe you."

"Well," he'd said, obligingly, as if she'd pushed him into saying something beyond what he'd intended. "A lot of other dancers have it, too. Most of your friends have it, you must know how common this is. It's not out of the ordinary, at all."

"Nobody has this. Nobody I know."

"Sweetheart," he said, "you're wrong."

He brought a consolation gift of two dozen blousy silk panties from Stockmann's department store downtown. That may sound like a deliberately cruel gift, under the circumstances, but it wasn't. She was pleased, because those panties were as soft and as comfortable as bloomers, and she was grateful to be made comfortable in any way.

Here Julia pauses again, and her frown deepens as she watches Sunny write. "This is what I meant," she says.

Sunny looks up, waiting.

"I'm describing things an unmarried woman can't understand. You think it's strange and repulsive that he gave me a gift of panties. I can see that you do."

"I don't," says Sunny. "I have no opinion about it."

"I loved him," says Julia. "Maybe that's what you don't understand."

Sunny readjusts the pages of her notes; almost imperceptibly she tilts her wrist while doing so, possibly to glance at her watch.

"I do understand," says Sunny. "What you're describing isn't unusual."

Julia pauses, reevaluating the effect of her words before continuing.

Over time, she says, the lesions changed, creeping down cannily to where they were no longer hidden by the blousy panties; under her nightgown she covered herself with a pair of jersey dancer's pants. Mr. Dey didn't always come home to sleep in the bed beside her, because of her fever and the shivering sweats, because of her restless movements all night long, because of her tendency now more than before to roll up against his back and press her legs against his, and because of the possibility of her sticky skin touching his during this contagious interlude. Did he have it, or didn't he? Yes or no? Oh, probably, who knew; she grew tired of his inconclusive answers. When she got up regularly during the night to move aside the soft dressings and reapply the topical treatments she would listen for him in the apartment and look for him in the living room, but he seemed to stay out all night after working at the cafés and halls. Or was staying elsewhere altogether, and she could hardly blame him, and she almost wanted him to disappear, because she hated him, yes, very much.

Sunny makes a note of this: *Patient hates her husband.*

Sometimes she was hungry and then she scrambled eggs carelessly, using the same red-patterned plate again and again, and drank vodka, even though she'd been warned that alcohol was a depressant. She cried regularly when Mr. Dey was gone, but no longer in front of him, never. When bathing she put her face down and wept over the water, afraid of her body now, afraid of anything more, afraid of the damage spreading beyond her aching back, her swollen lymph nodes, her fever from her scalp to her freezing, humid feet . . . and of course the first place. There was an odor as well, and she knew that someday she would catch this odor lifting from someone else, some stranger in a crowd, and she would recognize it. Or else someone would recognize this odor lifting from her, and turn to look. She also believed the disease would move up and outward onto her face, out from her mouth, her nostrils, her eyes, and then everyone in the world who saw her would know that she was carrying this particularly dreadful kind of private pox.

It would be a year until she could touch herself while bathing without weeping. It's a well-known mystery of the body, she has since heard, that there are stations in the nerves that bring up outrage and despair when touched, like pressing a switch.

The hardness cracked and bled, urination was painful and difficult. Mr. Dey still did not come home early for a long time; when there was a live band the dancing would continue all night, if he allowed it. She used water to prolong the vodka and then ran out. She lay on her back in the bed and felt the weight of her eyes sinking backward into her skull. There was a framed mirror on the wall, reflecting the ceiling, and beside it an advertisement she had especially liked, and kept, a sketch of herself and him, three-quarter profile, printed in red and black on white. It was for an event long since past.

When Mr. Dey did arrive one evening while she was still awake he touched her head and went out again to bring the doctor. In the background he opened the windows to dispel the odors of depression.

"Yes," the doctor said, "you're moving through the primary attack. It will stay with you, but you'll probably never feel this bad again." She neither believed him nor disbelieved him; it seemed to her then that nothing could possibly change, that the trouble, the pain, would be a constant and permanent presence. The doctor rubbed his hands with strong-smelling antiseptic fluid as she rolled back into the bedding.

"You're uncomfortable. I'll give you something for the pain." He sat on the edge of the bed. "Don't worry. It's more common than you might think."

And then, as an afterthought, "It won't leave any scars."

As he prepared the sedative from his bag, plaid-lined where she looked into it, Mr. Dey, in the corner, discreetly shifted her soiled laundry out of sight with his foot.

It was a long time until the pain and also the depression passed. Then he took her out again, in cabs right to the doorsteps of more restaurants, so that she would not have to walk much. And she accepted fish again, or fowl, or pork, or other whitish meats, and glasses of imported sparkling wine that were frighteningly expensive. He ordered light, bright meals that he liked to see her eating, and he was pleased.

"Can't you admit it?" she said. "Where did it come from?"

"No," he said. "I don't know. But how could I tell you if I did?"

To flake apart a fish, or cut pale flesh, to chew, to try to swallow, to receive this as an answer. She did want someone to blame, but he was elusive.

So she stayed home and would not go dancing, would not work with him at all anymore, would not be his partner, pretty, tiny, would not help to teach any private or public lessons to those who wanted to learn the Nordic tango. She would not touch his hand, his arm, his back, his shoulder, his leg with hers, none of it, she would not go to the cafés with him, not to the ballrooms, never, and if the money ran out she did not care. And he accepted the change and this, she privately felt, was an acknowledgment that he'd brought the disease home to her. Wasn't it?

She had no appetite to cook a big meal ever again and in any case she still hated him, and so, continually, they went out for dinner, and spent the money he earned, and she would not eat enough, and then he would take her home and go out again to work in the cafés and ballrooms, returning late in early morning. He was teaching with another partner now, a Russian woman from Petersburg, or so he said. She brought her accordion player with her. A little bit of Yiddish in the tunes now, throbbing. But Julia did not want to be told anything. If she woke up when he came home then she might fix something small, very small for them to eat at the table, bread and cheese, or an egg, small and meager because she hated him, and then they slept. In the mornings, awake before him, she read books and magazines. He woke late, dressed slowly, and took her again for dinner. The differences in their sleeping schedules meant less and less time awake together.

She threw out the dancer's pants and yes, they were together sometimes again, and she knew through the way that he touched her, which seemed the same in all regards as before, that he loved her and was not repulsed. He kissed her in the dark bedroom, very sincerely he kissed her eyelids, her temples, but her eyes were silvered, glinting slits; did he not see her suspicion? Perhaps. He said that he loved her. He sounded truthful. She still had thoughts of soaking the white sheets and mattress with his blood, of putting the scissors into his neck, his back, his chest, or maybe into the side of his face, aiming for bones and back teeth. Not really. Once or twice, a few times. Because if he did not bring it, how could he touch her now?

She continued with the sedatives, without which she could not sleep, she said. And although he often looked at her for long seconds when he caught a diminished coordination, when she fumbled her fork, not eating anyway, he did not interfere.

And this is how acceptance dropped into place, each day a slow weight like a pendant hanging with many others around the throat, hung to distract from the fissure with a red-black center that couldn't be coaxed shut or ignored.

"Nurse Taylor," says Julia. "I can sense that I've upset you."

"Me?" says Sunny, looking up. "No, Julia, you haven't upset me."

"Really?" says Julia. "Are you certain?"

"I've heard similiar stories before," says Sunny, "many times. Don't be embarrassed."

"I'm not embarrassed. I think you're more embarrassed than I am."

"I'm not embarrassed at all," says Sunny. "But you were, at first."

"I was trying to soften the effect, for you," says Julia.

"For me?" And Sunny doesn't laugh, but she does smile, and the smile means, *As promised, you haven't shocked me.*

"Yes, for you," Julia says. "I imagine this is awkward for you, eavesdropping on the private lives of normal people. It's not fair that you have to listen, over and over, when other women talk about their marital habits, and what they do in their beds with their husbands. How can you bear everybody else's happiness?"

"There's plenty of unhappiness, too," says Sunny, with a seeming detachment that causes Julia to close her mouth, and to sit, sucking at her front teeth.

"I was young when I married him," says Julia, experimentally. "Much younger than you are now. But when you were that age, you were still in school, sleeping in a dormitory. You probably never got to find out about sex, except from your nursing books. I mean, it's all academic, to you, I would think."

Perhaps there is a small shift, here, as Sunny smiles, formally recognizing that Julia is needling her, and trying to—what, to offend her? To find an exposed nerve?

"Sunny," Julia continues, and the sound of her given name in Julia's mouth is unexpectedly improper. "I hope you won't hold this against me. But I'm not sure how much you know about these things, so maybe I shouldn't be talking to you, maybe I should talk to someone else, because I can see that you're probably . . . I assume you are . . . intact?" Julia's smile is really no more than a slightly open mouth over a slightly pendulous lip, and two expectantly filthy eyes.

Is there any good way to answer a woman as rude as Julia? Sunny could meet this creeping question with irritation, with anger, but that is, presumably, what Julia is expecting, hoping to make this exchange personal and repellent even though Sunny will not be drawn into acknowledging the needling, nor into confirming in any way that yes, indeed, Julia is behaving appallingly and that yes, in fact, Julia is right to loathe certain parts of herself, because she is loathsome. Because surely self-loathing is at the root of this exchange. Or alternatively Sunny could dismiss the question with equanimity and a word of mind-your-own-business, leaving Julia to feel perhaps frustrated, yet certainly still pleased by the rebuff. But because Sunny is professional, and detached, she merely smiles, again.

"You've led an interesting life," says Sunny, gently. "Let's try not to put too much weight on your misfortune."

Julia's nose wrinkles, and her teeth appear briefly in her mouth like those of an irritated dog, above which her nostrils dilate involuntarily. "Why not?" she says.

"Because now we can approach this in a practical way, rather than making the whole subject too emotional. Your husband was right, you could have been infected long before you felt sick, maybe years before. You'll never know for certain. But six or eight weeks of incubation is normal, when it gets in through a sexual wound. Tell me again when you were infected. How long ago?"

"It was years ago," says Julia. "I've told you that already."

"How many? At least make a guess."

"I don't know. Thirty years."

"And do you still suffer actively?"

Muscles move in Julia's face. "I am aware of it," she says. "At times."

"So, it's still with you," says Sunny, and she makes another note.

"Cross that out," says Julia. "I didn't say I was sick now."

"Yes, you did," says Sunny. "And I can't cross it out. These files are like legal documents. I can draw a line through parts, but I can't erase anything once it's been written. Pretty soon it won't matter anyway." Here Sunny puts down her pen and folds her hands on the tabletop. "Most importantly, Julia, I really ought to take a quick look at you, now, so that I'll have more complete notes to send ahead for your appointment tomorrow." And Sunny smiles, blandly.

Julia doesn't move; this was not the outcome she'd intended.

"Come now," says Sunny, rising from her chair, indicating the bed as she moves to close the door more firmly. "Just lift your slip, there's no need to undress further."

"What?" says Julia, without moving. "You want to look at my privates? Now?"

"At your vagina, yes. Get up, and show me your vagina."

Sunny pauses, with her hand on the door handle. Julia's eyes move from Sunny to the door, considering the hall beyond, considering, no doubt, the availability and proximity of Nurse Todd as a helper, and whether or not it is easier and less humiliating to simply submit. An aide passes in the hall, and Sunny stops her with a quiet word.

"Julia, don't worry. You can't repulse me. I see this all the time," says Sunny, waiting. "For me, it's all academic. Don't forget." The aide hands in a sterilized exam kit, and Sunny pushes the door shut.

And that's all it will be, just a quick look, very informal, as uninvasive as possible under the circumstances. But the look is proof that Sunny will not be drawn into nonsense, and a reminder that she carries enough of the weight of the institution in her person that, at least here in the ward, when Sunny gives directions, Julia must follow.

"I don't see what you described," says Sunny; as she turns away to remove her gloves she is matter-of-fact and courteous, as she has been throughout, and this will be the tone used between them now. "In any case, it can be cured."

Julia sits up, smoothing her slip back into place, ready, perhaps, with some sarcastic answer, but this makes her too honestly curious to continue that way. "Really?" she says, in a normal-sounding voice. "I was told I'd have to live with it, forever."

"Not anymore. You'll find out tomorrow. And you're lucky, Julia, luckier than a lot of others, because you could have been struck anywhere, any time, in your liver, your lungs, your muscles. Eventually it gets to the brain. And babies born to sick mothers still die, all the time." Sunny is carefully folding the gloves away in their wrappings to be re-sterilized. "And stillbirths," she says.

"I know that," says Julia, looking away.

Sunny asks for another tub of warm soapy water, and again they walk the hall, with Nurse Todd glancing at them over her glasses, and Julia, in profile, ignoring her.

Maybe it really was, partially, shame and the fear of being contagious that Julia suffers, since she is not afraid of nudity itself, Sunny soon discovers. Julia drops her dressing gown and clothes when prompted and sinks well enough into the warm bath, watching as Sunny gently shakes her undergarments over a wastebasket, releasing the last of the amber glass.

"Don't kick me again," Sunny says. "Understand? I mean it." But she is in control, and all is well. She smoothes a fatty cold cream over all that makeup, from the bridge of Julia's nose outward, taking it off gently with a yellow cotton cloth. Julia stares up at Sunny until she has to close her eyes to be rinsed. And then with her eyes closed and the water running off her face she seems embarrassed again, and she tightens her fingers over the edges of the tub to keep from slipping.

"That's not so bad," says Sunny absently, wiping Julia's face and hairline and the tiny cuts with rosewater afterward.

Julia tries to stand, drops of water caught in her chignon. But no, sit back again in the warm water and relax, and Sunny will pull out all the pins and shake shampoo powder into the long black hair. She'll pour water and carefully massage the dirty, neglected scalp, feeling very gently for any more hidden glass.

This is still the first day, after all, and it has been a long day. Julia's eyes are closing and they begin to water while Sunny rinses her hair. She helps her out of the tub, wraps her in a large white towel, and helps her into a cotton hospital nightdress. She puts her into the bed with a heat lamp over her hair, combed and spread out magnificently behind her on its own second pillow.

Julia's feet are pale and puckered after the softening effects of the water and Sunny had might as well, because somebody will have to, she'd might as well just get the initial foot care out of the way, so she folds back the blanket and slips a towel under Julia's feet. Julia is tired now, too tired to resist when Sunny runs the foot razor over the heels and the hard calluses, shucking off strips of dead skin into a pile of withered yellow shavings. After, she rubs balsam into Julia's fresh, sensitive soles, while Julia tries hard not to twitch, certainly not to kick.

At this latitude it is still light outside and Sunny pulls the dark summer shade across the window. Julia looks different now. Clean and prepared. Her eyes are closing, but she watches Sunny turn out the overhead light, pull the door shut softly.

Sunny stops in the hall to tell Nurse Todd to collect the heat lamp later.

"Cold water would have been good enough," says Nurse Todd, loudly enough for Sunny to hear, but not quite loudly enough to expect a response.

"She's difficult," says Sunny. "Don't encourage that."

Nurse Todd's laugh is a shallow, derisive sound. "Don't worry. They can't get to me."

"You demean yourself if you let them."

Nurse Todd says, "I know that."

"I hope so," says Sunny.

Nurse Todd says, again, "They don't get to me."

Sunny takes her cardigan from the chair, ready to leave, finally, at the end of a longer day than she'd anticipated. She doesn't go immediately, though. Some glimmer prevents her, something bigger than any of the many small oversights caught in the course of a normal day. It's probably nothing. She's tired. And her room is waiting, her bed, her book, her slippers, the privacy of evening. So go on, Sunny, go to bed. Everything is in order here. She believes this, and turns to go; it is surprising, the pull of that private room, a destination at the end of the days, a distraction sometimes during.

"Who is responsible for the unpacking?" she asks.

Nurse Todd gives a name, but the girl is a day worker, already gone. Sunny will sharpen the tones of responsibility overnight, and will speak to the girl tomorrow.

Three

Something serious would be one thing, of course—though there hasn't been an emergency on the upper floor in so long—but Sunny missed her dinner and her evening to herself only due to a mess that ought to have been caught. She speaks to the girl Marja in her office, out of earshot of the others.

"No, Nurse Taylor, I didn't see it."

"You didn't see the broken pill bottle?"

Actually, yes, that had been found when the largest suitcase was unpacked. Marja had done as done before and left the medicines together until someone came to look in on rounds. The medicines, and some accessories accompanying them. She'd thrown out the pieces of glass. She thought she'd gotten them all.

"You didn't shake out the clothing?"

Sunny recognizes her role, including the lack of temper. Isn't it more effective to bring about remorse, regret, feelings that will stay and bother? Yes, in fact, it feels much worse to be on the other end of Sunny's disappointment than to be the target of her anger, because everyone knows she is too tightly controlled to ever indulge in real cruelty. There's been no reason to think otherwise, nothing said, nothing seen.

"It was your responsibility," she says, "and you should go, now, and apologize to Mrs. Dey, tell her you're sorry she was hurt by our carelessness on her first day here. Ask if she'd like a cup of coffee, and help her get dressed if she wants your help."

Marja goes, trying to shrug off this interview as she walks down the corridor toward Room 527. She taps Julia's door and allows a moment, as is customary, before opening it; she is surprised enough by what she sees to bypass the nurses' station (and Nurse Todd) and to report right back to Sunny, saying, "She's ruined her nightdress, and she's naked."

Sunny lifts the nightdress from the floor, torn at the buttons and under the arms. Julia turns over, burrowing in the bed, her soft clean hair loose around her shoulders. Her sheets are bunched to one side, however, and do not quite conceal her small gray backside.

"Yes, we've seen you," says Sunny. "Go ahead and cover yourself now."

"That nightie smells of dirty old women," Julia says.

Sunny's hands are on her hips, another role. "Julia, listen to me," she says, invisibly irked; she'd assumed the question of bad behavior had been settled the evening before. "You can't destroy what isn't yours."

"I'm sorry," says Julia, with a small, apologetic smile. She won't sustain Sunny's gaze, though, and looks up at the ceiling, contritely, to avoid it.

Sunny offers a second garment. "Julia, look at me," she says, and waits until Julia does. "This is what the ladies call a bunnysuit." She pulls the fabric taut to show the shape. "It looks soft, but it can't be torn. Stronger women than you have tried." She turns it around to show a row of tiny buttons up the back, unreachable. The garment is white, infantile, made of strong courduroy, with long sleeves and tight trouser legs that end in flopping booties. There is a flap in the seat, for the toilet. Sunny parts it, demonstrating, and Julia looks away again.

"Your clothing will be back from the laundry today," says Sunny. She shakes the bunnysuit and leaves it conspicuously on the chair, an empty seated figure.

"Would you like help getting dressed? Your evaluation with the doctor is in half an hour. And, incidentally, he can examine you through the bunnysuit, if need be."

Sunny gives the orderly the file containing all of her notes thus far and the letter from Julia's Finnish doctor in the city. She has worked her way through it at her desk with her dictionary, her *sanakirja,* and has made out what seem to be the following: *väsymys,* fatigue; *sekavuus,* confusion or maybe incoherence—nothing strong enough to mean dementia, she assumes; *emätin,* vagina; *diagnoosi,* diagnosis? Nouns only, because the complicated verbs are very difficult indeed.

Suvanto is not only a winter retreat where English-speaking wives hide from the frozen streets and golden buildings of the Finnish cities and the darkness and silence of the outlying timber towns, and it probably did make sense to send Julia here. Especially since Suvanto can now afford to admit the chronics, the low-grade incurables, and will take on some of those refused at other hospitals pinched harder by the need to save valuable bed space for the acutely ill. It is not obvious, from a distance, how serious this is, how many are dead here now, in Finland, how many young people are dead here now. Eight thousand a year dying of tuberculosis alone, in a country of two million, young and otherwise healthy people dying in their beds. The war set everything running backward . . . in light of which it had seemed like a good thing, to let the timber concern push extra money into the hospital budget.

The result of Julia's evaluation is as expected: prolapse of the uterus, and the other old problem, to be dealt with discreetly. Dormant, yes, that's fine, we'll kill it. But the prolapse should be dealt with now.

"And that means what?" says Julia. An explanation is given, in short, that she is falling slightly inside out, a question of muscle tone, of age, of plain bad luck. Julia has discovered that Sunny's patience with her exceeds what she can expect in the clinical wing, where she was surprised by a more thorough, much more pelvic examination. She folds her hands furiously in her lap, knees crossed at the memory.

"You mean something is coming out?"

"Your muscles aren't strong enough anymore to hold everything in place, where it should be," says Sunny. "It's not uncommon."

"Holding what in place?"

"Your uterus is dropping."

"What can those men do about it?"

"You'll see one of the consultants, Dr. Ruotsalainen. He'll look at your records, I'm sure he'll examine you, and then he can tell you what they'll do next."

"But what will that be?"

Julia is seated at the small table before the window. Sunny moves the other chair and sits, just on the edge, just for a moment.

"He's the doctor, not me," she says, and the memory of yesterday's brief examination is there, in the room with them. "It's better to wait and hear his advice, not mine. But of course I can answer any other questions you think of later or forget to ask him. All right?"

"Does it matter whether I agree?"

"I don't see why you wouldn't. Dr. Ruotsalainen is a kind man."

"This is terrible," says Julia.

"It will all go well," says Sunny. "You'll see."

And then every day moves forward, even a day on which our fates are set in motion. What's for lunch? Beef and root vegetables for lunch. Julia cuts her meat in half and hides the excess in her coffee cup. She chews and chews and watches the others eat and surreptitiously she spits. Then it is time for a short rest in her room, strongly encouraged whether she is tired or not. Nurse Todd finds her sitting on the edge of her bed, awake. There's a candy from the communal dish in Julia's mouth, still in the foil wrapper.

Evelyn Todd shakes a pill out of a white cup.

"Spit it out," she says, holding the cup to Julia's lips, and then she pokes the dry pill into Julia's mouth with her index finger.

"Don't be tempted into biting me," she says, finger between Julia's teeth.

"Give back my candy," says Julia.

She cracks the candy between her molars and would like to spit it onto Nurse Todd's back as she goes. Beyond her window a bird appears briefly, a reminder of the large dark flocks that occasionally appear in the sky with a magnified sound of wings.

Nearly forgotten, and quickly, the animals, until you step outside and remember them. The mosquitoes, tiresome, and the red-tufted squirrels, and field mice that scatter across the grass. And the one small hedgehog, the *siili* that seems to live in the bushes near the hospital entrance, whom one of the patients tries to entice and feed with napkinfuls of crumbled cake, crouching to follow slowly as it trundles away to hide.

The routine has not evolved without compassion. These are individuals, and Julia is not a representation of anything but herself grown older, and she'd no doubt rather be remembered as she might have been earlier and not at the age that takes her to Suvanto, the age at which she is obliged to sit down to heavy dinners with strangers who seem genuinely happy to inflict on her, at great length, the boring vicissitudes of their daily lives and the dull details of their innards. She would prefer the further past, and she interrupts the conversation at her table when she's heard enough speculation about the consistency of the pudding or the weight of the cake. Surely, good god, they could come up with something interesting? If not, she would rather remember herself, with Mr. Dey, before the trouble, standing in front of musicians who frown as they tune up in white cotton shirts and black jackets. Her own smile was a frown as well. She had loved those nights, she loved to dance, ballroom dancing was the only thing she had ever felt expert at; she was small, light, deft, and it came to her easily. Blue veins throbbing at the jaw when they finished the warm-up, the introduction, both slim, both in black, turning outward, away from one another. She looked to the next partner ready to practice new steps. She was the hostess, and Mr. Dey was the host.

Julia and her husband, they were among those first Danish couples who came to teach the Nordic tango over and over and over in the Finnish cafés. Pointed, particular, she was good as a dance teacher, a little impatient maybe but she was not cruel and the owner of the Café Pohjoisesplanadi called her, as a nickname, Mrs. Velvet, because she held all of those shy, silent Finnish hands without embarrassment, through her soft black gloves. But he also called her *Pieni Sydän,* which means Little Heart. In her room, corsages brought as thanks, sometimes even from her husband. Her eyebrows then as later grew together, a soft dark line, and her gentlemen partners stared away from there intently. She tells a story sometimes about someone sending a bottle of champagne, chilled, which instead of drinking she soaked her feet in; she means it to be funny, because of course it isn't true. A temperance joke, you know: Oh holy rollers! I may dance, but I wouldn't dream of drinking.

She'd change out of her dancing shoes, obviously, after, and then step out into the cold, well-wrapped and pretty in a set of silky furs. In the darkness think of deep red velvet, spread like a cape, tossed against evenings of pale blue snow, and this is something like that kind of cold tango, formal, fluid, intangibly feral, a way to touch your partner, to stare away in another direction, and never to have to speak.

But even respecting the past, situations change: who loved her by the time of her arrival, except a few old dancer friends with tiny tight chignons, retired to the Helsinki suburbs, or a few old men, musicians with stiff hands now living in the spas in Germany? And perhaps that same invisible Mr. Dey who presumably put her into the cab on the morning of her arrival? Poor Julia, early retirement and increasing age brought humiliation, cramping her into a lonely apartment in the city of Turku, within sight of the massive Protestant cathedral on the heavy brown river, in those rooms cluttered with Mr. Dey's hobbies, including photographic chemicals and the odor of urine-dampened wood chips from the toilet box of two blue cats, small rooms where she was deprived of the chance to exercise wit except at her own expense. She still hated him, of course. So it is maybe a relief to come to Suvanto, even though, as she says, she expects to go back to him when she is better. Even though she seems to look forward to this. The others at her dining table open their mouths a little and watch her with mild mistrust held in check by her celebrity. Because why? Because Sunny has asked to borrow one of the photographs from Julia's suitcase and has put it near the first-floor crafts case, below the aerial shots of the grounds, the plaque with the names of benefactors, a thank-you to the timber concern, and a large dun-colored drawing from Laimi Lehti's original draft of the building plan. And in the photo Julia is posing, her skirt a satin circle, hands draped wearily on her knee, long black eyelashes and a dying grace, and none of the women who see this photo quite know how to find fault afterward.

At the lunch table Julia frowns, lifts the butter and inhales: "Someone in the kitchen has left the butter too close to strong cheese. And onions."

"Don't you care for strong cheese?" says her table companion.

"That's beside the point," she says grandly. "When we want strong cheese and onions, we'll ask for them."

And the Americans at her table willingly agree, and one scrapes her butter aside, now that she knows it's tainted.

The principal work of the medical staff happens almost always behind the swinging steel doors of the clinical wing. One sees the doctors in their circuits, on their rounds, but not nearly as much as expected: they are not concerned with the routine tasks of bedside nursing. But there are evaluations, consultations, visits, and in getting down to the business of treatment—is there any other reason to be here?—Dr. Ruotsalainen orders a pessary to be fitted for Julia, since clearly, as predicted in the letter from the Finnish doctor and confirmed now here, she is suffering from the genital prolapse that hangs, a pink and pulsing intrusion of drooping private tissue. It is, perhaps, slightly worse than expected, but not as bad as it could be.

"Good," he says, in Finnish, by which he means, *You'll feel much better.*

But during Sunny's rounds and subsequent interpretation of the doctor's orders it becomes clear that a pessary is something Julia has avoided purposely; that though it had been possible to avoid this before coming to Suvanto, now, living under the institutional clock, her pessary must be fitted and worn, and she is not happy. She's been returned to her room, where she sits in a way that shows that she is finished now with being touched.

Small wonder that she had taken pains to avoid it: Sunny discovers that Julia does not know what the pessary is, or how it works. She has closed her ears in all previous discussions. She did not understand Dr. Ruotsalainen at all.

"I don't want it," she says. "It's intolerable."

"You should want it," says Sunny. "It will make you feel better."

"No, not after what I told you. Please," she says. "Take it away."

"This is the best option. You can wear the pessary instead of having a surgery."

And Sunny explains, with the help of a quick sketch, the form and function of the pessary, nothing more than a coil of wire in a rubber ring, firm and flexible, to be worn high in the vagina in order to set things right and to persuade the uterus and other parts not to drop down from their proper positions. It's just a ring, just another ring to wear, albeit in a different place . . .

"All the unpleasantness you've been feeling—problems passing water?"

Julia would in fact prefer not to answer. But, yes, problems like that.

"Problems with your motions?"

"I'm not answering," she says.

"A feeling of fullness like a lump down there between your legs?"

No more, no more questions.

"I thought so. This device is going to lift that pressure away, back up to where it belongs, and you won't feel anything like that anymore."

"Is it attached?"

"No, it's not attached to anything, it can be removed, but you should ignore it other than getting a replacement every few months. Pretty soon you'll forget it's there."

"And do you think I'll be able to . . ." says Julia, but she does not finish.

"You'll feel much better," says Sunny again.

"And I can take walks outside and never be uncomfortable?"

"That's right. After a while you won't notice it."

After checking that the door is closed tightly for privacy, Sunny opens the case that she has brought with her—opens it and lets Julia see the harmless, almost cheerfully smooth red rubber ring that has, in the back of her mind, resembled a blunt fish hook, made of iron.

"This isn't for you," says Sunny. "The doctor will take measurements and show you how to insert the one they'll give you. I'm just letting you know what to expect, and then later we'll talk about hygiene—there's an alum douche, for example—and anything else you think you want to know."

Julia looks at the thing with disgust, but she's also clearly fascinated, and now another part of her problem, spoken of rationally here in the clean blue room, begins to lose its weight of secrecy.

"What more should I expect?" she says. "Am I the worst you've seen?"

Sunny knows that some would be reassured most if the answer were yes.

"No," she says, "you certainly are not."

She has made time for Julia, time to help her settle, but this will change. The busy season of repetitive activity is coming. Admissions and orientations take time. New ward maids have been hired to replace those who have married and left over the summer, and these must be trained, supervised, corrected.

Those staff members who do not leave are mostly good-natured and don't begrudge their labor, and they bring their relatives to work as well. The longtimers, practical nurses and ward maids with seniority, bring their nieces to be their juniors, their nephews to be orderlies. They ride to town or home for visits together. They sit together over coffee in the *kahvila,* and they linger a long time in the staff sauna, and must surely gossip, too. Don't they? They sometimes seem so quiet to Sunny, so reserved, or maybe that's just the stereotype: the quiet Finn. Sunny understands words here and there, but sets her face as though not over-hearing. She understands more than she gives herself credit for. Like what she knows has been said about Nurse Todd. That Nurse Todd did her schooling in England, that she likes abusing those who work below her. That she still believes in the old rules of her English school: she calls to her juniors to bring bread to her in the *kahvila.* She calls for it in Finnish: *Leipa! Leipa!* The Finnish staff nurses turn their faces away without blushing, graduates of Baroness Mannerheim's nursing school in Helsinki, some of them, and all with far better manners than this.

Also, there are hints that Nurse Todd might dream of climbing the ranks. She would probably like Sunny to leave, because inertia might then keep the Head from finding an external replacement, so that every-one moves up a step, Evelyn Todd herself not least. And then eventu-ally, when there is a new girl, she will belong to Nurse Todd completely. A first real underling. Not an enviable position. Those aren't Sunny's concerns, though. She just doesn't like certain things, like the way that Nurse Todd will shave an old woman's feet too closely with a dull blade that skips and catches, leaving deep red dimples that are sore and hard to walk on. They go their separate ways after work, and it occurs to Sunny, as she walks to the staff sauna, that she has never, not once, seen Evelyn Todd there. Which is fine. But where does Evelyn spend her free time? This is one among many stray thoughts, flashing away in the trees before Sunny recognizes that she's thought them.

In the sauna, a new girl sits naturally, half covering her body with a towel.

Someone asks her where she will be working.

"Päivänkakkara," she says, which in English means *daisy*; the units in the wards have the names of flowers, Päivänkakkara, Ruusu,

Krookus. And Sunny's own Orvokki. Which means *violet*. "I'll be on nights."

"Oh," says one. "Bring a stack of fresh nightgowns with you down there, and linens too." The other women smile, not unkindly.

This girl will be partnered with her aunt, strong and unsurprisable, and together they will sign and initial whenever something is done, in this case, a hundred seeming initials in the night for incontinence: front, back, and double.

"You'll be checking every bed and if you find anything, then you take care of it."

"Do they wake up?"

"Some might. Some might fight you when you put the fresh clothes on. There's one in Päivänkakkara who will try to get out of bed in her sleep. There's nothing wrong in her head. She just sleepwalks."

"It's the same on Orvokki too sometimes," Sunny says, haltingly and not totally correctly but nonetheless in Finnish. There is silence after she speaks, and then she is self-conscious, trying not to be too aware of how this must appear—that she is listening to them, observing them. But it seems the women accept her, or at least they don't reject her input. They lean easily back so that anything said is spoken out into the warmth of the dimly lit communal space before them.

"Strange," says the aunt, shifting; her arms are dense and strong from the repetitive movements of lifting and pulling, shifting and tucking. "I don't walk in my sleep. Do you?"

"No," says Sunny, and no one else can remember doing so, either. "Is it uncommon?"

"*Anteeksi*—excuse me," says the new girl; she goes out for a drink of water.

The aunt leaves her towel behind on the bench to throw a ladleful of water from the wooden bucket onto the hot sauna stones, which squeal and hiss and send up steam. She climbs back to her place on the bench, unembarrassed, nude and rosy, her dark hair wet and falling. She ties it back in a knot. "I thought they were different, on your floor," she says, a long moment later, when the hiss subsides.

"They're more—independent," Sunny wants to say, but she doesn't know the right word. *"Itse?"* she says, knowing it is the word for *self* and wanting to say something that would mean something like self-sufficient, more self-reliant.

"Itsekäs," someone offers, and Sunny is still embarrassed, and nods.

Later, with her *sanakirja* in hand, she looks for that word, *itsekäs,* and realizes that it means not independent, not self-reliant, but only self-centered. Which, on consideration, fits as well as anything.

Four

Late summer passes slowly under a dark blue sky that merges in the distance with the sea. It's peaceful, yet in these last clear weeks before the convalescent season will begin, in the three weeks following Julia's arrival, someone begins to creep down into the kitchen at night and to stoke the industrial stove, whose long metal surfaces, new and appealing, are the special responsibility of Mrs. Anderson, the Swedish-speaking kitchen supervisor. First once, then twice, and now three times she has either discovered the stove already glowing in the morning, its belly full of leaping blue and orange flame, hot and wasteful, or was told of it by the girl whose early-morning job it is to stoke both the stove and the wood- and peat-fired baking oven first thing in the morning before boiling gallons of water and popping in loaves for the staff breakfast. It would be fair to say Mrs. Anderson had privately wondered at first whether she or someone else could have forgotten to rake down the embers the night before . . . but no, the fire had clearly been fed, and anyone working in a kitchen knows the routine, the dangers there encountered, no one would purposefully leave the vents open, everyone is careful because everyone knows of someone who has been badly or even mortally burned (usually of course a young woman with too much skirt, too much swinging hair) and she has even, herself, seen a kitchen on fire, and it was even more frightening than you can imagine. This careful, competent Mrs. Anderson would not leave anything burning, and the girls know they aren't to feed the flames again until the start of the day shift.

And there are signs of smoked fish and meat sizzled, herring and ham taken from the cooler and eaten from the pan directly with a small sharp knife.

Aside from this real risk of fire it is not nice to think of the intrusion, the theft of meat, and the waste of wood, all of which go against her affable institutional grain. It is not nice to think of someone coming into the kitchen, silent feet on the hard cold flooring, rustling in the kindling cupboard . . . mostly, it is the breach of the normal way of doing things that disturbs Mrs. Anderson.

The lines of authority leading to and from the kitchen don't necessarily cross those of the wards, but Mrs. Anderson comes to Sunny because, well, what if it's a patient? It would need to be somebody pretty ambulatory, wouldn't it? She leans forward. The braided bun in her dark gold and gray hair is, as always, canted to the side of her head, over the ear, a little habit begun in girlhood that is still girlish even now.

"Right," says Sunny from the yellow desk chair in her office. Mrs. Anderson is sitting in the second chair, resting after coming across from the third building, a vast white square containing all the domestic workrooms, the laundry and the needle rooms, the staff *kahvila,* the kitchen and the kitchen dorms. (Where Mrs. Anderson does not live. She herself lives a little way off in the pines, in a house that was there already when Suvanto came to be built. She lives there with Sister Tutor, and she likes it very well.)

Sunny looks through her calendar.

"I hope you're not angry that I ask you," says Mrs. Anderson, slightly disappointed that she isn't more outraged. "It may be an accident. Maybe Kusti should take a look at the stove . . ."

"But three times means it's not an accident." Sunny glances up over her magnifiers. "And you would know, if something is out of place."

"Who's doing it, I wonder," says Mrs. Anderson, well pleased by this, putting her glasses on to better participate in the moment. Sunny slides the calendar between neat stacks of papers and files, turning it with her fingertips and pointing. Mrs. Anderson notes with approval that Sunny's nails are buffed and smooth, well tended despite the rigors of constant obligatory hand washing.

"Mark for me when you think the three times were," she says.

Mrs. Anderson makes three careful x's by the appropriate dates while Sunny turns aside on her wheeled chair and pours two cups of coffee from a pot left standing on a side table, snug in a cozy given by one of the knitting up-patients.

Mrs. Anderson takes sugar and is further pleased to sit like this, for the moment. It is early in the morning and she likes having a few minutes of quiet conversation. And also she and Sister Tutor have spoken between themselves about Sunny, as they do in fact about everyone, in their little living room. Both agree she lives too much in the professional way, too courteous and too removed, too reserved even here, where reserve is the norm. It's unnatural for an American. It could make her crazy, over time. They agree that she might benefit from interaction, especially here in the woods without access to outside friends. Because imagine, just imagine spending all your time up on that floor; she really shouldn't be willing to take those upstairs ladies seriously. They're patients, remember, not friends, and furthermore they are not, Mrs. Anderson might privately suggest, entirely normal.

Living here is not easy, they agree; Sister Tutor lived abroad, and even taught abroad for years and years, and she remembers that feeling of being foreign. She remembers the thrill, also the exasperation, but most of all she remembers coming back and seeing, with new perspective, that it can be very hard to make friends here.

"So," says Sunny, "why not lock the kitchen after a certain hour?"

"I lock some cupboards overnight already," says Mrs. Anderson, who like anyone at her level carries a ring of keys audibly on her person, and Sunny nods absently without asking which ones: anything resembling spirits, anything expensive, and the knives.

"You have your master key, then?" And Sunny has hers as well, not on her daily ring but on a heavy chain locked in her bottom drawer. She'll switch it over now.

Mrs. Anderson hesitates.

"Well, good-bye," she says.

Sunny, smiling distantly, nods and says, "See you."

Alone afterward, Sunny lifts her blotter and beneath it is the Suvanto plan. As an aid to memory she looks to think again of which centers are too populated all night, preventing passage by patients, looking, perhaps, with special attention at the routes one might take down from her own top floor. It was not possible to go invisibly past the lit nurses' stations in the centers of the wards, to the main stairs, during sleeping hours. Or possible, but not all that likely.

But there were stairwells used for the convenience of the staff at the far ends, and then, from the dining room, it would be easy to find the service passages to the kitchen. It could be done from any of the floors. Because, in deference to the winter, the buildings here are all internally linked, either underground or by covered walkways. All it would take to find them is determination and an urge to mischief, which have somehow never surfaced, not until now.

Meanwhile everything continues, as most have no choice but to continue; the wards downstairs are kept for proper medical cases, and one is only for patients requiring surgery. Many of those patients are treated by private doctors, but these are still difficult times, moneywise, both for indivuals and for institutions, and normal patients, meaning local patients, must usually sleep in the open wards rather than the privately subsidized rooms upstairs. Those who fall somewhere in between, economically speaking, can stay in rooms for five or six, snugged into metal beds close enough to touch one another with an outstretched hand. There are always some who have lucky surgeries and then sleep and sleep for a short time only, regardless of which ward they're in, until they're feeling better sooner than expected and then it's time to get up, bags all packed, the car waiting in the drive. Shake hands good-bye. And say thank you to the nurses. Or anyway this is what Sunny and the other foreign nurses see from the local patients. The American patients are more effusive in their hellos and good-byes; sometimes, they'll try to kiss the nurses.

With the local women, the Finnish women, Sunny tries to communicate warmth in less intrusive ways. Tries not to touch them too much. Tries not to interrupt them when they are speaking. A Finn won't interrupt you; an American almost certainly will, without even realizing, and so Sunny is careful, always careful. And she notices now, she can't help but notice and withdraw from the confident volume of the American voices. She's an American too, of course, and this is why she understands them in an instant, and why it is deceptively easy to relax, a little, when she is dealing with them. But they are a group, remember, while she is on her own.

Some less tough might not be ready to leave, and some could use more time to recuperate, but life intervenes, the money runs out, the patience at home runs out, the children want their mother back and then your husband starts to think that it's time to have a normal life again. The doctors schedule your day of discharge and talk to you about the important things, the specifics of your aftercare. If you're weak, the nurses hold your hands down the steps and to the car. Or someone will sit with you in reception until the bus comes right to the front door of the hospital, and of course your family will have ridden out to help you home.

But for those who stay longer, there is danger in getting accustomed to care. For the lonely foreign wives from the mill outposts, any long stay provokes a cultish mystique, an attachment to the place and the people one meets inside. Then trinkets are exchanged, locks of hair, a scrap of lace cut from someplace sentimental or a ribbon tied in a bow to commemorate a day when something was realized. Either that you would eventually get well and go back! Or that you would not get well very quickly and so nothing, nothing is expected of you! In the latter case, there is breakfast, there is lunch, there is dinner to look forward to, perhaps it will be fresh pork again, and cake with fruit, and cups of coffee in which cream is probably permissible. Some things are forbidden, for some, but leave it to the doctors and Anneli, the diet nurse, to say what's harmful and what's not. When you feel up to dining in the dining room, take your diet card with you. Observe the honor system and stick to the diet nurse's orders.

Departures and arrivals are normal, rotations don't trouble, but it is a real wrinkle in the fabric when something out of order repeats itself. Variations might well make up the routine here, man ministering to nature, watching the course of an infection, a decline, a swinging temperature . . . it is not possible to accurately predict for all eventualities . . . but the wrinkle of the episode of the secretly eaten herrings and ham and the secretively heated stove rises again and again in Sunny's mind like the selfsame tongues of flame. It could be the prank of a kitchen maid, maybe some girl resentful of her orders by day to clean it back to the original, a task given seriously as this was an excellent industrial-sized range, as new and stainless as in any of the hotels downtown, a focal point of sorts. Or was someone simply too hungry to sleep? But then why not clean up after, to hide the taking of the meat?

A nagging intuition suggests to Sunny that she knows someone with dipping moods, someone relatively new here whose sleep is often interrupted by uneasiness and nightmares. Someone who is always happy to be difficult.

"Tell me the truth, now, do you walk around at night?"

"No," says Julia, but with a defensive inflection that as good as says, *I might*.

She's in an old-fashioned but nicely cut black suit with a full, dragging skirt—where did it come from? In her wardrobe, as in her toilette, she is not quite typical, and there is something in the vanity of the hairpins, the face powder that hurts Sunny a little. Her own mother would be younger than Julia, though less lucky, and she had not left the house for a long time before she died. There had been no new suits, no hats, but there had been a box of powder, yes, powder with a puff in the drawer by the bed, in case a visitor ever came. Just in case. But that's enough. Sunny avoids these memories now. Plenty of time later, someday, when the distance of time might muffle the unbearable parts. What was the point of a life so wounded? Not fate, not a lesson of some kind, that's nonsense, and horrible and cruel. But if it was only an unlucky accident, then everything is only an accident, only a stark grid of cause and effect. And if that's the case, then nothing has meaning beyond the question of whether an event will cause pain; the only thing that can matter is to be free of pain, just as in the life of an animal, and to avoid causing or allowing unnecessary pain, which is the responsibility of humans.

This afternoon, like many others in these last few weeks, Julia has been out following the paths through the pines, around the meadows, or maybe out to an observation point on the rocky beach. She walks slowly. She stops, cane propped. Looks back at the trees. Looks up at the sky. With her cramped fingers she has stripped off a lighter green tip of that year's growth and pinned it, with a hat pin tipped in jet, to her fur coat, now showing a few dark licks of pitch. Her walking shoes (made in town for the swollen, broad-knuckled feet of older, outdoorsy ladies) have been brought upstairs against the rules and kicked into an untidy mess near her door. Robust green needles are sticking to the flat heels. How she hates the flat heels. But the days of higher heels have passed. Nurse Todd has taken them all away.

"You've been in the woods, I see," says Sunny.

"No I haven't," says Julia, turning away and filling a water glass at the small round sink in her room. She fumbles with the greenery and Sunny helps her take it off, puts it into the water glass where the water magnifies the pale, torn end. As Julia settles into a routine she collects souvenirs from the grounds: pinecones, sticks, and feathers that Nurse Todd wants to throw out because surely they harbor lice.

"I know you've been in the woods, silly. Look at your shoes."

Julia stares at her shoes, the nightmares of the previous night showing in her slow, dry, still heavily painted eyes.

"I'm not saying you shouldn't go out," says Sunny, gently. "Just stay on the paths, that's all. I wouldn't want you to get lost."

On her bureau, Julia keeps an enameled box especially for hat pins, with a velvet head inside for sticking. Sunny sinks the pin and squints, seeing there a butter knife lifted from the morning coffee service. And this is not the first time in these three weeks of adjustment that Sunny has found a butter knife hidden in Julia's room. Their bluntness and seeming harmlessness make them more sad than dangerous, and each time Sunny has simply removed them. Now Julia, looking at her from the mirror above the sink, smiles impulsively, without an explanation.

Ultimately, Sunny decides, this is her floor, and these are her patients, and suspicion of bad behavior is only a suspicion until proof appears. She leaves the butter knife (after discreetly verifying its bluntness once more against her thumb) and does not acknowledge it in words— why not preserve dignity, because it could have been, and probably has been, borrowed for some legitimate purpose, to open a letter maybe, or like when many of the ladies bring bread and even butter away from the table to be hidden in their rooms, where it usually grows stale in a drawer until the ward maids eventually discover and discard it. Sunny won't mention the knife or the nocturnal kitchen visits to Nurse Todd, who would happily and roughly ransack every possession in Julia's room given half a reason. She will maybe walk the passage, though, once in a while, maybe late at night, just to see if anyone else is up. And she double-checks the lockup of explosives: ether, naphtha, alcohol, oxygen. Of course it's not all the same thing. But these are the normal precautions.

And then one morning it is September already: *syyskuu,* meaning the fall month, when the trees begin to turn yellow and the days are full of light but growing shorter, moving slowly toward *syyspäiväntasaus,* the fall equinox. By the end of the month the paths might whiten overnight, and if that happens then soon afterward Kusti will set the young men pushing wheeled boxes along them to dispense gravel and salt. You can't, you wouldn't forbid the patients who are able to walk from doing so. It would be too cruel. And there are necessary paths that must be kept clear and safe, for example, those to the staff residences, the nurses' pavilion, and the row of houses where the doctors live with wives and children. These need to be cleared along with those on the other side leading to the main road. The Doctors and the Mrs. Doctors are of course under no obligation to stay in place. And soon Pearl Weber will be arriving back again, with her friend Laimi Lehti, and last year those two liked to walk to the beach in any kind of weather, or anyway Laimi did, whenever she could.

Work and attention to details of comfort are a constant in this life, and the ward maid who did the careless unpacking stands out in Sunny's vision, and this is evidence that Sunny, though she takes pains to appear impartial, can hold a grudge. On a few occasions she has now given this girl, this Marja, a talking-to out of proportion with the offenses committed. Today it is a less than heartfelt treatment of the flooring of the stairs. It is a surprise lecture, provoked by an ambivalent day outside that Sunny has not yet had time to walk out into, but through the windows and on the porch she's found the smell of ozone in the air, the promise of wood smoke and genuine cold as yet undelivered in the distance.

The girl is stinging silently now whenever Sunny addresses her. It is out of scale for Sunny to be quite so disappointed in the small shortcomings of the staff at any level, so it's clear that this comes from the earlier mistake. More ordinarily it is a small neutral correction offered, or a word about a better way to do a task. Of course she learned hierarchy at home in school, but it doesn't feel right here. She is embarrassed to be speaking English, for one thing, but she can't say what she wants to say in Finnish and they both know this. That the girl understands as much English as she does further embarrasses Sunny. Anyway, it is not like Sunny to register her disappointment before a nineteen-year-old ward maid, feeding the floor with an insufficient layer of paste wax. But other factors conspire.

"I don't believe this is what they taught you in housekeeping," she says, looking down at the floor, down at the girl, and then over to the window. They are paused together on an upper landing of the Buttermilk stair, the one the nurses use to avoid the wards when coming or going from any level of nursing supervisors' apartments. The stair separates the quarters of Sunny and others from their assigned floors by soundproof doors and broad landings, a wide light borderland with a thick rubbery linoleum floor much scuffed by the soles of quick shoes. But something else is happening too, something has been irritable in Sunny all day, a growling irritation that will spread itself through her to the girl and onward to anyone that the girl, so much lower on the staff, can find to take it out on in turn.

Sunny may be coming down with a slight fever, or may not have slept well, or both. Something is turning itself over within. She stands, crepe-soled shoes only inches from where the girl sits back now on her heels—it begins to penetrate that a strange minute is unraveling between them on the landing. Sunny is still looking out of the window. Sometime in the last few minutes the sky has begun to shed intermittent snowflakes, and now everything will stop momentarily.

And Sunny, with the square panes reflected on the profiled surface of her eye, looks confused, uneasy. Maybe she should be gentler toward Marja. But she has no idea how many young people are dead here now . . . Sunny thinks, am I on this landing again? Why do I feel I'm always pausing at this window? She touches her knuckles to the window and stands, looking out, allowing the cold from the other side of the glass to seep slowly into her hand. The Buttermilk stairs are drafty, more so than anyplace else in the building, a margin between the wards and privacy, and whenever she swings open the door and feels the chill here she remembers that her own rooms are close by, waiting, warm, quiet and comfortable. Is there any chance to go into them and rest for a spell, for a nap, maybe this afternoon? Maybe she can get away, even for half an hour, even for fifteen minutes . . . but then Sister Tutor comes in through the muffling door of the landing just below and calls up gleefully into empty space, "It's snowing!"

"Of course it is," says Sunny, down now to Marja as if the girl herself had spoken. "Use your judgment," she says. "Use it better than you have been." In passing on her way down to Sister Tutor—who, in her dark dress, is casting a shadow up the steps—Sunny rests her hand on the girl's shoulder by way of strange acknowledgment.

Not sure how to interpret, the girl pushes what she thinks is too much wax across the floor, which feels wasteful, but which is in actuality as much as Sunny wanted. In any case, she will eventually be moved to the needle room, where her new job will be to turn over faded or ruined linens into menstrual pads; worn out by the hot alkaline wash of the foul laundry process, these are constantly needed, as you can probably imagine.

Life here changes utterly with the snowfall. Or so they say. There is excitement when it first comes drifting into the air from a high blanket of cloud. It won't last, of course, this is just a brief hint of winter to come. Fall will be golden again tomorrow and the real snow is weeks away.

Nonetheless, in the Solarium they look to the windows. Some stand right against the glass, pulling their cardigans up around their necks. And some are laughing a little. And others are concerned: *Will they make us go out into it?* These include the delicate southern timber wives from other climates, and others blessed with weak chests, newly adjusting to the temperatures of autumn, the pressures of the towering northern sky.

They turn off the lights to watch the windows without reflection. The late afternoon seems beautiful, seems full of activity, and even the perennial darkness between the pressing pines seems to flicker with white movement.

"Will the saltwater freeze?"

"This will never stick, the ground isn't cold enough, give it a few more weeks—"

Step away from the cool glass of the windows now. The panel heaters are clicking softly. It will be comfortable because Kusti predicts the weather changing, from a stiff joint or from the barometer or from the almanac.

Kusti? A Finland-Swede, an engineer supervising the grounds, keeping up the boilers in another wing of the hospital complex. It is due to his attention, his adjustments to the heating inside that the first snow outside brings comfortable excitement, novelty, and a load of letters written home, especially if there are patients who've never seen snow before, those who have traveled here from warmer, duller places. It also brings relief and, in the beginning, increased sleep, for some.

For Julia, the cold, even when it is controlled, affects her toes, her poor circulation in evidence. Lying tenderly between the sheets while she sleeps under the ceiling heater, they are dark, a little thick, and they hurt. She sleeps deeply but not peacefully, separate from the institutional bed, which is just a bed and not her own bed, the pillow not her own either. She wakes during the night, sometimes a few times. She shifts her feet. She pushes the button in the wall beside her head so that a nurse will come to check.

"What is it, dear? Do you need something?"

"I'm cold," she might say. "My joints are so cold, I'm afraid my heart is going to stop." She speaks without lifting her head from the pillow, eyes to the ceiling. "I can hear my heart stopping. Call Nurse Taylor to come and see me."

"No, you'll see her tomorrow, go back to sleep, that's all you need."

But that little bell will ring and ring and ring all through the evening, continuing throughout the night, unless someone crosses the stair to find Sunny.

But falling, falling backward, Sunny herself has a talent for falling deeply asleep. A good sleeper, all of her life, preferring sleep to dinner if forced to choose, preferring sleep to an evening out, wanting a solid nine hours at a time (utterly impossible during the dreadful years of private duty), occasionally augmented by a snatched midafternoon catnap. Nursing is not the natural vocation for a good sleeper; your time will never again be your own. But now, recently, in the afternoons Sunny will increasingly drift away from Orvokki toward the sitting room attached to her bedroom, where anyone knows to find her if they need her, and from which she might, just might sometimes drift toward the actual bed, well-sprung and perfectly supportive under a padding of wool felt, as broad and comfortable as any she's ever slept on. Maybe she shouldn't. But privacy is available when she swings the muffled door to the Buttermilk stair, unlocks her apartment with the key, and locks it shut behind her. This is very different from the dormitories she briefly knew at school, before giving up even that small independence to move back home, into the familiar miasma of her mother's situation. This apartment, the physical separation, is a mark of responsibility, and she never fails to appreciate it.

So it is not peculiar she should be there now on the day of the first snow, standing on the oval rug and stepping out of her house shoes, then stretching against the blue wool bedspread, not even pausing to unfold the extra blanket at the foot, merely slipping her feet under to cover the line of a stocking's reinforced toe. On her back, she lifts her wrist above her eyes to find the silver-plated watch, still the same old graduation gift from her parents. The red hands indicate it is just after 5:00. Make that 17:00, it's a twelve-hour watch, not twenty-four . . . disorienting here when she wakes in winter's long darkness or summer's white nights. Especially later when the daylight hours will seem precious and so shrinkingly indistinct. She gently winds the watch, an every-evening habit. The back, pressed to the skin of her wrist, is engraved with a date and the words *Women's Medical College, Philadelphia*. Her mother had kept the graduation photo that was taken that day: Sunny in starched uniform with a new white apron, white stockings, white cap, hands held lightly at her waist, fingers interlaced. Like a wedding photo. More accurately, like the bridal half of a wedding photo.

The snow is coming down, and the year is slipping into a lower, working gear. She drops her wrist to the pillow above her head and sinks as into water, multicolored on the way down. There is a suspension palpable all around. But then you hear her breathing and know that all is well, at least on this side of the privacy doors.

Sister Tutor sends a junior nurse to look for Sunny. This nurse really doesn't want to disturb, but can't help it, she's been told to, and Sunny

has made it clear: *Anything strange, anything dramatic, come find me.*
The nurse knocks once, twice. And is surprised to hear the answering
voice from within startled, as if woken.

"Yes," says Sunny from her bedroom at the far side of the sitting
room, kicking off the blanket and crossing to the door. "What's wrong?"
she says. Her cap is off, her hair is covering her ears, and this may be a
different Nurse Taylor than most have previously seen, much younger
than we thought.

"Sister Tutor says she's sorry, but Julia's making trouble. She had a
nightmare."

Is that all? Sunny nearly says to go fetch Nurse Todd and let her sort
this out, but then looks again at her watch—a hundred times in a day,
the same gesture repeating, the fingers slack, the angle—and she says,
"It's already seven o'clock." But then, suddenly more awake: "Is it seven
in the morning?"

"No, miss," says the graduate, and wonders if she can smile. "It's
still tonight."

And for a moment Sunny had felt herself skipped ahead into the next
morning, but then pulled back into the different twilight of evening.

"All right," says Sunny. "I'll look in on her."

"Yes, miss," says the girl.

Evening, then, early, early for bed anyway, but then they try to tire
Julia out by day to keep her in her bed at night. Oh, yes, there have one
or two further suggestions that this might be a good idea, accidents,
one or two little ones.

"I guess I'm still in time for dinner," says Sunny, tucking her hair
back behind her ears. And the new nurse will never again be quite as
intimidated by Nurse Taylor as she was before, even if she ought to be.

"What's wrong now, Julia?" Sunny says, not for the first time.

Julia is lying on the bed in a black kimono-style dressing gown,
with the belt tied around her waist tightly, too tightly, knotted repeatedly into an unsalvageable mess.

"I can't breathe," says Julia. "I'm cold again."

"Cold joints are normal, remember, we talked about that," says Sunny. "It's a leftover feeling, from what made you sick before you got here."

And Sunny, woken and cynical, wonders why there seems to be no structure in Julia's bad behavior, why it seems that Julia makes up ideas for trouble out of whatever materials come to hand. Although, to be fair, her nightmares are clearly real. Sunny recognizes the look of residual horror that Julia conceals by looking down, and Sunny understands that the bad dreams are, in fact, not something Julia herself controls.

"Don't you remember what we had to do before?" says Sunny, meaning, *When you had to hold your breath so that I could cut the belt off with a pair of scissors? When you were so upset at ruining it, and afterward Mrs. Numminen or someone picked apart your knots and sewed your belt back together, but I told you I'd take it away if it happened again? Do you see that I brought the scissors with me, expecting this?*

"I know I'm going to have that dream," says Julia, in a quiet, unaffected voice that Sunny has rarely heard from her. "I feel that dream coming, about the man. Look." She holds up her hands, elderly in the air, trembling.

"You'll be all right," says Sunny, pushing aside the bedclothes. "It will be easy for you to sleep tonight. It's cozy, don't you think? Cozy enough to sleep in peace, when it snows." As she says this, a half thought flickers like a frame of film spliced into the room by mistake, a flicker of peace, of sleep, and of snow coming down to cover you. That's just a little excess short-term memory from the graveyard, of course, turning over in Sunny's brain, still present from her evening walk. Details from her time spent out-of-doors appear like this after she comes back inside, all the time. Sometimes it's the bay, or its frozen surface, a black sky, a pale foreground. The trees appear most often, though sometimes ephemeral things come back, too, such as when she saw wasps from the orchard crawling on the walls for weeks. Passing images that come and go, the same as for any of us.

"No," says Julia. "He'll be at the foot of my bed by midnight with a little ax in each hand." She exhales deeply, holding her breath when

Sunny slips a scissors blade under her belt and clips it in two, revealing large white underpants and nothing else as the dressing gown falls open. Sunny takes the belt away as threatened, but realizes that if Julia will not wear a nightgown, much less a bra, they will need some other solution. Not the bunnysuit; that's an empty threat. Mostly. Tonight it's not worth the argument of suggesting to Julia that she put on more clothing. Sunny pulls the bedcovers up and looks briefly at the chart; Julia's injection has already been given.

"Your hair's too tight as well, goose," she says, slipping a finger into Julia's topknot and pulling gently. And with the other hand, she offers tonight's solution, already accounted for in the orders: a genuine soother in a waxed white cup. The welcome smell of rotting apples.

"No dreams this way," says Sunny.

Julia lifts her hand, smiling, with a happy darkness opening between her teeth.

Five

Everybody takes *piirakka* for breakfast, hot and shining with butter across the dimpled surface, a thin wheat shell filled with rice or potato. They're Karelian pies, from Karelia, the lost part of Finland, the torn-out heart of Finland. It's a real part of Russia now. The Finns are gone, they've been relocated. Or you could say forced, removed, transferred, deported. Replaced by Russians. Nonetheless, *piirakka* make people happy here, taken with a chopped egg and butter on top, because with a cup of coffee they're the best reason to get out of bed. Breakfast without chopped egg is too simple and too thin to mark the break between being sleepy and being ready for fresh air and a stroll outside. Except Pearl Weber, not here yet, who will push away the butter dish without licking a greased fingertip. Just an egg, that's all for her. Or just un-buttered brown bread so dense and dark it's nearly black, nearly sweet, nearly bitter, nearly as if there were bits of unsweetened chocolate baked in, though there aren't.

Meals and fresh air punctuate the day, but arrivals and departures mark the passage of larger time. Some go and are not seen back again, it's true, but for others with the luxury of decision there are itineraries and the choice of when to come and take a rest and see the doctors, the staff, the other residents. This year, it seems that many of the up-patients will return with a permanent wave in their hair, having discovered that the Beauty Room at Suvanto is not really a salon, just a room with a barber's chair from which a girl offers the most basic of haircuts. A perm saves on headache since the humidity in the sauna can have surprising effects. Thank goodness for the girls down there who do manicures. Thank goodness it can be easy! Just show them your fingers . . . It's not really the Beauty Room, but the up-patients call it that because they cannot pronounce the real name, and they don't try: *Kampaamo.* They rename places to suit themselves, like the *Lepohuone,* literally the Resting Room. They call the *Lepohuone* the Green Room because of the potted plants that line the walls and windows, soft succulents and rubber trees, but also tall, spiky green spears called, in Finnish, mother-in-law's-tongue, but of course no one can pronounce that. Most retain only the words that sound a little more familiar: *laakrits* for licorice, *sukulaa* for chocolate, *kahvi* for coffee.

Mrs. Minder plans an arrival in red wool: skirt, shoes, jacket, and a cap that looks very nice on her newly curly hair. Has Mrs. Weber arrived yet? No? It's a pity she and the others aren't there to see Mrs. Minder being led by the orderly into reception with her red leather suitcases and shoes dyed to match. She shows the smooth clean soles to the charge nurse, meaning, *These are for wearing indoors!* Upstairs, she runs on the balls of her feet, darting, chick-like flights punctuated with disappointment in the doorways of certain empty rooms.

"Am I early?" she says. "It smells so clean here. I love hospitals!" But then, as she senses the emptiness, she turns in small circles of sadness. "Where's Pearl and everyone? I love them. I miss them. Do you think they love and miss me too?"

What to pack, what to bring, it was in fact the very root of hesitation though we didn't know it was true of Mrs. Weber. She always comes in *syyskuu*. This marks her as a foreigner; she doesn't realize or maybe doesn't care that summer is the best time of year here. In summer, Finnish families arrive and reopen summer cottages everywhere in the shifting green trees, on the rocky shores of the clear cold water, but the cottages are so discreetly situated on the islands, on the coast, on the shores of the lakes that even from a boat you might not see them, might miss them except for the docks and the small moored boats. And there are the meadows for picnics and for picking berries and mushrooms, the forests for walking, the inlets and the lakes for swimming, provided one can withstand the mosquitoes, of course. The lakes are lovely for strolling around and then for taking naps beside on wool summer blankets under the deep, sunny sky. The locals quietly appreciate a good hard winter—of course!—but they don't fully understand why others might come *only* for the winter, when the summer is as it is.

Pearl Weber, though, has been traveling elsewhere with William, and Miss Lehti has come to meet them in Helsinki, having accepted William's kind invitation, well, more accurately, having agreed to his veiled request to travel northwest together with Pearl. Because they're great friends, aren't they, these two women! William thinks so. He assumes they are. Why wouldn't they be? He'd been introduced to Laimi during Pearl's first winter at Suvanto, and, over the course of the season, he'd inititated a comfortably distant conversational exchange with her, in Finnish, at an appropriately leisurely pace determined by the infrequency of his visits. Laimi had been quite cordial; this had somehow reassured him of the appropriateness of Suvanto for Pearl. He was pleased, relieved, that she'd made a Finnish friend for herself. *And how is Miss Lehti?* he would ask in his letters. *Is Miss Lehti still there?* And Pearl, as an investment in William's good opinion of the place, would reply, *Oh yes, funny you should ask! We just took a little walk together. Laimi and I often step out for a little fresh air.* It was the sort of ongoing fib that kept everybody happy. Except Laimi, unaware that she and Pearl were becoming such intimates.

Mr. Weber was upstanding, Laimi had determined, and he was, in a distant sense, a co-worker, if one considers that they both, technically, work for the timber concern. So there is this mingling of a personal invitation with a professional invitation, and the only correspondingly decent response is to accept his offer/request, with polite thanks, since clearly the man needed help with his wife. Laimi, understanding belatedly, will not disabuse him of his incorrect estimation that she and Pearl are friends. Or might ever become friends. And naturally she won't do him the grave insult of repudiating his offer of hospitality, either. She has to go back to Suvanto, anyway, more's the pity. She is perfectly capable of traveling there on her own. Pearl, however, is less capable. In light of which, yes, they can go together.

Thank you, Miss Lehti.

Don't mention it.

Pearl likes to take enough time before departure to finger what the shops might offer in the way of clothing. She does not care for wallpapers, fabrics, and furnishings, all of which she used to love; she's disengaged her attention from their company house. It's mostly only a repository now for old ideas, for clothing that no longer fits. Who cares anymore about the house? Well, William cares. She doesn't.

What do you love now?

I love to love myself, it is my prerogative to do so.

Pearl is a pretty woman. She smiles at her reflection and her face is meticulous in clinging powder, her cheeks peony-pink. Her lips are careful, coral, and from a distance do not divulge their actual shape under the liner and the lipstick.

To love to love oneself is possible in shops far removed from the reeking horror of steel traps and the cruelty of cages grown rusted and sticky with bloody resin, and in the weeks before her arrival Pearl had been sliding her arms into the cool tunnels of satin-lined fur coats. Her hands had been overly warm for days despite the calming efforts of cooling lotion but somehow the languid action of shopping was the main thing to make her feel more comfortable; it psychologically cooled her to cock various fox hats, to see their colors with her own coloring. She felt arctic. She wanted to be smothered in blond fox and black fox.

She was helped in and helped out, in the hot showroom of August, in the warmth of *elokuu* (the month of the harvest of course) by a gentleman with correct posture and dry but complimentary behavior. There are no other customers and he appears to subtly, distantly enjoy holding open the coats, lifting the hats with both hands. This is the way Pearl likes to be appreciated. She sits before a row of artificial heads on the counter, featureless to accentuate the hats, which he lifts down onto her blond waves one by one, culminating in a puff of bleached pink fox and she says, *No, it's really too much . . . my head looks absolutely tiny inside, don't you think . . . but then again . . .* She turns her head and looks into the triple mirror, turning, examining herself in a way that is not exactly sly, but sidelong, certainly, to try to see herself as others will, later, against the backdrop of winter. She adjusts the panels of the mirror to find herself in true profile. The hat more than doubles the silhouette of her head, but she mostly only sees her own face, unfamiliar and intriguing because she is looking away, and all that fur is merely the boost of a flattering frame. She doesn't feel the absurdity of so much more fur than face, or that, from behind, the hat above her collar is as roundly unruly as an allium gone to seed.

"Yes," she says, "this is the one."

The salesman inclines his head, maybe in agreement.

Yes, the pink fox, a pink fox lined to disguise its own papery pulling skin rolled away and hidden now but nonetheless hugging her skull through a layer of clinging satin liner, emanating into her late-summer hair a smell of—is it recognizable, this smell of fur, as something other than fur? The thin beige odor of desiccation. The salesman lifts the pink fox away from Pearl's head with the smallest twitch of revulsion as her hair clings to it, falling damply back against her suddenly humid forehead.

The pink fox makes her think of so many places that she would like to see . . . someday, when she is less physically uncomfortable, perhaps . . .

Shopping afterward for the fingers: a yellow sapphire, a blue ruby, an amethyst that at first seems altogether too brown, too much the color of tea at the heart, but that finally charms her anyway, and a citrine, and a peridot, and, best of all, amber. White amber, green amber, yellow amber, lovely Russian and Baltic amber washed up on the tumbling rocky shores. One little polished globular pendant with a very small, very ancient mosquito embedded inside. Ha! For the throat: variegated beads of garnet, amber, tourmaline, pearl. Pearl! She turns her head before the mirror, she knows her throat is flattered by these, knows her throat to be quite beautiful because it is unlined and well preserved. And this is because she takes care of herself, because she does not, has not for years slept with her head on a pillow because pillows will ruin the neck, will pleat the skin into folds like a sheet of used tissue paper found wadded in the morning.

And for the breast: an ornament on a gleaming pin, a blue cameo, a classical face in profile, with a pointedly feminine jaw, suspiciously similar to her own.

Over cold sliced sausage and cheese Pearl rounds down the prices to coax Laimi into agreeing that each purchase, based on merit, is not an outrageous expenditure. Laimi nods, politely, entirely without interest. Pearl has been told about the lean times, the civil war, she remembers something about a white party and a red party, the Russia problem, and some diseases; it has been mentioned to her more than once that tens of thousands of Finns have died within memory from illness and from ideological conflict. She shouldn't have to be told that most Finns are not wealthy, even though most people work hard and often. Laimi herself wears no jewelry at all. Laimi herself works and works, Laimi has been at her desk in the planning office for many weeks and she would be there now, if she wasn't destined for Dr. Ruotsalainen's radiography treatments, again. But Laimi says nothing of any of this now.

"Oh Lummi, guess what stone this is."

"Amethyst," she says, and is correct.

In the evening Pearl in the cocked pink fox sits on William's knee and must listen to the descriptions he gives Laimi of some new log being peeled for veneer, of what the clipperman does with clippings, of how a conveyor belt should shunt lumber, of what the green chain made of men does next. Her skull gently sweats while she fingers her beads and wishes ardently that William would shut up and stop talking, soon, please, and that Laimi will not ask any more questions, wishing and wishing until he sees her boredom and kisses her knuckles. He calls her a little czarina. She laughs, overturns a small table with her foot, and orders vodka. Perhaps she will have had the good grace, under the circumstances, not to do this in front of Laimi, perhaps she will have remembered at least vaguely that there are complicated bad feelings about the looming neighbor to the east— and Laimi's two brothers in the Finnish army, after all. Or perhaps Laimi has already excused herself and gone into another room, with a swishing, diminishing sound, disappearing to write a letter or two, in Finnish, of course. She'd have written in Finnish anyway, but especially now, having seen Pearl looking at the pages once, uninvited. If she refers to Pearl in letters she calls her Helmi, also a woman's name, also meaning, of course, pearl.

"Read to me in Finnish, Lummi, please."

"I don't see why, Pearl. You could listen to Finnish any time, if you wanted to."

Pearl persists, though, and so Laimi obliges, a few words anyway, a brief commentary on the size and shape of the hat, wryly enough to startle a chortle out of William, which was indeed her intention.

Pearl, laughing, not having understood, says, "Maybe you can teach me a little."

Laimi doesn't try. She doesn't see the point of reminding Pearl that the accent falls on the first syllable in spoken Finnish, because she's already been told so, to make it easier for her to at least pronounce people's names correctly. She won't even try the Finnish r, rolling and deep, admittedly a challenge for foreigners. And most likely Pearl doesn't know that there are two versions of Finnish, the spoken and the written. Why would she? Laimi politely says only, "It's a difficult language to learn, I'm told."

"Oh, everyone says that."

"There are fifteen cases in Finnish," says William.

"Really? Is that a lot? I have no idea what that means."

William stays awake longer than the women. He goes down to the bar in the hotel, comes back hours later. He is not drunk, just comfortably filled with Estonian stout, and he sits on the edge of the bed. He puts a hand on Pearl's sheeted shoulder. The heat of his hand wakes her. He wants to tell her something.

He says, "Pearl. I love you."

She is sleepy in the bed, sleepy in her nightgown, and wants to affect being sleepier still. *Go away, William.* But she says, in a faint voice, that she loves him, too. And she does, of course she does, but what she feels, mostly, is a dread particular to moments such as this. She is almost gone, almost away; please, in the meantime, please don't ask me for anything, William. Please don't insist on waking me, don't try to kiss me, and please, don't come looking for anything else, either. Because I want to sleep, and I'm looking forward to sleeping alone after tomorrow, in my own small room where I won't feel guilty for having nothing much to say to you.

He bends to take off his shoes. He stops with his hands on his ankles. Blood rushes to his shaven cheeks, pads his voice. In the darkness he says, "Can you tell me, Pearl, why do you love me?"

It is not meant as a trick, getting her to make the declaration so that then she must explain herself, and if it has that effect he doesn't know it. Soon she will be leaving for Suvanto, and they will not see one another for several weeks. Instead of being impatient with him now she answers, but carefully; she is momentarily afraid of being unable to answer. She is afraid of not having any reasons at hand, yet those she manages, more awake now, are actually true: good, kind, patient, generous William who sees the best in people. So that is something to be glad of. And he must recognize some truthfulness too because then he takes off his other shoe, and then his pants, and once he is in bed he says, "I'm sorry. I didn't mean to put you on the spot."

He draws her into an embrace, kisses her good night, and then he falls asleep. And though a moment before she had felt afraid of being exposed as an empty heart, she almost immediately falls asleep too. This is what she will remember when she looks back, after going away from him: this brief success, this partial communication.

September as the time for arrivals is a pattern from school days, and there is a sense of expectation, the beginning of the unknown . . . though it has two sides, this expectation. Because, after all, what is being anticipated? The return to Suvanto of those who've left for summer, of course, who now come back with new stories, new anecdotes. But after that? The winter, the snow, the cold that will extend until the end of March or April or May—there was even a spring blizzard not too long ago. The feeling is deceptive, it is a sense of expectation culminating in no real event, leading only into a long period of anticlimax against which some will struggle without realizing where the small, aching disappointment or the fear of futility comes from: from the air itself, from the chilly granite underfoot that erupts through the soil in places, hinting at massive unseen layers.

Some feel winter approaching already. Previously, in the quiet late summer evenings, some of our number taught each other new patterns for knitting or embroidering, and a small, committed group of them continue and continue to keep their hands busy with their needles now. It's a reasonable habit, one they can pick up and take anywhere, and some sit down by the windows hardly looking at what their hands have begun earlier during afternoons before the chill, afternoons spent in the sun with eyes closed behind blue sunglasses. They've already long since begun to lay in stocks of socks, scarves, mittens. Some will be worn, some will be given as gifts, and some will always be donated. During the war, some of these ladies—the Finnish ladies—made and rolled untold scores of bandages with the same restless fingers. The deep showcase in reception has in past months held examples of crafts, a selection of samplers and cozies. Now in September it contains a light yellow shawl for baby, on a stuffed paper model so that it resembles an impossibly upright shrouded newborn, like a featureless little phantom pinned out behind the glass.

The Dr. Webers arrive in September just a few weeks before the sticking snows that will come this year in the dirty month of *lokakuu,* or October, which is too bad but not serious because they've come in permanence, and will see the summer next year, presumably? He has been here already before, Dr. Peter Weber, he's had previous thoughts of joining the staff, of bringing Mrs. Dr. Peter and the children into the community, if it seemed a good opportunity for him, in the specific outline of his larger plan. These years are quickly passing, full of change. Dr. Peter can do things now that would not have been possible a decade ago; he has more or less perfected the idea of a new type of uterine stitch, for example, using catgut inside, silk outside, that will save the lives of many women, many mothers, after cesarean sections. William Weber is the connection, of course, the reason Peter comes to Finland now. For research. And practice. In a quiet place. The stitch will be named for them both: a Weber stitch. It will be a good thing. He is confident of this.

They have been given the second doctor's villa, a pine house behind a dense black thicket that tumbles in a long dark line along the grassy slope toward the path. It is a calm house, with a long rectilinear face and two round dormer windows closely set into the hipped roof, between four square, dark chimneys. And below, a deeply sheltered porch.

The patients do not come this close to the house, not legitimately. It is a relatively private property, off-limits, unfortunately for those who are curious about how authority lives in private. And who among us isn't? When the doctors are away, inside the clinical wing during the day, it doesn't hurt to try for a glimpse of that other daytime life, the one unspooled by their wives, their children, the life that ticks along, parallel to ours, yet awfully different. Their premises are separated from the hospital complex by a modest wooden fence and gate that is left unlocked, at least in the beginning, but its presence is a gentle reminder to us to observe the separation, to turn aside when strolling. The gate is on one of two paths connecting the doctor villas and the row of junior doctor houses to the hospital proper, a path that winds through the trees and more dividing, screening thickets, and is the route the doctors' wives might take if they are coming down for some special event, like a Christmas party, or something with a similar charitable feeling. There is another way, a second way, evidence of discreet convenience, a covered walkway with a pitched roof leading from the villas on their subtly higher ground. This walkway terminates at the private, sheltered rear entrance of the clinical wing, which is locked in the evenings, and for which each physician carries a key. This walkway can only be taken to and from the private clinic door, and if you cannot find the private door then you cannot find the second path to the villas; there is no other way of access unless by climbing up a ravine through dead leaves and sharp broken stones, and taking hold of the wooden handrail, and heaving oneself over . . . but why would anyone ever do that? If one was bent on getting to the villas one would naturally take the obvious path, toward the politely unlocked obstacle of the gate and the gentle climb up and around the bend.

Continuing hierarchy, more subtle here than elsewhere because it is suggested by the natural landscape: the first doctor villa, which is the house of the medical superintendent, is the highest on the residential hill, though all of the residences are situated with pleasing prospects. Laimi and the other staff architects of the company did what seemed natural to them and no resident need now look directly down into another's windows; the goal in the Finnish forests is to never see a neighbor's house, except by intention, and the trees and thickets make this possible. The bedrooms are generally placed with windows to the southeast, the pantries to the north to borrow cold, and one might at most see a bit of kitchen window glinting on a sunny day. Maybe, if one was walking near enough, Mrs. Dr. Peter there, decanting boiled drinking water to remove the minerals before making Dr. Peter and herself a cup of coffee. And maybe this scene, the arm lifting, the pitcher of water, is only visible because of recent changes, because the original hedge would have given better privacy, as well as serving the second purpose of reducing wind problems on that side of the house. But Dr. Peter, newly arrived now and happy in the autumnal sun, having only visited in summer and speculating about the darker months to come, has insisted that Kusti tear out some of the hedge.

Mrs. Dr. Ruotsalainen, in the villa above, purposely does not look down as Dr. Peter blights the layout. Dr. Ruotsalainen agrees; he is partially deaf now, but so well grounded that he pulls unspoken words out of the air quite easily. And so that evening he steps outside and lights his pipe. Without looking, he sees that Kusti's workers, gone for the day, have left behind a raw hole and a pile of splintered roots dug out of the soil. He knows that he can see Dr. Peter through the window, drinking his coffee, and so he stands and stares the other way, and smokes, until Dr. Peter feels obliged to look at him. And then Dr. Ruotsalainen turns further away and looks out in another direction, offering only the side of his head. And this seems somehow aggressive to Dr. Peter, at odds with the apparent shyness he has been told to expect from his Finnish colleagues. He stands and waits for his chance to nod in greeting, but still Dr. Ruotsalainen stares off into the distance, and smokes, and although he looks neither comfortable nor uncomfortable he will not go away, so that Dr. Peter steps outside also, wanting to be polite, but also wanting to find out what is happening; he has a lot to do in the next few weeks, and hopes he won't have to respond to this kind of thing very often, this feeling of having stepped on toes without realizing. Not that he has a problem with getting along. But getting along with his colleagues isn't why he's here, and he'd rather not spend too much time trying.

"It's very private here," Dr. Ruotsalainen says quietly. He points with the stem of his pipe at the trees, then puts it back in his mouth, but not stupidly so, not that way at all.

"We're trying to capitalize on the sunlight," says Dr. Peter, though Dr. Ruotsalainen certainly can't hear him at that range.

The next day the work is halted. Kusti's workers, working slowly, expecting to be intervened upon, will now have just the one patch of hedge to replace. But winter is coming and the replacement corner of the hedge will fail to thrive once it is replanted, and the leaves will wither and hang so that the corner continues to impose itself. ("*Voi Jumalauta,*" says Mrs. Dr. Ruotsalainen, privately: *God Almighty, what a fool.*) The Peters will hear the wind picking at the side of the house in consequence and can also see, from one corner, the gate, and occasional patients walking along the path, pausing and looking up at them, or sometimes lingering in the trees as if hiding.

For just a little while longer the upstairs corridors will be underpopulated and conversation will lapse into periods of quiet. It is so nice like this. The water of the bay is compellingly dark blue in the background, three shades deeper than the sky, one shade deeper than the islands in the distance.

There is ample time now to follow Julia, who sleeps by day but not by night, who fidgets her snakeskin gloves until they peel, who writes frequent, clandestine letters to Mr. Dey. She goes up to the outdoor promenade to sit in a reclining chair and to watch the grounds, to watch the paths and the beach where water seethes on stones. She often watches those who walk below, where the beach path is suitable for the slow perambulations of invalids, packed tight enough for the wheels of wheelchairs. Sometimes she stands at the rail with her cane, made even more public now after a near fall on the steps. She clicks it against the railing, irritatingly.

She has made herself unpopular by pushing Mrs. Minder in the buttocks with the dirty end of this rubber-toed cane, pushing and prodding her enough times that Mrs. Minder felt obliged to complain to Sunny. Julia says she couldn't help herself, that Mrs. Minder was staring and staring at the cane, trying to embarrass Julia, her rude behavior calling for some kind of answer; furthermore, says Julia, Mary Minder sometimes follows her around, even outside, even on her walks, and this makes her feel extremely uncomfortable. She never knows if Mary might be creeping up on her, at any time. The others have not learned to appreciate Julia's sense of humor, and she knows this.

"Mrs. Minder is probably lonely," says Sunny. "Has it occurred to you that she wants be your friend?"

"No," says Julia.

She comes to Mrs. Minder's room to leave a note on the pad of paper stuck there for messages, something cryptic in place of the conciliatory conversation that Sunny has suggested. Mary Minder opens the door quickly. She sees the pencil in Julia's hand and, confused, lets her in with a nervous little cry of "You can't smoke in here!" And yet there is a small odor of cigarettes from Mary Minder herself.

"Why not?" says Julia.

"It's against the rules."

What she means is that although she will sometimes sneak a self-conscious cigarette outside or on the promenade, she will never again sneak one in her room, and this is because she has—accidentally!—started two small fires in the bedding, one at home and one here last year, and now she worries that no one trusts her.

"But you're breaking the rules anyway, even if you smoke outside," says Julia.

"Not exactly," says Mary Minder, brushing her gauzy hair, stone blond, same color as the sand Kusti scatters in the snow. "I'm on my best behavior, aren't you? Good intentions count, don't they? I mean, we're all doing our best."

Julia takes the better chair, rests her chin on her cane, resisting the urge to leave a dark bull's-eye print on Mary Minder's forehead, below the place where she is brushing and brushing her hair. And the more she stares, the more Mary Minder brushes, as if brushing will speed Julia out the door.

"Go to lunch!" she says finally. "Please go to lunch."

"Why? So that you can follow me down to the dining room?"

"Just go!"

"Tell me why you follow me."

"No reason. I get bored, that's all."

"Boredom is the mark of a small mind."

"Well you're a small—you have a small—" says Mrs. Minder, grop-ing. "You have a small head, and a small appetite!"

"Well spoken, Mary," says Julia. "You've hurt me deeply."

Mrs. Minder says something, quietly hissing under cover of the hairbrush.

"I can't hear you," says Julia.

"I hope you die," says Mrs. Minder.

"That's what I thought you said," says Julia, smiling.

With the cane Julia walks along the curving corridor, takes the stairs down to the dining room. She likes to look at the photographs on the walls: the founding medical superintendent. The benefactor. One of the original site before construction, and beside it an aerial view of the hospital complex, curving along the coastline. Also, the brownish framed copy of a building sketch—the facade, the familiar front steps—lettered in careful, professional block script. She whistles between her teeth, a small sound. Sunny withholds judgment but she knows, sometimes this is happiness, this passive acceptance, and sometimes it is the beginning of decline. In the daytime notes she records: spirits, mostly good. Though the same cannot be said in the night notes. Howlers, writes Sunny. Increasingly frequent nightmares of a man standing at the foot of the bed, holding a four-foot knife pointed toward Julia, and the knife, she says, the knife has two distinct tips.

"Like this," Julia says at night, demonstrating with her fingers, though her joints are thickened and cannot point as she intends. The ruby rings need cleaning but will not come off. She sits in bed, sipping a sleep aid and pointing, pointing to mimic the knife.

"He stood where you are now," she says.

"Did you have these dreams before you came here?"

Julia weighs the question, guessing that her answer will affect her credibility.

"Not quite the same," she says, sipping.

Saturday afternoon, and Sunny takes her bicycle out onto the paths, as she normally does, heading away from the building for the sake of air and exercise. She slows down to cross one of the service lanes, looking both ways for safety; the trees are thinner here, affronted, maybe, by the passing of occasional delivery trucks. The scant sunlight has starved the lower branches, and she can tell that there are clearings nearby, open spots that have been cut and maintained. She can hear someone chopping wood close at hand in one of them.

There is a quick flash of color down the lane as she passes, scarcely seen. Unexpected, though normal enough. People work down there. And it must be awful work. She won't ride that way. The lane passes through the outbuildings, too near the clinging, bilious atmosphere of the pig barn and its stink of liquid excrement that not even the pines can filter from the air.

But Sunny rarely sees anyone on foot this far from the yard. She stops, backs up. The coat and hat had been red.

"Mrs. Minder?" Sunny calls, and gets no answer.

She rides on, but it troubles, and in a few minutes she turns back. The sound of chopping from the clearing has ceased, and she hears nothing when she pauses except boughs moving, brushing together.

She pushes her bicycle down the lane, face pinched in preparation for the smell, but there is nothing, only wood smoke, which makes her pause again; in such quiet the sounds of fire stand out, hissing, as from greenish wood, and the smoke grows stronger as she walks. Sunny props her bike against a tree and steps into the shade, onto a footpath, walking suspiciously over soft needles.

The clearing is unexpectedly close, and immediately she sees—not Mrs. Minder, but Julia, with her back to the lane, cane in one gloved hand and the other steadied against the rough bark of the nearest tree. She is looking out into the clearing, where there is a traditional log smokehouse, its door standing open, and a man, working alone, keeping warm beside an outdoor fire. He wears the same kind of sturdy blue coverall that Kusti wears, but with a full apron tied over, and this is spotted, because he's busy cutting meat on a makeshift board-and-sawhorse table.

A pig, and particularly a sow, and particularly one watched from behind while it walks, is burlesque in the way of a zaftig and very naked lady, because of the rump, of course, and also because of the way that the thighs touch, mincing on hooves that are not unlike small, fancy shoes. There is also, similiarly, the striking approximation of a human smile on the face of every pig, even a slaughtered one hung upside down by the hocks: the small eyes close tight in mirth and the mouth hangs open in a pleasant expression made worse by the color of the face, which, in its pallor, approximates the color of Nordic human flesh.

The cold carcass of such a pig hangs upside down from an iron frame beside the man's table, already bled and chilled and emptied of viscera. The man stoops to shift a slab of meat from the table onto his shoulder and takes it into the smokehouse. His eyes pass over the place where Julia stands, but without marking her, particularly; it's not the first time she's been there, watching. The fire in the fire pit makes a merry sound, steaming, and another column of smoke rises straight as a string from the chimney. A cat crouches comfortably beside the doorway, watching for the odd scrap of fat, which the man will often toss and the cat neatly consume, leaving only a damp spot behind on the sill.

The man comes back out, takes up his hatchet, and slides apart the hooks. He steadies the carcass, one hand in the cavity. As it turns, it reveals repellently familiar wrinkles in the usual places—the back of the pig's neck; under the short, hanging arms; and between the upended legs, now spread in an attitude of violence. The man lifts the hatchet and rests it, blade down, just there, moving the tail out of the way for accuracy, or delicacy, and with his other hand he raises a mallet and brings it down hard, making Sunny flinch, though Julia doesn't react. The blade sinks into the rump and stops at bone, and he hits it again, repeatedly, splitting into the pelvis, cutting down through the spine. He pauses to trade his grips and the body slowly butterflies open. The pig's head and neck are sturdy, but then the back of the skull gives way and only the fleshy, elongated face remains intact and connected. When the face is sundered the animal will no longer be an animal; with the last blow the pig will disappear and meat will hang instead. He taps gently through the cartilage of the snout, and then the two halves move independently, swinging and bumping haphazardly.

In cross section the body is surprisingly vivid, all pink and red and laced with white ribbons and pale chambers like a valentine or a split pomegranate. The head is full of tightly packed stuff, pearly, fresh, the jawbone lean, white, and very long. Buried in the sliced red meat of the cheek is a pattern of something pale—teeth?

The man lifts one of the sides and drops it heavily onto the table to portion out, some to smoke, some to send to the kitchen fresh, and a bucket of scraps for sausage. He tosses something more to the cat, the same cat that once hung around the back door of the kitchen. It cleans its face, rubbing and rubbing, until the man tosses it another scrap, and the cat breaks off, staring, already full.

Julia has been chewing something as she watches. It's candy, and she puts another piece into her mouth, dropping the foil wrapper at her feet among half a dozen others. As she does so she looks back over her shoulder.

"Smoked ham for Christmas," she says.

There is sudden laughter, and Sunny sees the red wool coat of Mrs. Minder in the clearing, a hundred yards from Julia but with her back to the trees, her mittens to her mouth, laughing, staccato, like a bird. The man glances at her, and then ignores her, until she throws a pinecone into his fire, scattering sparks. He speaks to her severely in Finnish and points the way back to the path, his face serious but unreadable.

"He's pointed twice now," says Julia. "I hope he hits her with the hatchet next."

Sunny wants to turn and be gone, back to the bike, leaning where she left it. But she feels pinned, perfunctory.

"Come away from there, Julia," she says.

"No," says Julia. "I'm watching out for Mary Minder."

"You're making fun of Mrs. Minder. It isn't very nice of you."

"She's enjoying herself."

"Did you bring her out here?"

"Not really. She followed me. I can't help that."

Julia, realizing Mary was behind her, had no doubt purposely changed her path, leading to a place with fire, a place of trouble. If

Mary gets burned, it's Mary's own fault, of course, but Julia will have helped.

"Maybe you can't help that, but you know better than to come out here," Sunny says. "You shouldn't walk this far from the building."

"Why not?"

And yes, why not? The up-patients aren't forbidden to walk the grounds. Yet for a moment Sunny weighs, with detachment, the difficulties of forcing Julia to go with her, the compelling, the pulling, the kicking, probably, and Mrs. Minder crying, no doubt, and for what? She passes a hand over her eyes, confused; she can't locate a reason for even considering this.

"I hope you aren't here when I check back in an hour," she says, but only because she feels that she must say something.

"Or what?" says Julia, amused.

Sunny rides away, down the path, as first intended. Her time outside in the midday air has been spoiled, though, and part of her attention drifts up from the path again and again. An hour, she has promised herself an hour. She takes the hour. She is at pains to take the hour. And then she turns back, rides past the lane, sees nothing, hears nothing, rides on, and eventually circles the hospital building, coming to a halt at the front entrance. She parks her bike and steps inside just long enough to check the book. Julia, Mrs. Minder, both signed in, a few minutes apart, Julia first, even given her slow pace compared to the red wool darting and rushing of Mary Minder. But then maybe she'd stayed longer, throwing more cones into the fire, not understanding when she was told to leave. And laughing, probably still laughing, not understanding the cultivation of boundaries—she has none—how could she understand that she wasn't welcome?

Sunny sees Mrs. Minder in the foyer that evening, and for a moment is obliged to stand with her among others waiting to enter the dining room. But nothing will come of it, no mention will be made, because even if Mrs. Minder had been aware of Sunny there, in the smokehouse meadow, she might not really remember, because Mrs. Minder lives in the moment, so close behind the glass of her own eyes that she has no distance to make use of, no perspective from which to contemplate, and so, as in the lives of animals, she just continues in her circles, in her routines, one day vanishing endlessly into the next without having registered in the first place.

"What's for dinner?" she says, stretching to see the specials.

Mrs. Minder, you ought to know already, but you don't, and this is proof.

The weather changes gradually, pressing an entire week of days down and down with the muggy pressure of a yellow washcloth, compacting toward thunder. It does not feel like a normal autumn, but it never does. Everything feels suspended, and so Pearl's arrival is a surprise, even though she's been expected, all this time. Much of this life has hung suspended, waiting for her, and now everyone is delighted, so delighted to see her. She is perspiring and uncomfortable in her nylons and shucks them off immediately in the lobby, waving them in the air like a skin-colored scarf.

"Hello, Sunny," she says. "Miserable weather, isn't it? I'd even prefer rain."

"It'll change," says Sunny.

If you weren't watching Sunny you would have missed the pained flush in her cheeks—uncontrolled and out of character—when she greets Pearl, and then Laimi, who stands slightly back. But then Laimi reaches forward, touching hands briefly with Sunny, a firm handshake, a nod of acknowledgment that says, *I acknowledge you, but nothing more.* It could be the memory of the misunderstanding between herself and Laimi in the summer. But maybe not, you'd never know, and the two are perfectly cordial; they will always be cordial, and whatever tensions passed between them remain unmentioned, because self-control and silence are the bywords of comfort for both.

Six

Mood is fed by climate, and everyone knows what happens in a closed environment when moods run unchecked by personal discipline. There has finally been thunder, audible through the panes of glass even if muffled by the concrete walls, and there has been lightning, high and far off, seen from the Green Room windows. Some hope it is the northern lights, but no . . . no one ever seems lucky enough to catch them here. This is only a sudden storm and a smell of ozone souring the milk in all the pitchers, leaving a thin, acidic odor of sadness rising from the coffee cups. But at dinner the rain adds some excitement, a little something to complain about.

Pearl is wearing a new dress, long and pleated, the slightest bit Grecian. She is telling a story to those sitting at her table about a rain forest, and endless rain, and inconveniences, and then abruptly about something else entirely, something seen in a museum, she can't remember where. Anyway, it was a necklace of shimmering green beetle carapaces from some Polynesian island, which contributes to the delight of Mrs. Minder, who has taken the seat beside her.

"On the neck?" says Mrs. Minder, making a show of brushing the idea away from her own neck. "Would you actually wear beetles up there on the neck?"

"Just here," says Pearl, tickling with one finger so that Mrs. Minder squeals.

At another table Julia chews the pale meat of her dinner. She is aware of Pearl, a stranger, and of the noises that Mrs. Minder makes. She notices when Pearl stops in midsentence, gratified by the sounds of Mary's laughter, but then, in time, she also notices that Pearl is slightly less gratified by their seemingly random distribution. Julia stares down at her plate, posing in an unflattering angle, the flesh of her jaw hanging and heavy. What's wrong now? Is she unsettled by thunder? Or annoyed by beetles? Maybe she doesn't care for the food? Or maybe Julia, now accustomed to the routine of the place, resents the sudden change, the sudden sparkling at the next table over. Pearl makes Mrs. Minder laugh and Mrs. Minder's laughter is loud and unforced. Julia waits with a mouth full of meat. She can't seem to swallow. She'll probably spit it into her napkin, which wouldn't be out of character.

Pearl says, "And the whole time I expected them to put out their hairy legs and scuttle away. You simply wouldn't believe they were dead, they were just too shiny and too beautiful."

Julia lets her head sink down onto one shoulder in a way peculiar enough to call attention. And then the others see that hot, thick tears suddenly fall from Julia's eyes and darken the shoulder of her green blouse, and that her mascara is leaving multiple black pollutions on her face. Such outbursts! They happen, they surely happen and she's not the only one, and what can be done, anyway? But the trouble here now is the contagion of these tears. Those seated with Julia stop talking to one another. Some go on eating, even if embarrassed, but find their own throats similarly constricting with the sudden grief, the sympathy. They are feeling second-best. Each is wishing she had chosen the other table, Pearl's table, where there is something new, where there is gaiety for no good reason, which they long for without being able to make it among themselves.

"There is nothing wrong with the meat," says Anneli, the diet nurse, not unkindly the first time, but she repeats it with irritation when she sees that it is not just Julia but the whole table of up-patients around her now looking down at their napkins, squeezed tight in ringed fingers; a choking, a sighing around the half-chewed meat that not one of them will explain to her. Pearl's table notices, goes quiet, and watches. And then Mrs. Minder, whose face is ordinarily so clear excepting the one wrinkle between her eyebrows, suddenly smiles, showing tiny even teeth, of which the front two are so discolored that they appear to have been capped in copper. And then as suddenly puts her hand up to stifle herself, her fingernails as clean as a baby's and as curiously thin and sharp.

"Mrs. Minder," says Anneli. "This is not funny." (Even though she herself may smile, later, in relating it to others in the staff sauna.)

Pearl pushes back her chair and comes elaborately around the table to Julia, looking down appraisingly before crouching beside her so that the glass beads at the hem of her skirt click against the floor. Even crouching, she is imposing, because she's wearing the absurdly tall pink fox fur hat. She smells of amber resin, and she is warm, and then Julia seems to enjoy the crying and the hot, fat tears. Her mouth is open slightly and her companions can see the grayish meat between her teeth. What is this? Most want to look away when Pearl, concerned, puts a finger to Julia's gums and sweeps the meat into a napkin. But then they do look away, pointedly, when Julia takes the meaty napkin and presses it to her eyes.

"The portions are too large," says Julia.

"Look, sweetheart," says Pearl. "What's your name? We'll cut the meat up small and manageable, and if you want, I'll even help you." Pearl leans to pick up the fork from the floor where Julia dropped it.

"You're not going to feed her!" says Mary Minder. But no one listens to her anymore, and, because they don't, Julia smiles, and accepts Pearl's help.

Pearl has brought a new game, a thinking game called Question, Challenge, and she teaches it later, in the Green Room. There are always a chosen few ladies around her, and always one in particular, sometimes the grossest, the most peculiar. Last year, this was Mrs. Minder. Now Pearl looks to Julia, the newcomer, and they sit side by side, to the open irritation of Mrs. Minder; she did not understand that abandonment is the fate of favorites. The kitchen has opened preserved milk and Mrs. Minder pours it from a steel pitcher. Trying to please, she turns the pitcher and holds it, handle first, to Pearl.

"Don't gag me, you know I can't stand it, darling."

"Sorry, sorry!"

Julia accepts the milk herself.

"Listen," Pearl says, slipping off her shoes and resting her feet on the ottoman, and for a moment those around her stop and hear the rain outside, the hissing of water on concrete, not realizing she wishes them to listen to her and nothing else. But there are voices beyond the rain, maybe. Or else it is the sound of the end of the late summer cough going around downstairs.

"First," says Pearl, "I'll think of something, anything, a thing or a place or a person, usually a thing, though, and I won't tell you what. And then you, Mary Minder, you'll say, It's like a *something*. You might say, *It's like a cathedral,* or *It's like a frog.* And then someone else will say something completely different, *It's like a fruit salad,* or whatever you choose. And then I, or whoever thought of the original thing, need to find the way to make it all true."

"It's like a bowl of agates from the beach," says Mrs. Minder promptly.

"No, give me a moment to think of something, otherwise you'll influence me," says Pearl. "Okay, now I'm ready."

"It's like a bowl of agates from the beach," says Mrs. Minder.

"It's like a refrigerator," says Julia.

"All right," says Pearl, flexing her pretty bare toes to crack the joints. "I was thinking of the mill William talks about and talks about." She lets her shimmering eyelids close, and says, "The new mill is like a bowl of agates because it shows man's desire to gather up the products of nature. The new sawmill is like a refrigerator because it's useful and reduces labor, compared to the past."

"I love new games," says Mrs. Minder. "I'm good at games."

"Then think of something now," says Pearl. "Julia, you go first."

And Julia moves her hand on the arm of the sofa, and frowns that she is ready, fingering the fabric of her dress.

"It's like a nail file," says Pearl.

"It's like a cane," says Mrs. Minder.

"I was thinking of pyromania," says Julia. "Pyromania is like a nail file because it's abrasive and vain. Pyromania is like a cane because it's a crutch for a sick person."

"I don't like this game," says Mrs. Minder.

"Yes you do," says Julia. "You just don't understand it."

At which Mary Minder frowns, nipping at her lips with her small dark teeth.

Sunny does not look in on Laimi; she had planned to, but after the train ride and the car ride and the long day, Laimi has gone up to her room and gone to bed without turning over the small red tag outside her door, the one she finds shameful and lazy, the one that means *I would like to stay in my room, I would like to receive my dinner in bed.* It is evening now and someone other than Sunny will be looking in on her later, because Sunny has buttoned up a raincoat and gone pedaling her bike along the paths. It's only rain, she tells herself, it's only rain, knowing that fairly soon it will be snow, and that snow might more easily discourage her from going through with the effort. Although why think about this now? In past years it has proved a better plan to avoid thinking of the snow, the shortened days, before they come.

But something is already different about this year, the atmosphere or the mix maybe, and some on the top floor are so passive that the

ward maids nearly have to change the bed linens around them. So dis-
tasteful, especially here. It shouldn't be allowed. But what can be done?
Not much. Sunny has come to dislike those up-patients too indolent to
move aside, the ones who won't get out for some fresh air. Yes, it's true:
she dislikes them. This is an oddly liberating and reckless admission,
because she has never said it outright before, having rarely applied this
standard to anyone in her care during all these years. She had assumed,
conveniently, that she couldn't really know any of them, because personality would always be hidden behind the presentation of a patient,
as far back from the center line where they met as Sunny herself. But
was it really possible, to be so impartial? Oh, yes, seemingly it had been,
before; she had not, for example, disliked her mother, nor resented her.
She may have disliked some aspects of the life they were obliged to live,
because of the circumstance, but that was entirely different. But here,
now, this year, some go too far into self-indulgence, they won't do much
more than eat cookies and make conversation with the nurses . . . some
of the ladies feel a compulsion to seek sympathy, and sometimes they
develop a new tic, an elusive pain . . . and oh, the things that come up
for review. The constipation, for example: constipation is a foolproof
way of getting attention. *Voi Jumalauta*. An enema, some bowel salts, and
a little assistance at the end of the process. Real need is one thing, but
choosing frailty is another, and Sunny herself has seen real frailty, un-
chosen, and as a result she would do anything to comfort real physical
pain, except cultivate and indulge it. Maybe this is what's wrong: some
are here only to have their pain—or their discomfort—cultivated and
indulged. And so Sunny, on her bicycle, declines to think of enemas,
not on her own time, not outside the building.

There must be some outlet for the exasperation of the healthy toward the infirm, especially if some improvement in the situation does
not seem imminent, and Sunny will try to find an outlet in exercise,
and will nearly always manage to keep her own frustrations out of
sight. Now in autumn there are apples growing in the trees of what was
once a small private orchard, grown over with berry bushes, that she
has found near a few abandoned outbuildings at some distance from

the hospital complex. It is a small recreation, a destination, to get off her bike and to turn the windfalls over with one foot, checking for wormholes in the slanting light. Those in reasonably good condition she takes to Mrs. Anderson and Sister Tutor. She doesn't like to leave them rotting on the rain-soaked ground after seeing them swelling on the trees all summer; they are only getting to a good picking size now, but the branches are over her head. And so she turns over the windfalls, in grass that is long and wet and full of slow insects boring slow holes through the green-and-red-streaked skins.

Where else to go? There aren't that many directions that lead anywhere in particular in the length of time she'd like to ride, perhaps an hour, possibly two. She crosses the bridge and follows the path along the coast in the direction of the long way around, toward the town and harbor, far away. Conversely, all destinations will seem closer later, when they are snowbound, if one is willing to walk out over the ice.

On the way home she stops at the small house with a bag of windfalls and interrupts Mrs. Anderson stripping her own bed—there is a laundry exchange, of course, but one must do the work oneself, and evening is the time. Sister Tutor comes out of a bedroom less bare than one would imagine, padded with a warm rug hung on the north wall, below which a little collection of icons glints on a dresser. Hanging from a chain in the corner is a golden lamp in which a flame is burning, about which Mrs. Anderson won't complain even though lately she is jumpy at the thought of fire. Sister Tutor's orthodoxy may not be entirely popular in these Protestant times, but Mrs. Anderson would never criticize her friend for it. Religion is private. Enough said.

Yes, all right, she'll take a cup of tea, to their surprise: often she says no thank you only out of habit. Mrs. Anderson is pleased and boils the kettle.

"I have new tea," she calls from their kitchen. "Tea from India."

"Oh," says Sister Tutor in Finnish. "Nice!"

Mrs. Anderson takes gingersnaps from the jar and gives the top one, stale and soft, to Sister Tutor, whose teeth are not strong, and who holds the cookie over her lips in a small anticipatory kiss. They both look at

Sunny. They'd never ask about her increasing bad moods directly, but she's restless, obviously. What options are there? Uprooting herself can't happen now. Change doesn't come naturally when the world is ramping down for winter. Maybe she's frustrated with the work, and the feelings will pass. They continue looking at her, across the table, Sister Tutor blinking over the gingersnap.

"I guess I'm restless tonight," Sunny says.

They are happy with this.

"Maybe you ought to go into town this week?" says Mrs. Anderson.

"That's a good idea!" says Sister Tutor. "It's the herring market all week."

"I don't like herring much," says Sunny.

"You don't?" says Sister Tutor, nonplussed. "Are you sure?"

"There's more than just herring," says Mrs. Anderson. "It's the season."

"You like smoked fish, don't you?" says Sister Tutor.

"Sometimes."

"Anyway, take the bus to the train platform, and then it's really only an hour and a quarter from there," says Mrs. Anderson. "Sometimes you just need to get away."

"Nurses in uniform ride for free," says Sister Tutor. "The market will be full of people. And wool. And bread and candy, lots of things, and the man who carves birds."

"No, he's only there for Christmas at the *joulumarkt*."

Sunny had accepted a ride last year in a car with some others who were going into town, quicker of course than the train and bus. It was snowy, and she sat in the middle of the backseat between two practical nurses, behind two silent orderlies who smoked cigarettes, barely cracking their windows, filling the built-in ashtrays. To her horror the driver had unexpectedly driven out over the frozen water, taking a shortcut not yet marked out for safety with markers of sawn branches. She had been nauseous with anxiety, feeling trapped, too firmly tucked away between the other nurses in their bulky town coats; she knew she would be unable to get out quickly if the ice cracked. She had expected the ice to fail, she'd waited for and expected the sharp terrifying sound, the tilt, the feel of ice water rising at her feet. She'd said nothing, though, staring ahead until they reached the opposite shore. She'd excused herself, and taken the train home alone.

"Maybe," she says, but knows that the time needed to get there is too much when she's only taking a day and a half off every week. And it seems, it often seems that she will never go into town again. Which is ridiculous.

The older women have learned how to be happy here, by doing what pleases them, slowly, if need be. But they are sympathetic anyway. Sister Tutor smiles as she stirs honey into her cup of tea. And Sunny wishes to be someone capable of enjoying stirring and stirring, someone more like Sister Tutor, a veteran nurse of the Balkan wars who somehow sleeps without nightmares.

They both watch Mrs. Anderson arrange the apples in a large glass bowl, where during the week the ripest will gather indents, the faint teeth marks of Sister Tutor's optimistic attempts. If she wants apples, though, she'll have to wait until Mrs. Anderson reduces them to applesauce, because tonight, even the cookies must be softened in her tea.

Somebody ought to yank those teeth out, thinks Sunny. But no: such a thought intrudes only because of what she'd seen earlier, at lunch, when two of the up-patients had proudly introduced new and unexpected dentures, dozens of beautiful teeth purchased abroad during the summer, for which both—one only partially, but the other more thoroughly—had elected to remove their natural (but weak!) teeth. Mrs. Minder, with her finger hovering, wanting to touch, had asked about the process. Was it painful? Oh, yes! Very painful. Did it take long? Not as long as you'd think. And the lady with the partial bridge had gone to her room to bring back a little jewel box containing her erstwhile upper incisors, each placed neatly into the box's velvet slits intended for rings, and each, when drawn out by Mrs. Minder, on a long yellowed root, intact and relatively healthy in appearance.

Sunny, in passing, half-attentive, had glanced down and mistaken the teeth for hoarded pills. "What have you got?" she'd said, sharply. "Show me."

Mrs. Minder had obligingly tipped what she held into Sunny's palm, and Sunny, not expecting the dry touch of the parsnip-colored roots, had nearly thrown the teeth to the floor. But she hadn't, she'd merely handed them back to their owner, and then stepped to the nearby sink to wash her hands, thoroughly and automatically. This must be some kind of a borrowed thought, like something contagious caught from the up-patients. Of course she'd never, ever suggest that Sister Tutor follow the example set by such as those, who love and hate themselves publicly in equal measure. If Sister Tutor wants her teeth pulled, then by all means pull them, thinks Sunny, pull them all and look for new ones, but do it under nobody's influence but her own.

Seven

Is there anything else for breakfast, beyond *piirakka,* chopped eggs, cheese? Well, there's porridge, of course. Rice, barley, rye, oat, whatever kind you like. But no, that's not what you meant, because weather turning cold provokes the appetite for meat, especially smoky meat to conjure memories of fire.

"Sausage and egg," says Anneli. "Pork in little cakes."

"Little cakes!" says Mrs. Minder. "I love little cakes."

"Do you know what's in them?" says Julia.

"Pork?" says Mrs. Minder hopefully.

"Snouts and sphincters," says Julia. "And whizzers."

"You can take *piirakka* instead if you want," says Anneli, ignoring her.

"Bread," says Julia. "And I'll take sausages," she says.

"But you said sphincters, you said it's little cakes made out of sphincters?" Mrs. Minder watches while Julia receives her breakfast plate.

"I like sphincters," says Julia. She picks up her fork and her knife.

"Smoked ones, especially, and I know you do, too. Go ahead. Enjoy them."

"You're disgusting!" says Mrs. Minder. "You ruin everything on purpose."

But in the end Mrs. Minder too of course will take the sausage, please, and will chew it well, putting the details out of mind.

Soon even those who are new this year and previously unaccustomed to sauna have begun to gravitate toward the heat in the dim wooden interior. They look forward to the whole process, to hanging their dresses and their underthings on hooks in the anteroom, to a mild tepid shower, and to opening the wooden door, eyes adjusting, looking for a place to sit along the benches. Then sitting on towels among their neighbors in a more natural state. It may have been hard for some to learn not to stare at the bodies of their fellows at first—just curiosity, it's normal—but soon it is surprisingly easy to sit in a room of nude women and not to actively look. There are the angles of arms, crossed legs, the exterior angles of bodies, and this is what meets the eye. Most of these up-patients are not Finns and have not previously known about sauna, and it is hard to judge how authentic their experiences here may be, but they seem to like it. Some like to feel natural, to notice their own bodies, their nudeness, but not their infirmity. At least, not at every moment.

Pearl wraps herself in a big white bath sheet, voluminous as a toga, and the soft dewlaps of her back and pink upper arms are a rosy contrast. She always takes a place on the medium tier. And Julia likes the sauna too, Julia, who doesn't like anything, whose skin has the undertone of ashes, but who is cured, cured! She ties her dark wet hair in a topknot, moving slowly and carefully, very carefully across the wet tile floor of the anteroom, her towel over her shoulder, nude and frowning. She sits on the highest level. She tries the upper corners, looking for the hottest places when the heat chases itself around the wooden sauna walls, repeating and renewing.

Pearl throws a ladleful of water, sending up steam with a hiss.

She has learned the word for this steam and tries to pronounce it in Finnish: *löyly?* Julia asks for more heat, more steam, settling into the sauna without drying off after showering, trying to make the sweat break out on her skin more quickly. She leans away from the red pine wall, leaning forward into the heat. When she asks for still more, Pearl clicks her tongue.

"It's harder to sweat at my age," says Julia. "It's been years." She leans forward, elbows on knees, staring down between her feet. Pearl splashes more water and the fresh heat comes forward. She takes up her sheet and steps out for some cooler air.

Sometimes Julia will drive the others out by throwing water for steam again and again. But they come back eventually, drifting in and out at their own pace, breaking away again when the heat is enough. They go out to the cooler anteroom to stand at the window and look out at the cold landscape, opening the window so that thick white steam rises from their skin and hair. They drink water from hexagonal plastic tumblers that do not break if dropped. They're of all different ages, hot and relaxed, and some do indeed open their towels to stand nude at the window, accepting the sharp cold air and the sanctioned thrill of exhibition. But it wouldn't be good to include a catalog of particulars, to succumb to the common descriptive terms for bodies, the tropes of age, the comparisons to objects from the natural world—no comparisons to fruits or flowers or animals. This may leave a gap in the picture. But it's enough to say that they can try to sweat out the pollutions accumulated in the flesh, to speak unguardedly, until the sauna attendant comes in at intervals to turn the hourglass mounted on the wall and to remind the more delicate individuals not to overdo it. And then they move back out into the anteroom and shampoo their hair into piles of pine-tar-scented foam and wash themselves with soft green soap that smells of birch leaves. The others finish, but Julia lingers behind, alone at the shower, her long dark hair twisted and held in one hand, the other braced against the tiles. She stands under the warm water for a long time, until the others are already leaving. Pearl smoothes various creams onto her face, her neck, her upper arms. Her back spills slightly over the strap of her brassiere like a second modest backward bosom. She's happy here, happy at Suvanto, among soft towels, clean sheets, flattering lighting, and nonjudgmental, attentive company; her life has not been as social or as easy as we may have first assumed, and the habits of real conversation do not come to her as easily as they might to the other Americans. The women put their dresses on and leave feeling cleaner than ever before in their lives, as they drift away in search of a glass of something cool and refreshing, a glass of something social.

When winter asserts itself routine is even more pleasant, expanding to occupy all the time there is, all the quarter-hour increments between glances at the watch face. Routine rolls forward until it is checked by change from without. Such as when on the first day of real, luxuriant snowfall, Dr. Peter requests an index of the treatments given by nurses to the patients of the top floor.

It is of course normal to keep records of this kind, and there are forms for this purpose, easily filled in by the charge nurses and taken by the head nurses daily for their meeting with the Head of Nursing, then turned over to the clerk to be added up at the end of every month. These records of treatments are arranged in tables to show the frequency of each action, to show how many pairs of hands are needed on average, and how skilled those hands need to be. But the doctors have never needed or wanted to see these lists before now.

"All treatment records?" Sunny asks.

"Yes, and the most time-consuming treatments especially," says Dr. Peter.

She is accurate and will do as he asks. She takes out carbon copies of the weekly and monthly tallies, and in looking at them with fresh eyes she sees that the lists do not look nearly as important or strenuous as those from the other floors will. Assisted bathing, foot soaks, enemas, mouth care, massage, changing dressings, vaginal douches: frequent. Catheterization, transfusions, intravenous medications, and other skilled work: not frequently found in the doctors' orders for the up-patients.

She knows this already anyway, has known for some time. Even the Head of Nursing scarcely wants to hear her reports anymore; it never used to be this way. In Sunny's other life, work had mattered. She had learned this during the nights when she was a student nurse in a women's surgical ward, checking and changing the dressings hourly, knowing by the character of the blood whether all was well, and that she was needed, in any case. That she was helping, and important. And everything at home. Everything she'd done for her mother had mattered. And for others, downstairs, work still mattered. Every morning at the meeting in the Head's sitting room each supervisor gives her report. The others report in Finnish; Sunny listens, picking out words that she understands, recognizing, maybe, unfamiliar forms of familiar words. Then she is given a minute, maybe two or three, to repeat the same thin information over and over. Unnecessarily. No one says this, but she feels it herself.

But she'd wanted this—wasn't this what she'd wanted? Not to be relied upon too acutely? It is uncomfortable to see that this is no better, that, in some ways, this is worse than the way she lived before. Here, without anything truly at risk, she feels like she's merely pretending, in everything. The work is nearly meaningless, and life is nothing but a search for meaning, yes? Isn't that right? And if these little purple carbon marks signify nothing more than many, many hours spent indulging the self-absorption of the up-patients, then doesn't that mean that for as long as she remains here, completing such tasks, she is wasting her energy? Wasting her life?

From the locked drawer she takes copies of the confidential records and tables these as well. Sulfur vapor baths for syphilis, acid treatments for genital growths: more frequent than you might suppose. Intimacy and contraceptive counseling: once in a while. Strange behavior: well, she doesn't think she's been asked to table that.

Ordinarily these records would go back into the file drawer and be locked away again, and the small key would be placed into its compartment in Sunny's desk drawer, and that too would be locked, because the habit of precaution is part of the routine. It feels late in the day, though. It feels late and Sunny is tired. She takes the paper out of her typewriter and leaves it for the clerk to pick up and send to Dr. Peter by internal mail so that he will receive it first thing in the morning. When she leaves her office she does not realize she has left the little key standing in the lock of her file drawer. Her mind is fixed toward a dose of warmth before sleep, and if she had the energy she would go over to the staff sauna in the nurses' pavilion, which she knows will be heated tonight, but she doesn't feel like putting on her coat and shoes. She goes instead along to the Radiant Room and draws aside the heavy red draft curtain. She pauses in the doorway when she sees that most of the couches are occupied.

This room, set apart from the rest, is the exception that proves the rule of quiet; there is a gleaming record player on one of the tables, along with a collection of records. Some are recordings of actors reading classics of poetry and drama, and some are just music, songs that the obsessive among them will play again and again. Pearl has already hidden "Ladies Are Running Wild," a particular favorite of Mrs. Minder's.

Julia wins here lately, by carrying down two records of tango music from her room, somber, and so exciting. The others look up when she places the needle, their heads lifting and pausing like interested deer. A voice swells, a fiddle throbs. The song is about nighttime, moonlight, summer, winter, birds, love, jealousy, snow, more love, more jealousy, more snow. Not everyone understands the words. But they understand the fiddle and the plaintive accordion, which should have sounded happy, yet doesn't. Julia herself doesn't appear particularly happy to hear these songs; her mouth opens, slack and shaky, as if she only half-remembers the words, occasionally revealing the nacreous gleam of her teeth when she tries to catch them.

Sunny could easily go in and sit down among the patients and it would appear that she is doing what she always does among them, circulating, watching, listening to their problems. But tonight she wants to sit in her own time, as herself, to sink into the feeling of enclosure in this room hung with red draft curtains, and to expand in the flickering firelight with her eyes closed and without speaking. This would be too strange, to sit there among them in silence as herself. And the music. She doesn't like it.

Pearl and Mrs. Minder, faces and arms still glowing from sauna, are playing cards. Mrs. Minder is humming along under her breath. She makes a mistake, and moves to cheat, a little. Pearl slaps her on the hand, before they see that Sunny is there.

Mrs. Minder holds up her hand to show the mark, but Sunny drops the draft curtain and goes without comment.

She turns on the lamps in her room, faintly disappointed in knowing that she will relax onto her bed and spill into sleep as soon as she can get out of her uniform, even though this is of course what she has always wanted. One hand is already busy with the buttons. She turns from slipping off her indoor shoes to see her small sitting room suddenly almost as she first saw it, and as it still might be underneath this present familiarity. On that day of introduction the door had opened in sunlight under her new key and she saw the greenish floor, the china-white walls, the evergreen trees outside the window, and she thought, *Yes, I will be happy living here.* The small inconveniences wouldn't have mattered anyway. Like the angle of the door to the bathroom, which when open obstructs, and when closed allows no chance to lose humidity, the result of a renovation to make self-contained apartments for the nursing supervisors and keep them closer to their wards. Which in retrospect might seem restrictive, a bad choice for quality of life. But the rooms are hers, and private, and rather than growing complacent about this privacy, rather than taking it for granted, she becomes increasingly aware that if and when she leaves Suvanto, she will lose these rooms, and the emptiness and quiet that they have afforded her. That may seem obvious. But it is a concern.

Without knowing the age of our girl Sunny it might be easy to again mistake her sudden flushing for a mood, but it is not emotion that leaves the fine hairs at the nape of her neck suddenly dark with perspiration. Maybe it's just stress, but maybe it's the first light fingerprint of the climacteric, a few headaches, a little dizziness, a slightly uneven heartbeat.

These are material signs, and it would explain the impatience, and the feverish discomfort that began in the spring, when she'd felt constantly exasperated, and the better the weather, the worse she felt. She had followed the paths with her feet, with her bicycle wheels. From June on she'd gone swimming almost every morning at a beach around the bend, out of sight of Suvanto. She had walked out into the water, which never got any warmer, sinking into the chill and then swimming out to the platform. Maybe it helped. But she still felt uneasy. And then she had, for the first time, been less than gentle with Laimi—a rare venting of that completely normal (in other circumstances) claustrophobic irritation of a healthy woman surrounded by the ill-minded. But Laimi was not ill-minded, and should not have been mishandled. The worst was on a morning when Laimi hadn't gotten out of bed for an appointment in the clinical wing, when she'd fallen back asleep, despite a cup of coffee brought to her room by the breakfast cart.

Sunny had been called to the phone and told to get the patient. She'd been a little too quick, a little too rough in pulling back the blanket and had found Laimi curled tight in the bed, asleep, and across the lap and back of her nightgown a scarlet and brown bloodstain of quiet reproach. She realized only then, just after she'd done it, that she'd lifted the blanket expecting to find something else, something old and familiar and frustrating, the damp sharp smell, her mother's yellowing skin, the usual inevitable mess. But she wouldn't have been so impatient then, either, and there was no excuse for it now. She had replaced the blanket more gently and turned away for fresh pads, clean clothing. Laimi had woken, of course, and there had been silence between them, the awkward heat of Laimi's pale skin, fresh from the bedding, the freckles on her legs, the rising and cooling odor of blood when she got out of her bed by herself and stood.

I'm sorry, Sunny had wanted to say, and yet hadn't, and now it had been half a year. And the sudden unbearable impatience was coming more often, flaring in her throat, heating her eyes, and sometimes she felt not just impatient but angry, out of all proportion. But she compresses that anger, immediately, every time. And then it passes. She gets tired more quickly now, too, and heavy sleep is always waiting for her at the edge. It feels ridiculous. She is only forty-two. *But when my mother was my age, I was already in Philadelphia.*

From her window she can see a clearing behind the main building, crossed with paths on freezing grass that disappear into the sparse edge of the trees. Her curtains are open. In town, in any city, she would have drawn them shut at nightfall. Here, it doesn't seem to matter. There are no city concerns of being watched by neighbors or prowlers. There are only the pines, and this outweighs many inconveniences. The solitude has given her room to unpack the years, spreading her thoughts out in a thin, widening circle. A little more time will be good. A little more silence. And so of course she will stay on. There's nothing for her elsewhere, nobody waiting for her in any other place. To leave, and to confront this, would be even more uncomfortable than staying.

Julia takes her cane and stretches her legs by strolling quietly along the halls after the others have brushed their teeth and settled into their beds. She has had her nap in the afternoon, and has not yet taken her sleep aid for the night, and she is not tired. She'll play the game of somnambulist, though it isn't funny when she shuffles, slowly, into Pearl's room with her eyes closed and her fingers outstretched, mouth open and tongue protruding like a ghastly old strawberry.

"Stop," says Pearl, propped up in the bed. She has taken off her rings to polish them with a tan chamois, and they sit scattered around her in the folds of the duvet. But as she collects them she relents, saying, "You're going to scare me sleepless."

"I'm not the one to be scared of. Mary Minder is the one," Julia says, sinking to her knees, arms on the bed, as if praying, so that Pearl cannot move her feet.

"Oh, stop," she says, kicking. "Mary's harmless."

Julia leans in close for a stage whisper. "Don't you know? Isn't it obvious? She's a pyromaniac. I saw it in the private files."

Pearl turns and turns a ring. "Really," she says, "I always thought so."

"I saw yours, too."

"Where was this?"

"In the fireplace."

"Originals, or copies?"

"Originals."

Pearl turns a ring in the cloth again, slips it back on. "You shouldn't ever touch the paperwork, Julia. It's not worth the trouble."

"I'm only wandering in my sleep," says Julia, tapping her temple with her finger, her voice quavery. "Can't a poor old woman wander in her sleep?" There is something restless in her tonight, more than usual; perhaps, finally, she too is growing bored.

"If you play at sleepwalking they'll give you the restraining board at night," says Pearl. She takes up Julia's hand. The ruby rings will not slide over her knuckles, and Pearl polishes one of them in situ. "But I do appreciate the gesture."

"Don't thank me. It was the poor pyromaniac who couldn't sleep and must have burned a few things," says Julia. "That sounds right, doesn't it?"

But Pearl knows that Mary Minder took her sleep aid ages ago.

"Did you see Mary's in the fireplace, too?"

"Of course not," says Julia.

"Did you read mine?" says Pearl, unconcerned, but asking.

"No. But I see why you won't touch milk, you poor infected thing, and I wouldn't either, if I was you."

"Don't say that!" Pearl slaps Julia's hand, hard.

Julia is surprised at this for a moment but then she slaps back against Pearl's strong fingers, an ineffectual, glancing slap that makes Pearl feel ashamed. She takes up Julia's hand again and separates out another finger, begins to polish again.

"Tell me what was in yours," Pearl says severely, "just to be fair."

"But I really don't remember, I'm only an old woman," says Julia, high, feeble, funny, swooning heavily against Pearl's knees so that her long, strangely fragrant hair drags across the bedding. And although Julia is small, and weighs very little, still there is a pained sound from under the blankets, a muffled report like the snapping sound of a wishbone pulled apart.

"You're hurting me," says Pearl, wincing, pushing, and Julia instantly leans away. Pearl looks almost ready to cry, and she hides her face by hugging her knees. Julia will apologize; rather, she looks like she wants to apologize.

"Do you want me to get someone?" she asks.

Pearl shakes her head, face still pressed to the comforter.

"Then you'll have to hit me," says Julia. "That's fair. Go on, hit me."

"No," says Pearl, muffled.

"Then stick me with a hat pin."

"Stop," says Pearl.

"I won't stop," says Julia, getting to her feet. She backs up, closely, portentiously, and bends over, gently bumping, until Pearl looks up to find Julia's rump in her face.

"Stick a pin in it!" Julia commands. "Or I'll stick myself and tell the nurses you're responsible. Hurry, or I'll pull up my nightie."

"No!" says Pearl, "don't do that!" She sits up, and then she's smiling, and though she's still cradling her knee, with the other hand she agrees to slap Julia's backside away, lightly, and the mysteriously fragile leg between them is never mentioned. It may be worth repeating: Julia alone among the rest of us knew what lay under the blanket, and she said nothing to Pearl, nothing, and it was this lack of proffered sympathy that Pearl appreciated most.

Eight

The new snow is soft and unbroken in the meadows, visible from the promenade through the bare black birches. A line of white stacked on every branch makes the sky beyond appear gray by comparison. It's best to go out and move the blood, and then come back to drop shoes and coat, tuck away your gloves, and in the warm rooms you'll feel your blood stinging in the cold red flesh of your face. The daily menu is, as always, chalked on the board and propped on an easel outside the dining room as an enticement.

"What does it say?" says Mrs. Minder. "What's special for lunch?"

"Fish casserole is the special," says Anneli, moving between the tables.

"I love fish casserole!" says Mrs. Minder. "What's in it?"

"Cod, parsley sauce, *katkarapu,* potato."

"Fish are filthy with the parasites and the worms, you know," says Julia.

"Don't sit beside me anymore," says Mary Minder. "Please get away from me."

"Shellfish including *katkarapu* keep their guts inside," says Julia, "and it's a known fact that you're eating their fecals."

"That's enough," says Anneli.

"Get away," whispers Mrs. Minder. "You're nasty, and I wish you were dead and couldn't talk anymore." This is only funny because she means it so vehemently.

"I'm just an old woman," says Julia, loudly enough that Anneli glances over at them. "Why are you threatening me, Mary? Do you want my cake, is that it?"

"You shut up," says Mrs. Minder, furious and embarrassed.

"But I love *katkarapu*," says Julia. "And I love to see you enjoying it, too."

"Well then I won't have any," Mary says, but then, of course, she does, pushing Julia away with her elbow each time she looks over at Mary's plate.

Quiet and routine settle even more firmly with the snow. Delivery trucks arrive at the complex regularly, despite the emphasis on frugality. The idea of isolation—the comments about the journey into town, the fears of running out of canned peaches, for example—is a habit from previous necessity.

"Do you know what will happen if we run out of canned peaches? Raisins for dessert. And prunes. Horrible things," says Pearl. "Horrible."

"I love them," says Julia. "They taste like scabs."

"Oh, honestly," says Mrs. Minder under her breath.

"I don't care what you think," says Julia. "You're a dumb cow."

"I don't care what you think either, you dumb cow yourself!"

"I don't want to hear that," says Pearl, lifting a finger in warning to them both.

The trucks arrive behind the screening trees, on the side away from the patients' windows. The staff speak in low tones and so do the guests, the patients, the visitors. The nurses walk in cork-soled shoes on the red rubber floor tiles and have the habit of closing doors behind them whenever they are leaving a room of activity; they handle equipment carefully, even in the clinking sterilizing rooms; the bells of the telephones are muffled and the paging system is so low that only those who have learned to listen will actually hear the calls.

It is known to happen, it is expected to happen, that the energy level and accordingly the sound level will fall off as the days grow shorter and darker, as the gold sideways light sharpens and then fades in the afternoon, as the dark hours press together earlier and earlier in horizontal layers outside the large double-glass windows . . . especially that Solarium window. It was once the largest plate of glass in all of Finland.

There is adjustment. Pay attention to details. You must, for example, have good house shoes and warm socks to see you through, otherwise you will feel the awkward memory of your toes in damp circumstances once you come inside after a stroll. The odor of damp wool and fur lingers near the coatroom, and that of wet leather in the shoe porch, where the steam-heated panels work all day and night. Not normal though is a whiff of decomposition, which is something else entirely; in the lower wards, where the windows are below the treetops, something might occasionally gather, a stale problem in the air. There are sick people there, after all, and surgical cases, too. The up-patients don't pass through. They say among themselves that under the odors of bleach and wax there is a stink of urine, of sepsis, of semiconscious individuals who haven't brushed their teeth in days. The windows have been designed exactly to prevent a miasma from forming, to let the air creep in slowly, without drafts, clean air taken far from the kitchens to prevent any odors of meat or vegetables from rising and depressing, but sometimes the fresh air is overwhelmed anyway.

The downstairs charge nurse stands on a chair to check the ventilation panels, and then asks Kusti to check outside, in case the condensation from so many sleeping bodies has frozen into a smothering cake of ice over the outlet. Kusti sends someone out with a stick and a rubber bladder full of hot water.

The nurses are accustomed to bad odors, of course, but the body in distress is one thing while unhygienic practices cannot be tolerated. Sunny offers a copy of the famous factors to watch for, to post in the nurses' sitting room: reduced oxygen, increased carbon dioxide, body odors, food in neglected mouths, increased room temperature from body heat, and increased humidity from breath and skin. She takes a copy from her files and sees that the key still stands in the confidential drawer, where she must have forgotten it the night before.

The drawer is slightly open. She looks through the files, looks for Julia's and finds it. The pages are complete. She closes the drawer and puts away the key, not without relief.

We used to think it was a difficult season to pass, the winter rest cure, but after returning more than once to the upper floor we believe that the slower days and longer nights will spread a smooth winter of extra time over our bodies and faces like butterfat. We haven't aged, and whatever plagues us abides in stasis. It might be difficult at first, to be alone in your room, with only the sky outside the window and your own thoughts. But isn't that some kind of statement, to stay the winter, and to come back for another?

Pearl and the others sleep late; there is little to do once awake except to step into a variety of undergarments, in which they will frequently glimpse one another before they muster the energy to get properly dressed. White lawn, pastel pinks and blues, and sometimes, not often, a little bit of precious black silk. And caps for morning hair; the ward maid with the tea and coffee cart sees them in nearly every upstairs room, pleated, gathered, with tassels sometimes, and, in Pearl's case, with beaded ribbons dangling extravagantly to the shoulders. The self-indulgence of such useless beadwork is lost only on themselves.

Pearl takes a long time to put on light clothes in layers. She'll go outside only briefly. She says the paths are untrustworthy and treacherous. She likes to go to the Solarium instead. It's a nice room, entered through a tall sliding accordion-style door that usually stands open during the day, when there is a view of pines and water beyond the plate glass. Or some would rather go up to the promenade, along the roof, where Kusti has used salt and gravel to make the surface safer. But there is no reason to hurry. You can do all of that later. No one comes to the private rooms until ten or eleven unless, upon waking, one puts a finger to the faint orange button in the wall beyond the pillow, which indicates to the nurses' station that someone inside the room is ready to begin the day, and legitimately in need of something. Often it is not even sleep that keeps them inside and quiet, but a heavy contemplative feeling. Pearl puts on her house shoes to pull open the curtains and then gets quickly back into bed, knees and toes cracking, dreaming for an hour before pushing the button. If it is Saturday she opens the pages of magazines and catalogs saved during the week. She looks for photos of full-length figures, real people, models, even drawings, and she takes scissors and cuts the figures out, preparing for games that evening.

Saturday is the day most anticipated for games and entertainment, because what they miss on Saturday, more than any other day, are their husbands, home in the past on weekends most likely. Some write letters. Some get letters in return. Treasure hunts are good, and so is any game giving a glimpse into someone else's room. They're nosy and love to see the repetition of everything the same but slightly different, dimensions and colors with small discrepancies, a streak in the beige flooring, a lighter-green curtain, a smaller chair. All the aspects and prospects. They run between rooms to stir up treasure hunt favorites: find a comb with a missing tooth, for example, and a string of green beads. *Does jade count? It's green, isn't it? Is it? Would you call that green?*

This morning Mrs. Minder runs down the hall in leather-soled slippers, shuffling without lifting her feet, her hair in two stubby pigtails. There's a newspaper in her hand and she's wearing only her white nightgown with a tiny dimple of fabric caught in the cleft of her buttocks.

"Put on your dressing gown!" calls Nurse Todd, but Mrs. Minder disappears into Pearl's room without knocking.

Others too have been scissoring through the papers. At the Solarium tables all the full-length figures have been snipped in two, neatly, at the waist. The two halves will be pasted onto cards, top and bottom separated, and later, in the evening, over coffee, these are dealt like playing cards.

"I've got a lady," says Pearl, "a young lady in a bathing suit."

Mrs. Minder says, "Blond hair?"

"Bathing cap."

"Is she at the beach?"

"She is. There's sand behind."

"Is she standing on her toes?"

"She might be, honey. I've got the top half, so I wouldn't know."

Mrs. Minder lays down a card, but the halves of the pictures do not match.

"I have a big bottom," says Julia. "I've got a big old bottom over here."

"I've got two enormous breasts to go with it," says Pearl, laying down a card.

"Those are mine, I cut them out," says Mrs. Minder. She has a kind word for nearly all of the cutout figures, nearly all the poor pretty dismembered ladies.

Julia keeps score, making an extra mark each time Mrs. Minder gets one wrong, which is often enough to be obvious.

And Sunny has to leave, to get out. There is no other way to occupy her own Saturday evening. She has had thick winter tires put on her bike and she pushes it along the path, past the area just underneath the windows where, after the unpacking of the vents, spilled water has become a plane of gray ice frozen solid around the slim trunks of ornamental bushes that will manage to survive despite their seeming fragility.

She knows that she is going someplace only to be going someplace, and feeling especially restless because tomorrow is her day off, her morning to sleep late, and yet tonight she has no plans. She feels, not for the first time but with a new explicitness, the tight, schooled expression on her face, which is never there in the mornings and always there at the end when she unties her cap. The tight face is a shield, it is the way her working self conceals this other, silent self, the one who roams alone out on the paths. It is a protection, but once she is out in the cold she feels it as pain across her forehead and jaw. She is ignoring the rustling memory of her own voice, and other voices that crowd into her mind to disrupt the quiet around her. It is precarious and loud, this humming act of ignoring the obsessive repetitions of the day.

Tension will grow to a loud, insistent crying in her head, if she lets it. She can't silence it. She can only release it, and to do so she rides out past the concrete buildings of the physical plant, passing the turnoffs for the hut where mushrooms are grown, the greenhouse, the chicken house, any direction but that of the pig barn. She rides toward the main road but will turn off onto another path, one that passes the graveyard, a gentle upward sloping field enclosed behind a low brick wall, peopled with dark, rectangular headstones upright in the snow under bare, reddish-black branches. Here she will dismount and push her bike, not liking to give insult by riding through. Sometimes in the dark afternoons each year around Christmas she rides in this direction specifically to see the long-burning candles that the Finns leave alight before the graves, eerie and lovely, each of which says, *Someone was just here, not long ago, and left this flame as proof.*

She dismounts, opens the gate, closing it carefully behind. The gravel cemetery path sends up the sound of her steps, a crisp crushing as one foot breaks into the snow and a squeak as she lifts the other, her tires making a slow susurration alongside. This is a familiar place, and a quiet place, and even if you were to meet other people here, brushing snow from the headstones, they would not acknowledge you, nor you them, because it is a private place. Sunny is not afraid of graveyards, and never has been, here or anywhere, and this stretch of her evening ride is a moment she looks forward to, a pause, a dismount, a moment of aimless contemplation while she is traversing it on foot. This place is merely . . . what is this place? Bodies are here, and so are the memories carried by the living who make visits, but that's all. She feels the emptiness in the same way that she can recognize, as can many of the other nurses, the almost imperceptible movement in the room when a person is in the actual stretch of dying, a movement like a layer of cooler, denser air at the level of her waist; she has felt this many times. One of her colleagues, working on another floor, is known to open the window, just after, in such rooms, as a way to release whatever it is that wants to be released. But that's downstairs, where patient deaths tend to happen more often, usually with advance warning.

She stops in the path, to listen; the silence is instant when her bicycle tires and feet are still. She looks down the faint slope at the rows of crowded dark stones. This evening they stand up out of the snow with unusual distinctness, each with a neat soft ledge of white along the top. She looks first at one, then the next, all the rows that she can make out in the fading light. So many? Were there always this many? It seems impossible. As she looks downslope she remembers that there are graves on the other side of the path as well, behind her, above her. Of course there are. And she can stand there as long as she likes, but nothing will move around her in the cold air, nothing other than her own absurdly warm exhalations. She stands on the cemetery path for some time, listening, before continuing through, unhurriedly.

Snow falls again later while she is riding, wet flakes that stick to her coat and leave water on her face. When she gets back to the hospital everything is smooth again below the windows, the fluffy new snow hiding the slippery frozen plane of ice. Though no one is in sight the path has been walked already in her absence and looks like a thick layer of crushed chalk, and she speculates, as she passes, about what other formations, what other oddities like the spilled water are hidden from sight under this newly fresh white surface.

It is enough exercise and Sunny falls asleep while reading a novelized biography in bed, the same as almost every other night. Usually it is the story of a surgeon, a researcher, a martyr for science, a wartime nurse. She reads what she reads to keep some perspective, to remember that it is a privilege to see changes in another person's life. The biographies say so, they're proof that life can glow with secular meaning, sometimes.

The change for Julia has been a big one, and a private one. The other up-patients do not know about the cure nor about the device under her skirt, the ring hidden in her belly. Her time alone no longer revolves around the trouble pushed back in the mind; there is no more sickening feeling that something is going badly, slowly, seriously wrong in the most private of places. Sunny is glad of this, even if it is now obvious that Julia is not . . . how to say it . . . not the nicest of women. Maybe she is horrible because of the twisting of personality that comes with chronic pain. We can hope that if she feels better she will behave better, now that she has settled in, now that she's part of the group and part of the routine. Sunny hopes so, but doubts it, and so it is both surprising and unsurprising that at census, well past midnight, the night nurse, having been told, of course, to wake her if anything strange ever happens, calls Sunny from her room where she has been dozing with her book in hand, with the message that Julia's bed is empty. Sunny dresses and goes along the quiet corridors, expecting mischief.

She begins at the top of the building. The Solarium is dark. She touches the switch by the door. The wall of black glass with nothing to see outside in the darkness gives it the feeling of a nighttime observation deck on an overnight ferry, looking out over limitlessly deep cold water. There is a chill despite the heaters. All of the gleaming surfaces—the red floor, the wood-framed chairs—encourage an upright posture easier to hold in sunlight, while writing letters, for example, while playing cards. It is the wrong room for right now and she draws the accordion door shut. The way to the promenade is locked; the railings there are disarmingly low, and even during her time here some have been tempted to let themselves step over, falling into the night. Only half of them have survived the fall. She shakes the padlock, inviolate. Down to the dining room. The night-lights are on but she touches the wall switch to be sure the room is empty, and it is; all quiet, with the tables set already for breakfast with folded napkins and small juice glasses upended to avoid any minute accumulation of overnight dust. She crosses the room to the connecting corridor, which is locked, as it should be.

But just in case, she opens it with her key and walks along, the floor and walls sloping down and then up again to the kitchens, a passageway painted white and layered with a pulpy insulation against the deep cold of the ground.

In the kitchen she pushes open the swinging door and stands in darkness. At the far end is the faint warm smell of embers in the stove, and nothing more. She can feel by the emptiness that Julia isn't here and hasn't been here tonight. Perhaps she ought to check the laundry and needle rooms, but all is quiet enough and dark enough that she frankly does not want to. She pushes back out through the swinging doors and back along the passage and stops in shock when the door won't yield, then remembers that at night it is set to relock automatically now. She unlocks it again and goes back into the familiar night dimness of the main floor. She raises a hand to the porter at reception, seated at the desk in a pool of yellow light. She passes reception, passes the row of office doors, passes the coatroom, official and tidy, but with no orderly at the desk at this hour waiting to take a room number and return a coat, including any gloves, any scarf tucked into sleeves or pockets.

There are several rows of familiar coats and Sunny looks for Julia's among the furs. There are hooks above, polished with trace oils from inside the hats. It is not so pleasant there in semidarkness, in the smell of old perspiration and taxidermy, when the coats fill out their shadows like mounted animals, the hats above like heads too far extended. Worse still when there is no hat and the hook is there, empty and grotesque.

Julia is not there and neither is her coat. Sunny follows the curve of the hall past rooms used for communal bathing, around the bend so that the extra light from reception behind her is blocked slowly, incrementally. The hall ahead of her then seems—suddenly in a flash much the opposite of déjà vu—to curve more severely than previously, and the lights themselves in their brushed, perforated metal shades seem dimmer and more yellow, and the darkness at the windows seems more intensely vacant than before, making the corridor as blind as another underground passage, another ship floating underwater in the night. Her cork heels make no sound on the rubber flooring. She casts no shadow on the walls. And then to the left the door of the Radiant Room is standing open. She pushes aside the draft curtain. The lights inside are dim, as elsewhere, and the fireplace is lit and glowing.

There is a slow uncurling movement on one of the couches. Julia, alone, is leaning back against the cushions, with her hair down and her dark fur coat tucked around her shoulders. She blinks, and in the firelight her pupils are green and glassy, her face smoothed by shadows. She has been blamelessly asleep, with her nightgown pulled up to expose her bare legs to the warmth. She moves her legs out of the way and for a time Sunny sits down on the couch beside her.

It is the first time in months that Sunny has visited the Radiant Room at night. And she does imagine that she feels relief, the touch of firelight in the blood. But there is a record turning on the phonograph, a violin and a voice, both terribly sad. A song in Finnish, again. Sunny catches a few of the words when they are drawn out enough: *full moon . . . love . . . how very much . . .*

Julia slides off the sofa and stands with one dry hand extended.

"I'll teach you how to dance to this one," she says.

"I can't dance," says Sunny.

"I know, I said I'll teach you."

And Julia waits, hand extended, and then her hand twitches with uncertainty.

Then it is only to prove to Julia that her flesh is not poisonous that Sunny stands, much taller, and accepts her hand. And now, newly, Sunny looks and she sees Julia, sees the darkness of her eyes and her nostrils and understands with a little sadness that she must have once been a warm brunette, a peachy Danish beauty. And the eyes that look back from behind Julia's face are not the eyes of an old person, just eyes, and ageless. Sunny accepts Julia's little hand, with its weight of dull gemstone rings, and she thinks that she takes up Julia's hand in order to be kind. But Julia is still looking at her, and her hand is firm against Sunny's, and there is a tension in the muscles as Julia moves to move

Sunny, to position her, because of course she wants to teach a step or two. It's what she's good at, the only thing. And she will of course be the one to lead. It seems true to Sunny—suddenly—that Julia is the one being kind here, by showing Sunny some human attention.

"It's time to go back up," Sunny says, gently, so as not to be hurtful in any case.

A missed opportunity here; when else, and where else, will she ever be asked to dance again? The answer is never, and nowhere.

Nine

And now it is November, now it is the dead month of *marraskuu,* and the pleasures of Suvanto spring from heat and cold firmly divided. There are photographs in the big album on the bookshelf in the Radiant Room to this effect, memories from the year before and the years before that, of invigorating walks taken on the glowing ice, photographs of patients and staff holding one another's elbows on brilliant white days. The staff of successive years recede, leaning back in their heavy sheepskin coats and looking away from the camera, but the patients come forward, wrapped in long furs that conceal their figures, dropping from shoulder to knee like warmer versions of the dressing gowns worn inside. The cold is a bracer, a stimulant, if you believe this photographic record. The familiar faces are flushed; Pearl with a previous favorite fox hat high on her head, a white one, the plump softness under her jaw protected by a matching collar. The faces, hers and all the others, oddly heightened but expressionless and candid. Black and white, the hectic undertone, the whites of the eyes and teeth, a few genuine smiles below flaps of fur that cover foreheads and cheekbones, concealing and flattening most of these faces so that they appear similar, as similar as sisters pacing out over the surface of the ice after a certain necessary depth in inches has hardened. Some, of course, do not pace, but prefer to be taken out in wheelchairs.

To actually walk out onto the real frozen bay is a fabulous and fearful delight, crisp under the boots but with the motion of water always underfoot, a subtle fullness, a shifting. There is often a brilliant sky, a bright sun illuminating the frozen surface like a froth of opaque, soapy water, a lighter crust over a darker, more transparent solidity. There is a swimming platform that some family forgot to bring in and stow away when leaving their summer home, a sudden wooden block standing in a dark socket from which the ice has retreated. Are we so far out already? Turn and look backward, there is the beach and above it the broad wall of Suvanto, the many windows, the curving rows of windows like ribbons of glass tied across the concrete surface, glinting.

There are the occasional twin tracks of sleds to show that others have already gone across and there are people visible farther out, dark figures at the horizon where the ice meets the trees far away on the town side. Through the binoculars a distant man pulls a distant child on a sled. There are cracks leading out from the swimming platform, parallel to the shore, and more cracks leading from the lumps of rock rising out of the ice, islands now accessible. It's stable, it's safe, but the cracks are deep and dark and go on for long distances, running out of sight, and the pressure of footsteps right alongside creates a sucking movement. Someone shrieks, and someone else says, *Shut up, just step over.* There is silt caught in the darkness, for those who get down on their knees to look.

Sunny walks the ice as well, and it is a relief to have more territory. She likes the somber green of the cracks. There are places where the fissures converge, triangular breaks that give way to reveal the reassuring thickness of the lip around the hole. Proof of the surface one stands on. The deep water is revealed, startling and dark, until new ice grows back and hardens into opacity.

She pushes the cracks with her foot.

"Aren't you afraid?" someone calls out.

She had been, when she first came. Not now.

"Follow the Finns," she says. "They'll know where it's safe."

In *marraskuu* William Weber puts on a warm hat and eyeglasses and drives the long route overland in a company car, even though the ice is strong enough to take the shortcut. He likes the trees, and he also likes passing the offshoots of logging roads, quick openings blinking at the sides of the car. From above, these roads must look like a pale network of veins branching and spreading in a frozen leaf. He likes that idea.

He comes to visit his wife after an absence of several weeks in which he has received typically affectionate letters reeking of distance and relief. The latest have been signed *Kiss, kiss,* which is new. He arrives in the afternoon and his bag is put into one of the downstairs rooms kept available for rural families coming a long way to visit their hospitalized relatives in serious circumstances. She could have met him in town, but she isn't feeling well, or so she says. He accommodates this as ever, and anyway there is something curious in the way the up-patients do not leave by themselves, but only in the company of someone from outside. A husband, a family member, a friend, at the very least a driver from the outside world is necessary first.

She wants a dinner, she says it is for him, and a kind of dinner party is arranged so that he will meet the new ladies whom she has taken up as friends and of course recognize the ladies from last year.

The Green Room is softly lit, filled with shade-loving plants, ferns and their familiars, and potted trees whose glossy broad leaves are regularly wiped with a dab of mayonnaise to make them gleam. Against the windows there are props of driftwood taller than William himself, from which cascades of long and leggy smilax vines hang like tangled green hair. A table has been assembled there so that others in the dining room will not feel slighted, seeing William, a guest, and not being asked to join. The table isn't big enough for everyone! But it will do for a dozen at least. Chairs are brought, and a tablecloth; at each place there is a stiff white napkin folded to resemble (accidentally, no doubt) the white cotton caps of the nurses who are still, at this hour as at any other, to be found elsewhere in the building, so that as the seats are being taken and before the settings are disturbed it appears that each person at this table will have a vague attendant of her very own.

Those invited sit waiting with their hands in their laps or their arms folded across their chests, with sassy expressions, glad to have been included. The potted trees are drawn closer to the table, making an intimate mood, but beyond them the clay-colored walls seem distant, and the windows are sweating with condensation. William lingers near the smilax, letting the seating order settle itself without him. The leaves of the vines are mingled light and dark green, with curly shoots at the joints, and tiny, soft-looking thorns. He knows that he is being watched. He continues to politely stand near the smilax. There are small pale spots at the crotches of the vines that, he finds, are small insects, oblong, powdery, and piled atop one another, each with a tail of two long hairs. They are motionless even when he blows on them.

He takes his seat. The ladies move their chairs incrementally, repeatedly, and William recognizes, as he does whenever he comes here, the sensitivity that grows in so much leisure. He doesn't understand this. He is embarrassed by this. It is so out of place, so *un-Finnish,* that although nothing has been said, he is sure that the doctors and the other managers of the timber concern must wonder what is wrong with these wives. Everything must be arranged perfectly for them, especially the distance between a plate, a hand, and a glass. They look as soft as poached eggs wrapped in dark dresses, with Pearl as a kind of invalid hostess excused from all responsibilities save conversation. She sits with the pink fox on her head, though it is warm indoors, and he detects on her a bloom of perspiration.

She is sitting beside him tonight, to his left. He had been told, before his first marriage, that he would probably never again be seated side by side with his wife at a dinner party—husbands next to wives, never— but here, it doesn't matter.

"Take off the hat," he says.

"No," she says, "I won't. We make a party for you."

"Speak properly," he says. "Good lord."

At his other side is Mary Minder, moving the closest candle a little closer to her plate. She's put on pink lipstick, and her hair is back-combed and big for this occasion, decorated with a few random, girlish hairpins. Her dress, despite the white collar, is a creamy beige unfortunately so near in color to her skin that for whole moments she appears peripherally nude. And yet in fact is quite concealed in her long sleeves when he turns to look at her directly. Still, it is unsettling.

Does he remember her from last year?

"Yes, of course. Nice to see you again." *Hard to forget those two front teeth.* "Has your stay been helpful?"

"Yes, definitely," she says. "These doctors are better than anyplace else."

Before him on the table are unbreakable steel bowls of pickles, stainless dishes of herrings in oil. A bottle of dark, stiff beer is produced and poured into a goblet before him; it is a gesture, and he must drink it. He hears toasts made, one in his honor, sees strangers clicking their water glasses together repeatedly, and realizes they have looked forward to this all day. This makes him unexpectedly sad. They smile at him along the length of the table. Their brows are thin, and fiercely arched, and plucked and penciled severely.

"In fact," says Mary Minder, "when I got here they asked me if I had ever been examined for discreet tumors. My mother and my grand-mother both had the discreet tumors, so it must run in my family, wouldn't you say?"

"I'm sorry to hear that," he says.

"I've been checked over now, though, thoroughly, and I found the attention absolutely gratifying. I felt very special." And she is reaching for the glass again, teeth clicking against the rim.

He sees a gold tooth, a nervous silver molar in the candlelight. Until now he had not noticed that the steady, recessed lighting of this and every other room allows no shadows to be cast, but tonight the small flames throw out points of light reflected from hairpins, from eyes and teeth, from wedding rings and other rings. From the yellow-gold band of Mary Minder, still adjusting the squat glass candle guard with her fingers, though it must be nearly too hot to touch. There are too many chairs around the table, too close together. Pearl shakes her napkin out of shape, belatedly. Smell of sweated silk.

He shifts, needing more room for his legs, afraid of making unintentional contact under the table. There has already been some agitation over the brown bread and butter being slow to arrive. Pearl's bracelets clink against her glass. Her nails are polished, shining. She tells a story he has heard before, about a ring, a brown amethyst from Brazil so large it nearly paralyzed her finger when she wore it. Across the table, Laimi gives no encouragement. She sits quietly with her hands resting behind a centerpiece of dried flowers. She has changed for dinner from the black dress and tie she normally wears, into a different dress, also plain, also dark. She returns his look, a wincing around the eyes. Surely she must feel as he does—trapped and repulsed by this atmosphere of overly intimate confidence—but she'll probably never say so. Good god, he thinks suddenly, what's it like for her, to be stuck here this long? Doing this every day? With these women? When she looks away he feels a nearly visceral pang of sympathy.

The salad, when it arrives, is cucumber from the greenhouse mostly and some canned fruit. There is a small amount of precious lettuce mixed in, another project of the Mrs. Doctors. He is glad to begin the process despite the diet nurse passing through with admonitions. She delivers a small white medication cup. His salad suddenly tastes of something unpleasant—ammonia?

Is it obvious already that this will be his last visit? He had believed, without phrasing it, in the hygiene, in the motivating idea of the place: a place for those who are not incapacitated but not ready to go home. But these are not sick people. These are bored women, powdered and perfumed for dinner. This is terrible. This is a life without surprises. This is torpor. They're letting themselves fall apart. They're even forgetting the art of conversation, even the ones who had seemed charming last year.

A dark chignon tilts down over a salad plate.

"What's wrong?" someone says.

"My salad has been cut with a knife," says Julia.

And it is true that there is slight discoloration seeping in along the veins. There is a sigh of disappointment, and then—he has never seen such behavior, though it is exactly what he expected—the dark-haired woman puts her chin down on her chest, and William sees tears in her eyes.

"What's wrong with her?" he says to Pearl.

"You can't understand, darling," she says, pushing her plate with her knuckles and leaning over to speak directly to his ear. "There isn't a lot to look forward to, for those of us who are in pain and who are uncomfortable. Every little detail means more to her than it does to you."

He eats his salad, all of it, on principle. But Pearl does not.

"Are you too sensitive to eat your salad?" he says.

She lifts her shoulders, disappointed. He looks down the length of the table. Some of the others are picking unhappily with their forks. Across, Laimi at least is finishing hers with no expression of displeasure.

"I might agree with you at a restaurant," he says. "But this is not a restaurant."

A server appears with dishes of replacement beans for those who are upset.

"This is a hospital," he says.

"Precisely," says Pearl.

Julia puts down her napkin. "Sorry," she says. "I don't know what's wrong with me." She lifts and sniffs the beans. "Do you think they're canned?" she says.

Mrs. Minder sees, does the same, then turns her beans over with her spoon.

The serving maid carries the salads away. William stops her to ask whether they'll be thrown out. He speaks in Finnish.

"*Anteeksi?*" she says, startled.

Pearl flips her napkin but says nothing. The neckline of her black silk dress moves across her collarbones, her beads shifting as well.

"Are you throwing out the salads?"

The girl hesitates. "They'll go to the pigs."

"Scraps for the pigs," he repeats in English.

"You see," says Pearl, "it's not really so bad, not really such a bad indulgence."

"Very pleasant for the pigs," he says.

"Excuse me!" says Mrs. Minder. "Are these beans from a can?"

"No, ma'am. Dried."

Mrs. Minder touches William's arm in relief.

"I'll never eat canned beans again," she says. "My father had botulism, and our family doctor said it was food poisoning, and he said don't worry, it'll pass normally. But it didn't. What do you think happened? He almost died!"

"Bad luck," says William.

Her words are tumbling, she clearly expects to be cut off but she wants to get as much out as she can. "He was stuck in the bed and we had to take turns because he was sick and windy and loose in the bowels and it was terrible, oh yes, it was terrible! My mother and I made diapers out of bath towels. Think about that. Man-sized. And then changing them." And she leaves a pause, for William to imagine.

"After a week we took him back to the hospital. They were amazed that he was still alive. He should have been dead. He nearly lost his kidneys. I was so worried, I nearly poodled in my pants myself—excuse my French."

"I'm sorry to hear that," says William; it has become his easiest answer.

"Mary Minder," says Julia from across and down the table, "don't be shy. You know it was yourself who had the bean poisoning and a full year of diarrhea. Don't blame your father."

"It was not me who had it."

"You know it was. I read it in your diarrhea diary."

"You did not!" Mrs. Minder leans around William, looking to Pearl for help.

"Ignore her, Mary," says Pearl. "Be the bigger person."

But it could be true, William thinks, she might really keep that kind of diary. It wouldn't surprise him. He glances at Julia, the instigator, to find her looking up from her plate, with a smile for him, and he sees that her eyes, in their dark hollows, are brighter and smarter than he'd thought. Was that really all makeup? Why would anyone do something like that to her own face, intentionally? He'd gone to school with an anemic boy, a sickly kid whose eyes had also been set in plum-colored sockets. One of Julia's eyes is more shadowed than the other. It could be the lighting. He meets her gaze perfunctorily, then looks back to his plate.

"I can be the bigger person than you, Julia," says Mrs. Minder. "That's easy."

"Good girl," says Julia. "But you're bigger than me already."

Down the table another napkin is shaken out, a chair moved. William catches a whiff of singed hair and a candle is moved out of the way. Laimi is quietly looking into the middle distance, her fork sitting slackly in her fingers. Her hair is held back behind her ears with silvery clips only visible when she turns her head, infrequently. She's only marking time, he realizes, waiting until it's late enough to go back up to her room and strike another day off the calendar, just as he would have been, in her place.

"He was all right again afterward," says Mrs. Minder.

"You're not all right," says Julia. "You still have it."

"Shut up!"

"And this came from badly canned beans?" asks William, politely.

"I'm certain. I mean I always assumed it did. He hardly ever ate anything else, so I guess it was bound to happen."

The serving maid loads plates onto a cart and goes through a soundless swinging door back along the passage to the kitchen. Mrs. Anderson looks at the plates as the girl bangs them on the edge of the tub reserved for animal scraps. If they'd been left untouched, if they hadn't been forked through, well, maybe someone working in the kitchen might want them, but now of course they are contaminated.

"What a waste," says Mrs. Anderson. "Full moon tomorrow, can't you tell?"

There is a toilet in the hall just before the Green Room doors, toward which William Weber excuses himself. He opens the door—it is unlocked—and catches a quick glimpse of a gray dress, a metal cane propped.

"I'm sorry," he says, stepping back immediately and pulling the door shut. But perhaps the door was unlocked because the occupant was coming out? In that case it's rude to shut the woman in again, if she's trying to get the door open around the impediment of the cane. And so he pushes the door fractionally ajar. Although this doesn't seem quite right either.

William Weber would like to find a different toilet but now the woman (someone he doesn't know and whom he does not think was seated in the Green Room at dinner) starts to shuffle out. He does not want to hurry or embarrass her but there isn't time for him to step far enough away to avoid her. She leaves the bathroom, leaning heavily on the cane, and looks at him. She's an American, then; her curiosity shows it.

"Hello," she says. "It would have been lovely to meet you."

As she moves aside he catches the distinct, unfortunate odor of urinary incontinence. He's sympathetic. For this, for something real, he is truly sympathetic, because we all lose ground, we all grow weak, eventually. *But there's sick, and then there's sick,* he thinks, with distaste. Imagine getting stuck here permanently, in the half light of the upstairs. *If I ever get addled,* he thinks, *if I ever get needy, just take me out behind the barn and shoot me, please.*

Pearl wants everyone to play cards in the Radiant Room. Mrs. Minder wants to smoke a cigarette, but not alone, and Pearl, with a sigh of protest, accepts one as well.

"But you don't smoke," says William.

Pearl says, "Good for the gander, good for the goose."

"But it's not allowed," he says.

Mrs. Minder crouches low, blows smoke up the chimney, past the fire, and Pearl does the same in a practiced way. They've obviously done this before.

Laimi is seated on a sofa. "William," she says, seeing his discomfiture. She lifts a dish of walnuts from the end table and offers it to him, with picks and a set of silver nutcrackers. She smiles, a little, with a small shrug.

"Not much else to do here, I'm afraid," she says. They sit on the sofa with the basket of nuts between them, cracking and extracting, tossing the shells into the fire and listening as the others chat about whether it will snow tonight, or tomorrow, or whether a thaw is coming. Of course there's no thaw coming, not for a good long while; he and Laimi are both noncommittally dismissive. His glasses are lowered on his nose, and his face in concentration is less tense, more neutral, the face of a habitually pleasant individual. He is methodical in his attempts to remove the walnut halves without breaking them, but his fingers are large, and the hook is quite slender, and success doesn't seem possible. He's trying not to have to pick the nutmeats out in pieces.

"Rather Egyptian process," says Laimi, without looking up.

"I got one," he says, holding the curly thing in his hand.

"Here," she says, and gives him two or three of hers. "I don't like them."

"You're not a knitter, are you?" he says, seeing that others, on other sofas, are engaged with their needles, yarn trailing into baskets on the floor beside their slippered feet. There is a faint but steamy odor of vegetables in the air, despite the fireplace, and he blames the baskets.

"I'll say good night," says Laimi, standing.

"Good night, good night," say the others.

"I'll say good night as well," says William, standing also. "I'm going to walk over to Peter's house, before it gets any later."

Pearl has tucked her skirt over her feet, crouching on the fireplace ledge. She is looking up at them, with a faint, sardonic smile, but no possessiveness, not a bit of concern at her husband's innocent conversation—if one can count a dozen words as such—with another woman. It's only Laimi. This is how the evenings go, when they do happen to see her: Pearl grows weary of William's interests, and Laimi either does not or will not show her boredom, and she and William engage in some trivial activity, and then Laimi says good night. If anything, Pearl's smile is encouraging: *Thank you, Laimi, you've done a good deed by taking him off my hands, even briefly.* What she fails to see is that Laimi likes William, that it is not a stretch for them to have a cordial interaction; that in fact William is the only normal, non-caretaking person Laimi has encountered in weeks. He stoops to kiss Pearl's cheek, as powdered and silky as a moth's wing. After all, he loves her, and she might get better.

William collects his things from the coatroom and his boots from the shoe porch and steps out into the fresh, still darkness. He takes the path that circles around the building and across the grounds and up to the gate before the doctor villas, with the intention of visiting Dr. Peter—who is his youngest brother, of course—and Peter's wife, Pamela. William will be sleeping separately in the hospital's family quarters, so there is no chance that he will wake Pearl when he returns; in any case, joining her in the same bed isn't as appealing as it once was.

He bites and spits the end of his cigar into the snow.

William is tired; he drove many hours that day, from the home he shares with Pearl in the cathedral-and-university city of Tampere, a city she hardly even visits now. (What's wrong with Tampere? Nothing is wrong with Tampere; she could have done a lot worse than Tampere. He now has a better question: What's wrong with Pearl?)

He strikes a match and smokes as he walks. He has not yet entirely given up on her, though it is true that their situation is changing, like the slow closing of a door willed shut from both sides. The only time he can look at her and still appreciate her presence without feeling unhappy is when she is asleep. Pearl is peaceful when she sleeps, not fidgeting her jewelery, not touching her hair, not correcting her lipstick after sipping from the small glass near to hand with a foggy reminder of sleeping powder crawling up the sides. In earlier times he had admired her stillness before lifting the duvet and joining her in bed. Her face was more beautiful without the makeup. When she stirred, as inevitably she would, with a small noise of complaint and a frowning movement across her eyelids, he would reach over and draw her closer to him. And in the beginning she had yielded to this with a seeming good-natured totality, and would press limply against his chest, dropping her arms, folding into him, and seeming to sleep even more soundly with one of his heavy legs thrown over her, weighting her into the unresisting feather of the new mattress she had asked for. And often enough she would open her eyes in the darkness and kiss him, and all seemed well, and it was all right then to pull the silky nightgown unhesitatingly up over her full, shapely thighs, though she always slept in stockings rolled up over the knee. For her circulation, she'd said, or for leg cramps. He could have done without hearing that. They'd been more appealing before he'd known their vaguely orthopedic purpose.

Had this been a trick, a misdirection? In that beginning she had even been willing to sleep nude with him, stockings excepted, in the small hours, with the sheets smooth and dense against their skin and the shades drawn. But then his life had resumed and he was soon out again in the evenings, which she took as an opportunity to have some time of her own, to soak in the bathtub, to paint her fingernails . . . but soon when he came home she said, with unmasked irritation, though hidden in the darkness, "You stink of alcohol."

He'd said nothing, reaching across the sheets with fingers that, to her sensitive nose, smelled filthy with smoke.

No, she didn't like the bad smells that she said came into the bed with him—alcohol, and smoke, and onions, and sausages, and other things, too. She complained. Constantly. And it was not only what she said, but the shrinking away that made her seem horrible. This meanness, this smallness was also clear in the way that she slept now when she was with him, with her head thrown back like a pelican in the effort, even while asleep, to avoid his breath. Which was really, in fairness, just breath, just normal breathing, the same as what everybody did. Wasn't it?

He is who he is and for a long time whenever they sleep together he has tried to draw her in, even when she squeals, reasoning that the initial passionate behavior of a woman who had been a virgin until the age of thirty might have faded away because of a self-consciousness, a hesitation not entirely abnormal.

"I've been married before," he reminds her, meaning to tell her not to worry, not to worry about anything. But he's beginning to admit now that she just simply hates the physical details, the smell of whiskers, of whiskey, of jackets and underpants, the rankness of another body close by . . . this, thinks William after a while, is what a late first marriage after an only-childhood will do, it will make a person possibly unfit to live with others. She has the faintly nasty taste of raisins baked into cake in a single-child household to preserve it, where in other more fertile homes the cake never lingers to need preserving. He has been patient. He has said that he will give her time. *I've been married. I understand.* He means to tell her all that having been married means, the adjustments, the knowledge of daily life, everything at once including his willingness to live with her, to be intimate and patient with her. She just has to do the same. And stop complaining about absolutely everything.

And the visits to Suvanto had been his idea. She'd been the reluctant one! (Or perhaps that, too, had been a misdirection?) She hadn't been well during their first winter in Finland. She'd been looking forward to the move, but William had not realized in time that this was because she was tired, so tired, that she wanted to get away because she didn't like people and had assumed that in Finland she would be left alone. She hated the responsibility of interacting with the people he knew, the people one has to see, at least sometimes, and the wives of colleagues, wives of clients. In Tampere, William accumulated colleagues, and clients, and even friends. She developed a headache, and then a backache. He'd suggested calling a doctor. She'd declined. He'd suggested it again, and she'd answered, delicately, and then sharply, that she didn't care for doctors very much. Don't be silly, he'd said. He'd deduced that whatever was bothering her had coincided with the cold weather; she'd begun spending the evenings (and, for all he knew, entire days) in an armchair brought so close to the ceramic hearth that he was compelled to feel it with his hand, repeatedly, to confirm that it wouldn't combust while she sat dozing. She still took the time to powder her face, to do her hair, so that was all right, wasn't it? Nothing too serious? Rheumatism, that kind of thing? Weeks passed. At Christmas he realized she hadn't asked him for gifts—no new boots, no new furs—and he'd called a local doctor, one who spoke some English.

"Get away," she'd said, hiding under her blanket and huddling uncooperatively in an armchair when he let the doctor in. "It's personal!"

William had been mortified.

"Why didn't you say so?" he asked, after the doctor had been seen out. "You could have told me it was personal. I wouldn't have pestered you."

She'd been crying then, poisonous tears that turned her cheeks red in streaks where they fell; he assumed, naturally enough, that by *personal* she must mean *female,* and that by *female* she must mean . . . *menstrual*? He didn't ask, and she didn't elaborate. Nor did she argue when, in the new year, he'd carried her down to the car, tucked a new fur coat around her, and driven her here, to Suvanto.

She'd been reluctant, true enough, but that had changed, pretty quickly. Inspired by the new environment, she began to tend her catalog of discomforts more carefully than any correspondence, writing down her symptoms as they occurred in a little leather-bound datebook kept among her toiletries. Sometimes she also wrote down any gratifying or perceptive comments from new friends. Not those who were actually really terribly ill, poor things, but those with whom she could comfortably discuss the slackness of bowel function, the bloating of the belly, the awful congestion of the menstrual blood, and headaches, headaches, headaches! It wasn't that he pried into her privacy. The little book kept surfacing, in and out of her piles of things, and he'd glimpsed terms private enough to warn him off. Plus, she'd made him listen to the entries, now and then, as she composed them. This had pruned his curiosity back considerably.

Now, every year, September comes and Pearl gets on a train and leaves him behind, on his own, in Tampere for the next few months. This September he'd kissed her on their last night together, and she'd rolled her eyes to the ceiling, not disguising the twitching of her skin even though he was deliberately undemanding as he pressed her to himself for sleeping; he did not even have an erection.

"There's nothing badly wrong with you, is there?" he'd said, not for the first time, settling her face against his chest, breathing into her hair. "You'd tell me?" He'd felt the heat of her contorted face against his chest, and knew by the movements of her lashes that her eyes were open.

"Your whiskers smell of dog," she said. "I can smell them from here."

And because whiskers had once been a playful euphemism between them, she disappoints him. He relaxed his hold and let her slither away. This was the last night they spent together before she came to Suvanto in September, and this is what he will remember when he thinks of her later, when he thinks of her from far away.

He finds the house behind the black hedge and lifts the knocker without taking off his heavy gloves. Dr. Peter opens the door, smiling, and stands aside as William kicks snow against the brushes on the step.

"Come in," says Dr. Peter, opening the door even more widely. William can feel ribbons of warm air flying past him, out into the dark. "Come in and speak some English to us, please. We've run out of topics." Behind him, a fire in a fireplace, and warm smells of coffee and of fruit baked for dessert.

"That's not true!" says Pamela, from another room.

"Are you hungry? Did you have a nice dinner over there?"

"It was terrible," says William. "Very unpleasant."

He wipes condensation from his mustache with a handkerchief. They can hear Pamela getting the children ready for bed, helping them say good night to the white mice who live in a vivarium among the plants of an indoor garden. They've been given their dinner of oats, beans. The mice, that is. A little white bread soaked in milk. A few peanuts that the children also like to eat. A few for the mice, a few for the brother and sister. *Good night, mice!*

He shrugs out of his coat, and says again, "Terrible." Unlaces his boots. Scarf tucked into a coat sleeve. He follows Peter into the sitting room and is given a tumbler of bourbon.

"Do you want ice?" says Peter. "We have plenty. That's a joke, by the way."

William leans back into the sofa, his reddened cheeks making him appear a bit bewildered. "I think they like it," he says.

"You think who likes what?"

"They like being sick. That's all they talk about. Even at dinner they keep talking about . . . personal details not appropriate for the dinner table."

"Pamela's got dinner for you, if you're interested."

"Thanks. I think I will be, in a bit."

"That's good news, by the way," says Peter. "It's good news for me, if they enjoy being patients, because I'm going to need them."

"No," says William. "These won't be having any babies."

"Ah, well," says Peter. "Maybe they'll like the idea of a little operation to keep life interesting. Maybe it'll catch on and be fashionable."

"That's awful!" says William. "But I wouldn't be surprised."

"I'm only half-serious. But I really could make those women into happier people."

"You mean by taking out the . . ." But William won't say it. Doesn't want to.

"The uterus. Don't be so melodramatic."

William watches as Peter fills both glasses again. "Peter," he says. "Do you think maybe she's not quite right?"

Peter hesitates, out of courtesy. "Who do you mean?" he asks.

"Pearl."

"I haven't seen much of Pearl, to be honest. I don't go up to that floor much."

"No? I hoped you were looking in on her, now and then," says William. "But I suppose you've been busy, doing the other thing."

"What other thing?" says Peter; this is the way of it. William understands what Peter does, of course, but he's not so comfortable with the vocabulary.

"The special babies—taking them out of the . . . uteruses."

"Not yet," says Peter, smiling into his glass. "In the new year."

William shifts his legs. "You're pretty sure it fixes female problems?" he asks. His socks are wet, and he points them toward the fire, looking down as he speaks. "The operation? Do you think it could help Pearl?"

Now it is Peter who hesitates. "You mean a hysterectomy? I don't think so. Pearl's not at that point in her life, William. She's not old enough."

"Good," says William, relieved. "I don't want her to know about it."

"I'm not her doctor," says Peter.

"I don't want her getting an operation just because others are doing it. Because—Jesus, Peter, it's disgusting. I don't know how can you do something so unnatural. Even taking the babies out that way doesn't sound very good."

Peter says, a little sharply, "I'm helping them. You know that."

"I know," says William. "I know. But it still seems so savage."

"Are you drunk?" says Peter. "Do you have any idea how many women die in childbirth, even in the hospitals?"

"No," says William. "A lot, I guess."

"Do you know what happens when we can't get the baby out normally through the birth canal?"

"I don't want to know."

"You're right, you don't want to know. We have to choose between the mother's life and the baby. You can't imagine what that really entails."

"No, I can't imagine," says William, agreeing, unhappily.

"I'm being serious," says Dr. Peter. "I want you to think about it. How do you get the baby out, when the baby won't come? What if the head's too big? How can you expect to get the baby out *in one piece* if the head's too big?"

William is silent. "That's terrible," he says finally.

"Yes. It's horrific. On my word, William, I'll never do it again. You think I'm a savage? Do you think crushing a baby's skull is more civilized? I don't think so," says Peter, reaching for the bottle. "This way the baby gets to live, too."

"Okay," says William, "you're right, I know."

"It's not the same procedure," says Dr. Peter, "but any time I can take one out over there, I'll do it, you bet I will. The Finns need time to learn the stitch, and I can't wait around for opportunities to show them."

"But then you won't need to do the stitch," says William. "Because it's all coming out, right?"

"If the uterus is coming out anyway," says Peter, "does an extra stitch really matter? Would even a dozen practice stitches matter?"

"Peter," says William, aghast.

"Weigh it up, and tell me, do you have a better way?"

William can't find an answer. "Not Pearl," he says, finally. "Please."

"I won't," says Peter. "Not until she legitimately needs a hysterectomy, and then it's in her best interest, too."

There are sounds from the kitchen, of cupboards being touched.

"She's got a plate of venison for you," says Peter. "Pam's got your dinner warming in the oven. She'll be out in a few minutes."

"For me?" says William, looking to the hall, realizing the sounds of bedtime for the children have gone quiet. "Very kind," he says. "Very kind of her."

He rests his head against the sofa, staring into the fire. He feels nauseated, and perhaps as far from physical appetite as he's ever been. He can't look at Peter for the moment. Isn't there some other way? There must be a better way. Peter knows what has to be done. But William can't agree. "Do the Finns know?" he says.

"Not yet," says Peter. "I need to make sure it's actually a good teaching opportunity. I'll confirm that pretty soon."

"How will you know?" says William.

"Do you really want to keep talking about this?" asks Peter.

"No," says William. "I don't think so." And he looks around the room for reassurance from the tidy surfaces, the neat books in the shelves, the chaste potted plants, the presence of Pamela, soon to join them and hopefully interrupt this terrible conversation. But he stops, sits up straight, and looks behind him, all around the room.

"Where's the *rjily*?" he says, checking the four walls.

"The what?"

It's a Finnish textile, wool woven with geometric patterns, deeply colored from natural dyes; it had hung on the north wall of the main room. But where is it now?

Dr. Peter hadn't liked it. He'd thought it would be too dusty. "That old rug?" he said. "It's rolled up in the attic."

That *rjily* is a sacred item, handwoven, well over a hundred years old and irreplaceable. It may look like something between a blanket and a rug, but it is neither, it is both and more. It insulates the room, bringing comfort and color in the cold months. The *rjily* is an old way to strengthen the north wall of the home and prevent the devil from entering there, from the north, his favorite direction of approach.

"I brought that for you," says William. "Don't you care? It's a house-warming present, so put it back up, all right? Put it back where you found it."

"Why are you so superstitious, all of a sudden?" says Dr. Peter, smiling again.

Pamela comes with coffee, and a warm plate of food, and sits down with them on the sofa. She's brought William a knife, and a fork, and he'll do his best to clean his plate.

"I mean it," says William. "Put it back up."

"I will," says Peter, even though he clearly won't.

In the morning William drinks his coffee and leaves without waking Pearl to say good-bye. He'll drive directly over the frozen bay using the tracks marked with sawn branches by the locals, the shortest, quickest route away from the place. He won't be back. He wants Pearl out. This is why he will send word within the week that Pearl should pack up if she wants to accompany him on a trip that will lead them to St. Petersburg, a destination she has been agitating toward for months, with her silly fox fur hat, her tourmalines and cameos, her sugar held between the teeth while drinking tea, and her feigned, affected, embarrassing taste for vodka, for caviar.

It's not common knowledge, but Dr. Peter has already invited a few delicate maternity patients for bed rest and observation. Babies will be born, as he told William, in the new year. The first of the mothers, in fact, is already preparing to arrive, and very soon she will come through the lobby, with her husband carrying her small suitcase, and she will move into a semiprivate room. And she will wait patiently to be moved upstairs into Pearl's place in her absence.

Pearl will want to know when the decision was made, and why she was not told.

Why would you be consulted? Why do you care? You're not even sick!

She must give up the room. Her attachment isn't healthy. This is a change in policy, that's all, not a decision to take away her retreat. No one intends to be cruel, but the room won't be there when they return from Russia. She'll have no choice but to come home. This is only part of a logical progression and you can't stand in the way of progress, personal or public. So just come along to Petersburg instead. See the palaces on the Neva. Walk with me, hold my arm, along the *prospekts*. I will buy you amber by the fistful and we will eat very well, we'll have wild game and cream and pepper and rare golden berries. And if you want vodka, or strong tea from a silver samovar, you can have that, and you can have many more things that you haven't even thought of yet. You can have everything you ask for, everything. And if that's not good enough . . .

He buttons his coat, adjusts his gloves, and departs over the ice into an open vista composed of harder lines, more definite perceptions.

Ten

Good-bye, for now! How exciting! St. Petersburg! Happy travels! Departure is a perfect excuse for a little merriment and movement. *Bon voyage! Hyvää matkaa!* Can anyone say it in Russian? Three bottles of secret champagne appear after dinner, provided by Pearl, and a shot of vodka apiece for those who think they want one.

"Give it back," she says, annoyed when Mary Minder hesitatingly touches her dark tongue to the rim of the glass. Pearl tips it back in one go, and oh, how it hurts!

It's another special occasion in the Green Room, and Pearl snaps her fingers to send two ladies to fetch the record player on a wheeled cart. Russian folk dances are played, and someone contributes a tin of caviar received as a gift, now given again. It sits opened on the table with the coffee, black, glistening, bulging, uneaten.

"Did you read about Faye's comet?" says Mrs. Numminen. Pearl turns away, too busy, leaving Mary Minder to listen. "It was in the newspaper. Faye's comet passes every eight years and we can see it from here, if the sky is clear."

"What's a comet, again?" Mary asks.

"Have you been to St. Petersburg?" Julia asks Laimi.

"Yes, of course," she says. "Several times."

"Did you enjoy yourself?"

"I was there as a student," says Laimi.

"I knew a man from St. Petersburg," says Julia. "He was teaching in Helsinki. Then he moved to Turku to teach Russian language and literature at the university. He hated it. And I agreed with him, because I found it hard living among you, too."

"You've been here long enough to understand that he should have gone home," says Laimi. "Nobody here wants to learn Russian. Especially not students."

"But Finland was part of Russia," Julia says, "whether you like it or not."

"Not technically true," says Laimi, "though I'm sure your friend said so."

Laimi is quite all right, quite unoffended; Laimi leans forward to take up the pot to refill her own cup of coffee, pausing first to offer some to Julia. You see? Unoffended. A few bars short of amused, maybe, but certainly not offended, and when Laimi looks fixedly at Julia it's clear she doesn't feel the touch of intimidation that some others might. It's as though she has already said to Julia, *Why are you being deliberately obtuse?* And as if Julia has answered, *I'm not.* To which Laimi has said, *You are, but you're lying, so I have to assume you're incapable of straightforward communication.* Laimi sits back again, watching Julia.

"Go on," says Laimi. "I'm somewhat curious to hear you."

The stack of records makes a waxy clatter when browsed. Someone finds sound effects to be used in pantomimes and drops the needle. There's the sound of a dog, barking in the distance.

"What's that?" says Pearl. "Turn up the volume."

The barking is joined by more barking, growing louder like a pack of dogs circling closer. The barking peaks, drops off, resumes. There's a howl, and a squeal, like a dog just kicked, which makes Mrs. Minder laugh. She uncrosses her legs and leans forward in her seat.

"Oh, my bladder!" she says. "Put it to the windows."

She rises and on tiptoe pushes the cart toward the glass-paned wall. Someone else cranks a window open and the sound of barking moves out into the quiet evening; it's easy to imagine someone imagining a pack of wolves running loose among the trees.

"You don't like dogs," says Julia.

"Not particularly," says Laimi.

"Did you get a bite, when you were little, maybe?"

"No, Julia, but it's nice that you ask. In fact I saw a pack of dogs bring down a bear once. It was a horrible thing to witness."

"Hunting is a natural outlet for animal urges," says Julia.

"That's sometimes true," says Laimi, "but these men tied up the bear, and I don't believe it was natural when they forced a pole between his jaws so that they could pry his mouth open, and leave him until his tongue cracked, and his voice went hoarse from crying. They were shaking the pole, in time to music. They meant to infuriate the bear, of course, and to torment him, and make him crazy with pain and confusion. It worked, and it was cruel and stupid."

"All people are cruel and stupid," says Julia. "I'm sure they put him out of his misery, eventually."

"They pierced a ring into his nose, first. Then they broke his paws, so he couldn't hurt them, and then they untied him, and then they shot him. For sport. It was quite impressive behavior, by some very brave men, clearly."

Even Julia looks down at this. "Is that a typical Finnish sport?" she says.

"Oh, no," says Laimi. "No, these were Russians on a hunting holiday. These were Russians, having a party, in Karelia."

Julia accepts another small glass of vodka, tipping it into her coffee. "How could you watch?" she asks. "I couldn't have stood by for that."

"Really?" says Laimi. "Do you think your tender feelings are that valuable? Or that ignoring something very bad means you're not participating in the cruelty?"

"And yet you did participate. You watched, and you keep a bearskin blanket folded in your room. I've seen it, when your door was standing open."

"Ah, Julia. That bear was shot cleanly by my uncle, years before I was born. There is a philosophical difference."

"But the end result is the same, for the bear."

"You can't be serious," says Laimi, and then she laughs, unguarded and incredulous. "How could you possibly think that?"

"I have nothing more to say to you," says Julia. "You're laughing at me. I'm just an old woman, and you should be ashamed. You should be ashamed of yourself."

"Strange," says Laimi. "I don't think I feel anything like that."

"Then that's what's wrong with you," says Julia. "No shame."

"I can't find any," says Laimi, looking thoughtful. "So it must be true, I haven't got any shame. I also don't have any of the—" and she pauses again, to find the right words in English. "I don't share your obvious feelings of self-hatred. All of you."

"But what if we frighten someone?" says Mrs. Minder suddenly. "What if we give someone out there a heart attack?" She turns down the volume. "Someone down in the regular rooms?" She whispers this, and then they are sorry, a little. But it was worth the fun while it was happening, wasn't it?

Until the silence, the deep silence after the needle is lifted. Then there is the night outside, and the ice in the air, and the moonlight. Something should be done or said, probably? To atone for the flippancy? They step out then, through the wide glass doors onto the swept concrete, to stand with arms crossed. But the atmosphere is impassive, and they have no effect. Their voices are absorbed, wicked away from their mouths, and it is clear that against the night they are very small, very insignificant indeed.

Parties notwithstanding, everybody wants to feel unflustered and calm. The ideal private hospital was a haven of rest, extremely clean by the contemporary standards, where all of the practical details of rest and recuperation would be taken care of by an efficient system. That the up-patients were able to live as they did marks out Suvanto as a hybrid, part hospital, part hotel, upstairs, anyway. Even the doctors did not include the up-patients in their daily rounds, leaving their observation more or less to Sunny and her staff—much as the Head of Nursing believed that nothing in Sunny's reports was likely to be of interest. All were in agreement that these patients weren't sick enough to be here; these patients were taking time they did not deserve, filling spaces and beds they did not need. But there was the agreement with the timber concern—when their North American employees came permanently, or for a few years at a time, the wives, and daughters if there were any, wanted English-speaking doctors. The men didn't care so much. The men were able to make do with local doctors. But in exchange, the annual contribution in American dollars spent treating their wives would ensure that more local women, including poor women, and rural women, could be taken into the downstairs wards, where all would remain normal. Where, just as in the States, ordinary patients had little control over their treatment, where female patients especially were told less, because anxiety might provoke new symptoms. Peter Weber, whom we call Dr. Peter, had been trained in that kind of regulated atmosphere. He had expectations of a certain kind of order, of protocol. It can hardly have been otherwise.

William Weber leaves for Russia, and Pearl goes as well. This is when Dr. Peter becomes immediately more present at Suvanto, walking in the halls with a slight limp left over from an accident in childhood. This is how babies will come to be born at Suvanto, and how plans will arise to remodel the top floor into a maternity ward.

There is more underneath than just casual agreements and the admission of the first expectant mothers. There is the fact of Dr. Peter's qualification in gynecology as a surgical specialist, and also his interest in obstetrics. There is also the proposition that he had made the year before: let him bring obstetrics into the routine at Suvanto, let him perfect the stitch, and in return Dr. Peter will invest some of his own money, as a gesture, taking the place of the timber subsidies for at least two years.

Not yet, though. He'll have to wait until the mothers are ready. But decisions made for the future give Dr. Peter a legitimate right to install a few problem maternity patients at Suvanto a bit early; this is how the change becomes inevitable.

Rumors are the first way in which Sunny is offended in the month of November. It is humiliating, to be asked for details at an Orvokki staff meeting: one of the nurses has heard in the sauna that changes are being discussed. Is it true that a few obstetrical cases will be brought experimentally to Suvanto? And that in time one of the wards will be given over to mothers needing care for complicated births? And that the babies might even be kept with their mothers, in the same room? And is it in any way true that Dr. Peter is perfecting a new version of a cesarean section? And that he'll be perfecting that surgery here?

"Well," says Sunny, who has not heard any of this until now, "nothing has been decided, but as we know, Dr. Weber is a specialist."

"There's no nursery."

"They'll keep the babies with the mothers the whole time," someone says.

"That will change everything." But this is said with a degree of fascination, a novelty that provokes some institutional pride. Not quite what Sunny herself is feeling.

"Is he bringing nurses from town?"

"Nothing has been decided," she says, and thinks, *He'd better be.*

In her office she thinks over the first few words of a letter of resignation, trying to compose it in Finnish, but she stops because these words would look so indulgent, so melodramatic, and because she is practical by nature and knows that the proposed change is just a rumor at the moment. And where would she suddenly go, anyway? Back to the States? In any case, she knows from experience that things do not change drastically here, not quickly, and not during the winter. *But if it happens,* she thinks, *I'll have to get out of here, before the babies come.*

Sunny has always made it clear that she cannot work with maternity cases. She accepted this position in faith that she would never have to.

Remember the story half-told, the birth of her younger sister and the injury suffered by her mother during a long, hard labor. Some injuries can never be fixed, or at that time could never be fixed, and one of these injuries, a terrible trauma, permanently disabling and intensely painful, was a certain kind of fistula, a bladder ruined by the grinding skull of a reluctant baby. What can you do, when the tissue is flayed, destroyed? All you can do is suffer, for years. Her mother's injury was long before the corrective surgery was perfected . . . and the pain, the dressings, the unbearable shame of the obvious, the slow horror of the undisguisable trickle of continual incontinence, the rotten smell of a ruined body, of spoilt bedding, the damp mattress, Sunny as a teenager going out to find linens, bandages, replacement rubber covers, and the pain, the pain, the pain . . . let us say simply that by the time Sunny was grown it seemed quite obvious that her experiences in the home would lead to a career in nursing. That she is disinclined to touch a pregnant woman. That she avoids them. She never speaks of it.

It is not long after the rumors of the change reach Sunny, accidentally and through her staff, that Dr. Peter lets Sunny know that he will be visiting her patients in their rooms. And would she accompany him? He would like to become much better acquainted with the workings of the residential floor.

Accustomed to her own routine, Sunny takes the hour needed to see how the residents are feeling . . . to make sure they're all clothed and presentable and in their own beds, and then she is in the supply room at the far end of the floor when Dr. Peter arrives. The charge nurse presses the small bell to get Sunny's attention while Dr. Peter waits at the nurses' station. He is writing something down; some kind of evaluation is already in progress. She walks toward him with an armful of charts, looking entirely correct, aware that she must be careful to play this role well today. He looks up at her and smiles and says, "Good morning, Nurse Taylor."

And Sunny also says good morning. Even though she has been awake since 4:30 and it does not feel like morning. She is polite, she is obliging, she is as courteous to him as she would be to any of the doctors, Finnish or American, but she will not be lulled by the ease of speaking a common language. She doesn't have reason yet to distrust his intentions, and being unaccommodating with the doctors would be, at best, counterproductive; actually it's hard to say what the reaction might be, as none of the nurses ever disagree with them outright. But Sunny sees that in contrast with his white coat, which is starched and ironed, he is wearing outdoor shoes and that the cuffs of his pants are damp. He hasn't yet realized the wisdom of changing wet, heavy outdoor shoes for dry, light indoor ones. There will be a trail of sand from the paths dropping behind him throughout the day every day of the winter until he looks around and notices that everyone else has left their outdoor shoes behind, arranged neatly by the doors.

He would like to see all of the patients, including those he has not yet seen in the clinical wing. Sunny looks at the side of his head as he is writing. His hair is clipped and smooth. His dark eyes flicker to brown only when he looks at her directly; his obvious curiosity about the layout of the floor feels judgmental, except that of course he has hardly been there before, and so curiosity is normal. She leads him along the curving hall. All of the doors ordinarily kept open midmornings as a nod to the nurses, from which daylight might angle weakly into the hall, are now closed. She might have expected to see this at Pearl's empty room, but here too is even Laimi's door, at the end, closed like all of the others.

Hadn't she, earlier that morning, spoken of Dr. Peter's rounds to the residents, and hadn't she said to make yourselves available?

At the door beside Julia's he taps once, a courtesy. "Doctor's rounds," he says, and opens the door, and there is no response because the room is empty.

"Occupied," he says to Sunny, "yet empty."

She gives him the chart and says, "Early riser."

He makes a note and the next room is Julia's. He taps the door once with a knuckle, again a courtesy warning, and turns the handle, and the door does not respond.

"Occupied?" he says, and Sunny is embarrassed. She hands him the chart, and he says, "Is Mrs. Dey also an early riser?"

"Not in my experience." Julia had been there earlier, still in the bed.

Dr. Weber raps again uncompromisingly, such that his knuckles must have felt pulpy and sore later, but the sound is deadened, and there's no answer.

"There was a going-away party last night for Pearl," says Sunny. "Some of them are sleeping late because of that."

"A party," he says. "That's interesting. Is Julia the one with the bad behavior?" He looks through Sunny's notes and although it is indeed what she has written, in abbreviated detail, she wants to soften it now.

"Mrs. Dey is more comfortable now, and she's doing much better."

"Do they take the keys with them?" he asks. There are keyholes and surely keys must exist someplace—on a ring in Sunny's office, for example—but even in times of petty theft they do not hand out keys for the doors of the up-patients. Invariably some would lose them, perhaps in the snow, and what would happen then? Endless copies being cut of endless keys.

"No, we don't give them room keys. I don't know how she can have locked it."

Sunny carries the master on her ring and tries it now in the keyhole.

"It must be barred from the inside," she says.

"Which means that she's in there, I suppose. Is there any good reason why she might lock herself in?"

"No, Doctor." *We'd prefer to avoid you, Doctor, no offense intended.*

"Wait here," he says. "And listen for her."

"Yes, Doctor."

At the nursing station he tells Nurse Todd to call someone to get the door open. Sunny stays where she is, waiting; she knocks once, and says her own name. Down the hall she can see Dr. Peter looking back at her, looking at her and seeing—not her, really, but only a woman in a blue uniform. He is assessing her, and he is not impressed.

"Julia, open the door," says Sunny, believing that she ought to submit, in her own best interests, because although the up-patients are well looked after, it is still the doctors' prerogative to see them. Of course it is. She puts one ear to the crack and simply stands, in her silent shoes, with the side of her white cap touching the door frame. It is very quiet within. She lifts her head, realizing belatedly that behind each door, someone is waiting. Waiting for Dr. Weber to leave, and Sunny too, though realistically of course they can't. Won't.

Sunny touches the key ring at her waist out of habit. The shadowy forms of the residents seem obvious behind those other closed doors, as if the walls are as membranously transparent as oiled paper. And most disturbing is the attitude of listening—each form seated at the edge of a bed or before a bureau, inclined a little forward, waiting, as she herself is waiting, to see what will happen when the doctor returns. Straining to hear in the controlled, muffled rooms. This has never seemed sinister to her before, the hidden presence of others up and down the hall. But today, it does. She can feel them, all around, in all directions, behind every wall and door.

He comes and says, "Is there a chance she might hurt herself?"

"No, Doctor." She almost laughs, but doesn't. Of course she does not laugh.

Dr. Peter puts his eye to the keyhole, but can see nothing. Sunny watches, keeping her face plain and opinionless. She can't bring herself to participate in this, although she knows that his intentions, his concerns, seem logical to him because he doesn't know Julia, doesn't know her personality at all.

And now soon here is Kusti, who of course has slipped off his boots for a pair of indoor rubber clogs, after zipping himself into a clean, dry set of coveralls. On seeing him in his clogs Sunny realizes that she does not know where he enters the building, whether he comes from one of the connecting underground passages, or where he leaves his shoes and his coat. At the foot of her own stair, for example, there is a door, and beside it a place for outdoor shoes and hooks on the wall for the supervisors' coats. Kusti holds his own ring of keys and doesn't look directly at Dr. Peter.

"This door," says Dr. Peter. Kusti squints at the hinges.

"Just open it, please," says Dr. Peter.

Kusti slowly flips through his keys, examining the numbers on each. "It's barred from the inside," says Sunny.

Kusti finds the appropriate key and tries it, but the door will not open.

"It's barred from the inside," she says again.

"Take it off the hinges," says Dr. Peter.

Kusti takes a screwdriver from a pocket of his blue worksuit and methodically removes the screws from the hinge plates, slipping them into another pocket, and then he gently lifts the door away from the frame. There is a sound of something metal falling to the floor inside.

Dr. Peter looks at the blankets of the unmade bed. He turns back to the door.

"Where's the inside bolt?"

"*Det finns inte,*" says Kusti. Meaning, there isn't one. And Sunny remembers that he's a Swedish speaker. She hasn't actually ever heard him speak before.

"Where is she?" says Dr. Peter. Kusti will not step into the room but waits at the threshold. Sunny goes to the window, though she knows that it will not open wide enough to permit exit.

The room is exactly as it was when Sunny had last been in it. On the bureau there are combs, a pair of gloves, and a bottle of cold cream with the lid screwed on incorrectly. And the smell of some perfume that reminded simultaneously of birthday cake and faint intestinal gas.

"This just isn't acceptable," says Dr. Peter to Sunny. "They shouldn't be able to lock these doors from the inside." He looks to the wardrobe and Sunny realizes that he still expects to find Julia, uncooperative, somewhere in the room.

"Yes, Doctor. This has never happened before. I'll speak to Mrs. Dey."

"It isn't up to Mrs. Dey," he says. "It's our responsibility to keep track of her. It's *your* responsibility. What if she falls? What if there was a fire? She needs to be accessible at all times, especially if she's any danger to herself."

"She isn't," says Sunny, who knows that there is no record in the charts of her suspicions about the nocturnal pranks, or the butter knife. She knows what will happen now if she ever tells Dr. Peter about them; at the very least, a restraining board will be tied to Julia's bed frame at night, and who knew what dreams this might inspire.

"Where do you think she is?" he says.

"She could be out for a walk, or she could be on the promenade. She might be in the dining room," says Sunny. "They come and go pretty much at will."

"Then when do you complete your rounds?"

"Early. I'm quicker than they are."

He smiles, but only to show that he does not understand, she can see that he does not understand, and he shakes his head slightly.

She says, "If you'd like to come with me at that time—"

"No," he says, almost gently, as if Sunny and everyone else were mistaken, as from his perspective they must certainly have seemed. "This is not a hotel. Tell them all that I'll see them in the afternoon."

When Dr. Peter leaves to visit his surgical cases downstairs Sunny gets into the elevator with him, to look for Julia, although she does not tell him this. Kusti is by then carefully replacing the door on its hinges, wiping the edges clear of his own invisible handprints.

In the elevator, he says, "Competent nursing should prevent this kind of chaos."

And Sunny says, "Yes, Doctor," because it is true.

It is nothing personal, it has only been a statement, Sunny can see this although Julia will not admit it. Back in the room later Sunny finds the bent butter knife on the floor near the wastebasket, and thinks that it had been wedged into the hinge somehow as Julia left the room that morning.

"How did you manage to block the door?" she asks.

"I didn't," says Julia.

"How did you expect to get back into your room?" says Sunny.

"I didn't."

"Dr. Weber will be back after lunch," says Sunny. "I'll be here with him."

"Fine," says Julia. "I'll be here with him too."

It would be wrong, though easy, to assume, as some of us did, that Dr. Peter's later advice to Julia is a response to this stressed beginning; that would imply an impulse to punish that wasn't ever there. At most, he might have wanted to cut through any silliness, misdirection, or waste of energy. His intentions were always good. And when Dr. Peter comes to Julia's room they speak about the pessary as if it were an orthopedic shoe, nothing more, something useful for a while, but not something to ever be proud of or very much attached to. There is a better solution. Surgery, he explains, will correct her problem permanently, and allow her to feel normal again.

"There's no reason to wear that pessary any longer than you have to. It's uncomfortable and unnecessary. And there is a remedy."

Julia sits at her table, hands in her lap. Her eyes are dull, turning inward like those of a fish pulled up and left to suffocate in the sun. She turns her head, looks at Sunny.

Sunny moves to answer him, but she has nothing to object with, nothing other than Julia's own previous fears of being tampered with. And Julia is not actually protesting; Julia says nothing. Anyway Sunny has not been asked, and the decision is settled as part of a story already determined.

"A hysterectomy will make her a lot more comfortable in the long run," he says, looking at Julia's chart later, and he smiles, now that a minimum of order has been established. Now he is walking in the hall quite naturally, as if he will never leave it. He turns his head, so solidly attached to his shoulders, and there is a nagging in Sunny's brain— perhaps a premonition of things to come—an observation of the contour where Dr. Peter's head would be most efficiently separated from his body. There is an invisible red line sketched below his chin, curving where his head would be most easily scooped away from his neck. The thought is a sudden effort to restore proportion, because the weight of all his intention is too heavy. But it's ridiculous to imagine that decapitating him could restore proportion because then, of course, he would be dead.

She hardly knows she's had the thought, so similar is it to the many other momentary, inchoate impulses, like the urge to cut down young trees, to lop off rosebushes at the ground. To ride her bicycle into the cemetery wall. To walk down to the shore and fall forward, at the edge of the water, splitting her skull and cracking a line to the cold mantle of the bedrock somewhere below.

Sunny parks her bicycle in the covered shed near the kitchens, protected from the waist-high snowdrifts on either side. It is dark after her evening ride and she has her personal key ring in her hand in readiness, though she feels perfectly comfortable in the darkened yard. She can see quite well by the lights of the circular front drive off to the side. The keys are ready in her hand and heavy because keys have been especially much on her mind today. She cuts across the yard, through the shadows toward the side door in the base of the supervisors' tower. Her fingers are cold and the ring of keys just simply slips away. She hears them click together in the air, but there is no sound of them hitting the ground. She stops. They have disappeared neatly into airy, porous snow, leaving no hole behind. Without moving her feet, she tries to reconstruct their trajectory. She is carrying a small flashlight as usual and she takes it from her coat pocket and turns it on, but can see nothing to help. And the light in her hand suddenly seems to call attention to herself. Above, she thinks that anyone passing in the hallways of the hospital can easily look out and see her sinking to her knees. Most of the windows are invisible behind drawn thermal shades, and those rooms whose lit ceilings she can see don't offer the silhouettes of any observers. Some of the upper rooms are dark, however, and invisible, with shades left undrawn, probably empty, since it's still the dinner hour. As she looks up she hears an unexplained sound, like ceramic against glass, from a high unidentifiable source, and this is so unaccountably disturbing that she shuts off her flashlight immediately. It's a little ridiculous; she can still be seen against the snow, after all. She'd felt an instinctual fear of something being dropped, or thrown at her, but of course that's ridiculous. And the windows don't open wide enough anyway. But isn't it strange? Isn't it strange that she feels nothing out of place while riding through the trees, even in the dark, even through the graveyard, but one small creaking sound this close to the building floods her mouth with the tinny taste of adrenaline?

She still needs her keys and she's got no choice but to begin in the only way she can think of, by brushing her hands, ungloved now, through the bottom layers nearest the ground in a sweeping circle, disrupting the snow and possibly burying the keys further, but what else to do? And after a long interval, after her hands have grown painful and wet and then numb, she finds them, suspended in a bank to one side of the path. She sits back on her heels for a moment, relieved, but a soft sound behind her, much closer than the first, makes her spring up and turn in time to see something, she's not sure what, drop quickly from near the roof and disappear almost silently into the snow near the building. Falling icicles, probably. Dangerous. They can impale you, easily. She'll tell Kusti, or someone. Not trusting her fingers now she puts the keys away in a pocket, from where they radiate cold, even inside later when she spreads them out on a towel to dry.

After a cup of tea she has still not entirely thrown off the cold. Nor has she thrown off that feeling of standing alone outside at night, a shrinking of the world down to her own body, a shrinking down to her own warmth in layers of wool and cotton, simultaneous with an expansion of the world out toward the remote, cold, inhuman expanses. On this night, in this state, she goes down and puts her coat and shoes back on, and walks across the grounds to the nurses' pavilion for a sauna among others.

She undresses in the anteroom, showers, and wraps herself in a clean white towel. She knows that she is not alone here, because there are silent dresses and sweaters hanging neatly on the hooks, shoes lined up inside the door, and the living quality of a shared sauna in the air. She knows there are others inside already, and this is a relief. In the early days Sunny felt anxious there in the darkness if, when alone, she heard the anteroom door open, imagining another woman unbuttoning a dress, slipping off her shoes, lifting a towel. Then the shower, the sound of water hitting the tiles. Waiting for the door to open. The outline of a body entering against the lit doorway. Then where to look, and whether to speak, and what to say if so? And if the other woman speaks, then how much to answer? To make eye contact or not? To try to speak in Finnish or not? Or to leave the other woman tactfully alone?

For them, the Finnish women, it seems easy. They are at ease here, and they seem at ease with themselves generally. Maybe they have learned to sit like this, comfortable in their nudity, from childhood? They can relax easily in the circumstance, but Sunny is still learning to be calm. To come and go from the heat and to stand without embarrassment at the wide-open windows, her flesh exposed to the ice, the stars. Recalibrating her core so that the cold won't touch her, can't enter her afterward when she steps out, ready to ride over to share whatever Sister Tutor and Mrs. Anderson are listening to on the radio.

She pulls open the wooden door and steps into the dark heat. At first she can't see the faces of the other women who are there. She steps up to the top tier, and as she relaxes in the warmth she feels the heat changing the contours of her face. The end of her nose begins to feels pinched, narrow, her cheeks seem to flatten, her ears are receding. It is like finding the natural expression that underlies all others. It is like turning back the changes that come over her face by degrees during the day.

The practical nurse and her niece who worked together in the Daisy ward have since been separated during work hours, but they are here together now. It is quiet for several minutes, and then the girl speaks of a woman in her new unit who, throughout the night, calls out from her bed.

"She says, 'Apu apu apu apu . . . help help help help.'"

"Some of them do that," says her aunt.

"But then she slaps me away. She won't stay in her bed. I find her half in and half out almost every night. She had a stroke."

"All you can do is dress her properly. Then put her in a chair, wrap her in a blanket, set the brake, and leave her someplace where she can look out the window into the trees. That's all you can do."

They're quiet then, and Sunny knows they are silently sympathizing with how much that woman would hate to see herself so reduced, so dependent and in need. The shame she would feel, if she understood. Much better if she doesn't.

A thickish sweat slips over her skin. The women on the tiers around her start speaking quietly again. They talk about work a little more, but then they drift away, toward other things, and the patients who consume the hours of their shifts are left behind. They've been to a movie in town. They've been out for lunch in town, to one of the department stores on the Kauppatori, to the tearoom on the third floor with a view of all the people shopping in the square. One of them says something funny that Sunny doesn't quite catch. It would have been nice if she'd been able to make friends here. Maybe it would have been nice. There had been Laimi. But Sunny herself was the obstacle, she knows.

The aunt stands and makes a gesture to the bucket of water—does Sunny mind?

"Thanks," she says, absurdly, because there's no word for *please*.

The water makes a shushing outburst when it vaporizes against the stones. As the vapor rises the heat pushes back at them, touching and scalding everything sensitive, Sunny's lips, her ears, her nipples, and she is afraid to breathe, to draw the heat in because it feels hot enough to scorch her lungs. But as it settles she feels her face tightening again, the daytime mask of artificial expression hardening and retracting even more, nearly ready to pop free so that her real face, humid, fresh, young again, can be restored to her. And wouldn't that be wonderful.

Eleven

December is *joulukuu,* named for Christmas, because Christmas itself is called *joulu.* We love to look forward, especially here, especially now, we love the excitement of the tree, the candles, the presents, the singing, and all the special treats of the season. Christmas prune tarts! Christmas prune rolls! Christmas prune soufflé! And of course lots of prune-filled Christmas cookies. But first, much more mysterious, comes the celebration of Lucia; the Christmas season here can only commence when the Swedish speakers celebrate Saint Lucy's day. She used to mark the solstice, so you'd thank her when the light came back, up north especially, but doesn't that mean her day was also the darkest, shortest day of the entire year? They used to wait for her and she used to wake them up, at dawn, with a crown of gentle flames in her hair, and then look, wake up, it's your eldest daughter bringing you the coffee, wearing candles. And so we'll wait, too, and count our twelve days of Christmas from then, as locals do, because Lucia takes place, now that we think about it, precisely twelve days before Christmas. Until then the days pass comfortably, because in *joulukuu* we've learned that warmth, distraction, and a comfortable indoor life are the answer to the darkness outside. Routine and leisure tick along best when small projects keep nervous or idle hands occupied. It's good to work at the craft tables in the Solarium. Take best advantage of the short daylight hours, when the ice of the bay is a mirror bouncing back the sun and everything in the room is illuminated. The knitters don't even need their glasses.

Some would like to go to church; services are held in the chapel of a Sunday. What else is there to do? There's the wood fire in the Radiant Room, stoked highest at midmorning into big yellow flames that bounce against the granite mantel in reflected points of blue, silver, graphite. You can make little fire starters there if you'd like, it's Mrs. Minder's pet project, little twists of newspapers torn and then burned unread. What else is there to see? A large display of Christmas boughs and berries and pinecones, put together by the staff. In the afternoons the patients gather near the boughs for coffee, and there are always piles of shiny round *pulla* bread, fatter than your fist, plain or with cardamom, or dimpled with a deep navel of glistening baked sugar. Sometimes there are sweet, nap-inducing prune puddings served around the fireplace. The others, downstairs, will of course get their pudding in little dishes, brought around on a trolley with the meals.

Are there more cookies? More *keksi*? Of course, there are always plates of cookies, more now than ever, would you imagine a Christmas season without them? No, thank you. *Ei, kittos.* Mrs. Anderson oversees the beating of scores of eggs while sweating buckets of butter stand softening beside the stove, where pots of fruit bubble down to hot dark syrup.

"Can I toss these lemons in the pig bin?" One of the girls taps a lemon, hard and dry as an old stiff shoe, against the counter.

"Absolutely not," says Mrs. Anderson, who methodically tenderizes them with a rolling pin so that, when cut, the shrunken and leathery lemons are wet and sweet once more. Mugs of hot lemon water are given that afternoon, pulpy flesh floating on ribbons of dark peel, studded with a clove to rinse germs from the throat. Some of the cookies turn out spicy—ginger, pepper, cumin—and tingle in the mouths of the sensitive. But such small burns are easily extinguished with a spoonful of cream, and no one cries, because suddenly it is Lucia.

This year Lucia is the eldest daughter from the doctor villas, and she is followed, in her procession, by other staff daughters, the last of which is Dr. Peter's little girl, so little that she doesn't walk with the others, or carry a candle, but sits in Mrs. Dr. Peter's arms, in a white dress, watching, like the rest of us. Lucia and the other girls bring candy, and ginger cookies, and they give these away as they proceed, walking slowly, in a well-balanced way, through the lobby, aiming for the corridor.

Mrs. Minder of course loves Lucia, loves Saint Lucy, doesn't know who she is but loves her celebration day, the white gown, the berries in her crown and the buns and cookies in her hands. She loves it all because obviously more than anything she loves that crown made of tall fat candles—very tall, very fat—and the way that their glow, thrown over the girl, makes the group into a court of angels, moving through the building together. Mrs. Minder's hands are raised, in hopes of receiving anything the girls might offer. This year, one of them gives her a *Lussekatt*—a double saffron bun, two swirls that meet, each with a gleaming dark prune in the center. She clutches the bun, watching them file into the corridor, Lucia herself already out of sight.

"Where are they going?" asks Mrs. Minder, disappointed.

The girls are going to the chapel. It's a saint's day, after all. Don't forget that Lucia was beheaded, or blinded, depending on who you ask, and that although by refusing to marry the pagan of her parents' choice she technically died *virgo intacta,* her eyes are nonetheless no longer with her. Her eyes have been removed, and are being kept elsewhere. Sometimes she displays them on a plate to indicate that she is also, remember, the patron of the blind. But she does that in paintings, not in person.

Julia passes Mary, still holding her *Lussekatt* to her chest.

"What's that?" Julia asks.

"I don't know," says Mary Minder, "but I'm supposed to eat it, for the holiday."

"Jesus, Mary," says Julia. "You'll eat anything."

"Isn't it rude not to?" says Mrs. Minder, puzzled.

"Don't you know what that is?"

Mrs. Minder does not.

"Those spots are eyeballs. Those are cat's eyes."

"Go away with that kind of lying," says Mrs. Minder.

"You saw it yourself, pigs and wild cats at the smokehouse. Ham and cat buns for the holidays. Loose cats. Ask Anneli. I dare you."

"I will," says Mrs. Minder, dubiously.

"Good girl," says Julia.

Mrs. Dr. Peter is among the last filing toward the chapel, bouncing the little girl, talking to one of the other wives, holding the little boy's hand. Her hair is braided, and held up with a large comb. Long hair used to be in fashion here. Now we bob ours, but she's the kind who never will, Mrs. Dr. Peter, even though she's stylishly modern-minded about other things, in her little leather walking boots, with her ears pierced, like an actress. We can't get close enough to see whether they're really pierced, but we're curious about her. We want to know but would never ask whether Dr. Peter himself delivered their two babies. She spends her days feeding them, in their high chairs, offering them puddings, soft vegetables, mashed meats. Diapering, stroking, bathing, and asking, *Where's Mousie? Is Mousie in the house?* This is the kind of exchange we strain to hear, from the path below their house, and if we can't, well, that life is not really so hard to invent. Because some of us have left just this behind, in other life, existences the same as hers, or the same as what we imagine hers to be. Except that she is, strangely enough, happy there. Happy in that life.

The up-patients take breaks from activities kept somewhat secret from one another, projects involving silver paper, sequins, glue. There are a few favorite possibilities for gifts to be made and exchanged: precious oranges sacrificed on the radiators, dried to be used as sachets for the closet or drawer. Hand-sewn bags of lavender and other herbs, stitched into dream pillows to increase lucidity. Knitted hats, scarves, socks, gloves. Some tear up magazines to make rolled paper beads that move lightly and quietly when dangled. Mrs. Minder makes a wreath of glued and painted rocks from the beach and hangs it on her door, there in the building surrounded by pines, and then she not-so-secretly strings bracelets of red and green beads, often dropped and regathered, to give away: *Surprise!*

At the craft cabinet in the Solarium there are bowls of hard red berries for stringing to hang on the tree in reception, a shapely fir sacrificed for the spectacle, to be decorated with small candles on aluminium clips—lit only under supervision, of course, and only on the day, much to the frustration and delight of at least one. What's the word for Christmas tree? *Tuotantoventtiilistö.* Can you pronounce that again? Just call it the *joulukuusi*—much easier. The bowls of berries must be replaced often as some will chew as they work. One of the day nurses has seen Julia putting them into her mouth and then spitting them back into the bowl, masticated and damp, for others to unwittingly touch. Julia is handed a scrap of tissue paper.

"Pick those up."

"No harm done," says Julia, showing her rough red tongue on purpose, like a melancholy chimpanzee, as if to say, *Have pity. The boredom here is killing me.*

Won't some go home for the holidays? Some do, most don't. Some families will visit. It depends, it all depends.

Laimi goes to spend the holidays with family, at her grandmother's apartment in Turku. Before leaving, she spends time with a paper knife in her room, with tracing paper, a ruler, a grid, cutting patterns that pop out into cards, which when opened present words in relief: *Hyvää Joulua ja Onnelista Uusi Vuotta.* Merry Christmas and Happy New Year. She makes a *joulukortti* for Sunny that opens into a circular stairwell, one door at the bottom, another at the top, strung with a garland. Sunny had hesitated over whether or not to make one for Laimi, and then over whether or not to actually give it to her. The up-patients usually made cards or gifts for the nurses, as small children do for their teachers, and it's odd to receive so many little things without quite knowing how or whether to reciprocate. It doesn't seem to matter, either way. Most of the nurses don't, just to be easy, neutral. Of course with Laimi it's different. Laimi is . . . what is Laimi? She's not really a patient, not really. She's just here, at times, for recurring treatments, staying afterward for a while and always already mentally on her way back to work. She doesn't want to be here. And this makes her something more like—not a colleague. What would you call it? Sunny can't say she's a mere aquaintance. She wouldn't presume to say she's a friend. Not now. Sunny makes a noncommittal card for her, not especially special, one that says, carefully, *Lykkyä tykö!*—and she hopes this means *Best Wishes!* She keeps it in her apron pocket, and is glad it's there when Laimi stops at the nurses' station, and says, "Sunny, I made you a card for Christmas."

"It's wonderful," says Sunny, as it unfolds in her hands.

"No, it's just, you know, with a paper knife it's possible."

Laimi smiles when she opens Sunny's card. "*Lykkyä tykö,*" she says. "And I'll wish the same to you."

"Is that wrong?" asks Sunny; she hadn't been sure, and she hadn't asked Sister Tutor, because making the card had embarrassed her. If her Finnish is wrong, she'll be more embarrassed still.

"No," says Laimi, "it's perfectly correct."

"But not quite right?"

"It's not wrong. Thank you."

The stairwell in the card from Laimi is very like the one near the promenade upstairs, near some crawl spaces full of spare porcelain pieces, but who else would know that? The card contains no message. No secret message, that is. Just *Hyvää Joulua ja Onnelista Uusi Vuotta.* And Laimi also makes one for Mrs. Minder, of the silhouette of a fir tree with tiny candles that rise from the card when it is opened, and one for absent Pearl, of the moon rising at the tree line.

Sunny thinks she might get herself a pair of ice skates for Christmas. She'd like to get out onto the grounds even more than she already does, because exercise is a protection against the threat of insomnia and she never wants to repeat the first year, when for many weeks before and during Christmas she shrunk to a rattling specter of fatigue. The other nurses had offered their best advice. Warm milk before bed, of course. A warm bath or a sauna to raise the body temperature, to produce the drop-off into coolness that the body seeks in sleep. Valerian tincture, lavender pillows, a glass of secret brandy. And, most persistently, the option of getting one of the doctors to give her a sleep aid—a real one. Or maybe just take something light from the pill room yourself. But you've got to do *something*.

It is the eagerness with which the patients take up their nighttime prescriptions that makes Sunny avoid them herself. The mildest of the sleep aids are brought around at nine o'clock on stainless steel trays, a dose apiece in waxed-paper cups with a chaser of spring water left on each bedside table for convenience. There is not much monitoring of these particular doses because they come in a sticky liquid form that can't be hoarded. They're mild, and voluntary, and truthfully the cups don't contain much more than herbal syrup (though some are given the real thing; Mary Minder, for example, is always given a real dose). The patients look forward to this end of the day. They go up and down the corridor in their dressing gowns, up and down from the bathing rooms. They could brush their teeth in their own rooms if they wanted to, each at a round white sink before a small round mirror, but they look forward to meeting at the communal basin instead. When the toothpaste runs low Nurse Todd snips off the end of the tube and they scrape the last bit onto their brushes dutifully. And then afterward they drift to bed. Good night, good night all around. They tie their ribbons into small bows, put back their hair, tucking curls into caps, releasing the smells of cold cream, hand lotion, and nightgowns.

No problems for them, seemingly, with sleeplessness. But Sunny's insomnia comes from without, from shortened daylight hours affecting her circadian rhythms. She thought she would get used to it. But sleeping doesn't get easier, neither by ignoring her wakefulness nor by trying to overcome it. She has to get up early enough and goes to bed early in turn to accommodate this, but she wakes again and again before midnight and cannot drift back. And the temptation to remain in bed hurts more than it helps, when she is trying to fall asleep again in the darkness with the pillow warming under her neck and the pointlessness pressing down.

Is it possible to lie in bed for several hours and not to fall asleep at all? Isn't it likely that she sometimes drifted off without knowing it? She couldn't be sure, because the darkness outside did not change in degree very much during the hours she spent lying in the bed with her eyes and curtains open, with the dark outside a pressure at the glass intimating that all was not well; she repressed the urge to get back up, get dressed, and go back to the floor to reassure herself simply that all was more or less the same as always. In the mornings her eyes were clicking and dry and there were sparks of phantom activity glimpsed in every corner, and there seemed no point in trying harder. She began to close her curtains and turn on her reading lamp and to read from the novels or biographies or novelized biographies until the clock by her bed said that it was time to get up and begin again. And her eyes felt like they were sinking backward and down, pulling her face grimly out of shape. Sometimes she would stop at her desk and suddenly press the heels of her hands against her eyelids, hard, so that afterward her vision blurred, taking as long as a minute to sharpen up again. Sister Tutor, noticing, had touched her arm once, in the hall.

"You need your bed," she'd said, sympathetically. "You don't look well."

"Thank you," said Sunny. "But I'll be fine."

When her concentration finally broke nothing could hold her attention, and she gave up the books as pointless. She couldn't remember whole pages at a time after reading them. It could be dangerous; she might make mistakes, misread the medication cards. Not sure what else to do, she had gotten dressed and drifted toward her office through the corridors, all quiet with the assistance of the placebo sleep aids. She walked the halls for no specific reason, with no destination, or so she'd thought. But the feelings of unease were prompting her farther into the building, to check that everything was as it should be. Like what?

Nothing in particular. She drifted deeper into corridors with patient doors closed for sleeping, through passages and supply rooms without windows. There was some false alarm sounding off in her, regularly and needlessly, probably a product of the insomnia, she decided, because nothing was ever really out of place here. Knowing this did not, however, diminish the compulsion to get up, get dressed, and walk. And this was the circumstance in which, during that first year, she had become friendly with Laimi Lehti.

Laimi wore her flannel nightgown and a woolen cardigan as long and warm as a dressing gown, and pointed house shoes lined with rabbit fur, and she walked slowly in the halls with her arms crossed over her chest. Sunny had paused and looked into her face; it is more or less standard, if at three o'clock in the morning a patient is roaming the halls, to check whether or not she is walking in her sleep.

"Don't worry," said Laimi. "The charge nurse knows I'm up." Sunny was in uniform, pressed for the day, but Laimi had known. "You can't sleep?" she'd said, in English, stopping. "You look tired."

Sunny had been surprised, because even then, just a few months into that first year, it was already clear that the up-patients didn't and wouldn't ever care about, or even notice, any difficulties Sunny might have. Laimi's question stops her, not least because Laimi is herself ordinarily so reticent.

"I sympathize," said Laimi. "It's hard to adjust to the darkness."

"I'm not adapting well."

Sunny's feet feel heavy on the floor at that moment, and she is nauseated with fatigue. From habit, she feels she ought to keep moving. Laimi is clearly comfortable enough in silence, comfortable left alone in the hall. But then she says, "I'm going to the Radiant Room. Have you tried that? It couldn't hurt."

Sunny had not considered this for herself; it seemed like something reserved for the patients, but they walk together slowly, taking the elevator downstairs. At this hour the room is empty but the lamps are on and the fire is burning as it always is at night there behind the special clay radiants, an experiment borrowed from the Swiss and designed to throw the benefits of healthy radiation straight into the red cells of the blood. Laimi settles in one of the armchairs, rests her feet on an otto- man. She is obviously in some discomfort and Sunny feels she should probably leave her to herself, but again she does not. She doesn't know where else to go. They sit before the fire and do not speak. Then it is as if they both doze, open-eyed, before the glow.

A long time later Laimi wakes, repositions her feet on the ottoman, and says, "Physical exercise is the only good cure for insomnia."

"Does that work for you?"

"Oh yes, it always worked for me. But at the moment . . ." She shrugs, her hands palm down on her thighs. "I used to go out on skis, and that was pretty good. Obviously I can't do much of that now, so I come here instead. You really should try it."

Had exercise helped Sunny? She'd started taking walks on the paths, every day, and that had helped a bit, enough anyway to avoid asking for a real sleep aid, as most of the foreign staff had already done. Sometimes she still got up, put on her uniform dress without an apron as a compro- mise, and found Laimi there on the couch. But sometimes she deliber- ately did not go to the Radiant Room, only because she did not want to intrude on the other woman's privacy.

Sometimes Laimi has a book or a magazine with her, but if Sunny comes she will not open it, even despite the silence between them. And Sunny thinks of bringing a magazine or book of her own along as well, to make it seem less awkward. It's a little strange for her to simply sit before the fire, doing nothing, saying little. She thinks too much about it. And then, having overthought it, she is too shy to bring a magazine, especially since she is partially in uniform.

"Sunny, I have a question," says Laimi.

Sunny is quick to say, "Of course."

"Why did you decide to come to Finland?"

And, having expected some other kind of question, she has no ready answer. And anyway there is no good answer. Why anywhere? Why anything?

"I was curious. I saw an article in a nursing magazine. I wrote the letter because I was curious and I wanted something different, and I'd heard that it was beautiful here, and peaceful." But this sounds so pale, so pathetic, not a good enough reason to have traveled so far. "And my mother died the year before."

"That's a good reason," says Laimi kindly. "It's important to know something about the world. To travel and to see new places. It helps with grief."

"Yes, but—" says Sunny. And what Sunny would like to say, but doesn't, is that she's afraid that after living here she'll go home no different. She'll be the same as she was, and she won't have learned anything about anything.

Laimi waits.

"I haven't seen much of Finland," Sunny says.

"But you're on the land a lot," says Laimi. "In the trees. That's good."

"Yes," says Sunny. "I suppose."

"What were you expecting? Something different?"

"I didn't know what to expect. But I didn't think it would be so difficult. I'm trying to learn Finnish, but the Americans aren't, so I can't practice, because every time I try to start a conversation with a Finnish person it's over before it begins. I ask a question, and Finnish people will be polite, and they'll say yes, or they'll say no, and that's all." Sunny stops herself; was that all too frank? Was she being insulting?

But Laimi laughs. "I'll tell you something about Finland," she says, in Finnish. "Don't feel bad if you don't fit in. People here won't seek you out or offer to help, unless you ask. They'll leave you alone and expect to be left alone, and that's not considered rude. That's considered polite. Keep this in mind, and don't be insulted if you feel like people are ignoring you. Everyone says Finnish people are quiet. But I'll talk to you. In Finnish, if you want. Can you understand anything I'm saying?"

"Yes, thank you," Sunny says, and wishes she could say more. But she doesn't, and can't, and feels bad about her own ineptitude. So she says, in English, "I got about 70 percent of what you said just now."

"Your Finnish isn't too bad," says Laimi. "Really, you're surprisingly good."

So they are friends, and they have conversations beyond what either would have had with anyone else at Suvanto, even if those conversations seem to emerge from a distance, taking place while seated side by side instead of face to face. Which is why it seems natural to mention it one evening when she sees an envelope between the pages of Laimi's magazine, unopened.

"You have a letter," says Sunny, and Laimi looks at it. "Please, go ahead and read it, if you like. I mean to yourself. Don't let me keep you from it."

But she already feels intrusive, her curiosity bright in the air.

"My fiancé," says Laimi. "He's working in Stockholm for the year."

"Your fiancé?" Sunny didn't know about an engagement, even after weeks in the Radiant Room. And she doesn't know all that much about the other woman's life beyond Suvanto. Or even at Suvanto. Maybe it only seems odd because one has the impression of knowing so much, so many private details, but not details of personality.

"I'm reluctant," says Laimi, rolling the r extravagantly. "Maybe I'll never get married," she says, looking into the flames. Sunny would like to say something reassuring, but can't seem to.

"If I can fix my health, then I'll go home and decide."

"You're going home?"

"Yes, of course." A quick look. "Of course," she says again. "I'm not going to stay here longer than I have to."

The fire before them makes a natural sound of burning, but the warmth seems intensified, penetrating. It is probably only the knowledge of the purpose of the clay radiants that creates this feeling.

"I've been here a long time. Long enough, it should be. My friends are sending pictures, to remind me of what they look like. It's nice, but then again it's not so nice, looking at the places I'd rather be. So no, I won't stay, I still have a life to go back to, after all. And my job. I like my job."

"I don't really know what you do. I mean, not exactly."

"I'm a draftsman. For architecture. But you still don't really know what that is, and it's all right, don't worry."

"You draw plans."

"More or less, yes. You saw one hanging in the lobby, didn't you?"

"Maybe sometime you'll show me another," says Sunny; she doesn't know what to say to express interest in Laimi's life.

"You're kind, to ask, Sunny, but it would be very boring."

"Then maybe you can show me some photos, sometime." There are limits to what all she can suggest as any further interaction, any other way to speak to each other. And everyone here seems to have photos, everyone except Sunny. The patients collect them, indiscriminately. *Look, look!* they say, on the days when mail arrives, their airmail envelopes slit open on the tables, trying to catch Sunny's elbow or apron as she passes. *Look! Here's a photo of my sister, and here's one of my sister's children, and here's one of their neighbor's new car, and here's one, wait, I don't know who this is, maybe somebody my sister knows.* Sunny now has the habit of skirting any table at which a photo album can be seen, lying in wait. And so this willingness to look at Laimi's photos is something of a sacrifice, a token of unspoken esteem.

"I'd be happy to show you," says Laimi. "If you like."

She seems to want the company tonight, though Sunny is as always overwatchful against taking this for granted, and would at any moment turn away rather than impose. Except that this is also, arguably, her job. She's really not sure, in these early hours, what their relation is to one another, except that Laimi is the only person in the building whom she honestly likes.

Laimi blinks at the flames, looking worn, and soon rises to go upstairs. Sunny is ready to go as well, finds herself going along, pushing the elevator buttons as if clearing the way. In Laimi's room, black-and-white photographs hang pinned in a neat line along one wall.

"I was learning," she says. "I took these myself."

A mole, a squirrel, a bird in a nest with an opaque eye, alarmed and flat.

It is not that Sunny has never been in the room before, because of course she enters it daily. But there is a difference between entering and being invited. On this occasion the belongings of the occupant seem more apparent, more important, resolving into a setting that is more human than at other times, when it has seemed, to Sunny anyway, quite appropriately impersonal and temporary. Just a room. But different women can make rooms into different rooms, at different times. The fur blanket is very black, startling, rolled at the foot of the bed.

"If you don't mind, can you lift out the album from the bottom of the wardrobe?"

It is a heavy album, with photographs carefully and evenly pasted. Sunny puts it on the table and Laimi turns on the reading lamp. She lowers herself onto one of the chairs, tucking her long cardigan around herself. She opens the album and looks at Sunny, and then with one hand questioningly invites her to the other chair.

"You said you'd like to see some pictures?" says Laimi. "I have two or three hundred to show you, so please, sit down. Make yourself comfortable. I'm kidding. Just a few, since you were kind enough to ask."

And Sunny had meant it as she said it, but considering Laimi's habit of privacy she had not truthfully expected to be shown, and had felt she'd overstepped herself by asking. But she is pleased, and she is careful to appear interested. Is interested, of course is interested.

After living in this functional building, designed in the urban architecture studio where Laimi worked, and now sitting in this starkly arranged room, Sunny imagines from the photos that the mirrors of the past must have tilted too far forward from those walls, too far toward the younger Laimi. The furniture must have been heavy, overwhelming, the mantel of the ceramic hearth too choked with photographs in ornate silver frames, distracting the eye away from the place where flames would burn.

"This is my grandmother's home. I live with her, in Turku."

In the photograph there is winter sun through gauzy curtains, a room with potted miniature palms. Great pale roses in the rugs like bleach poured out. Framed photographs. On the wall behind the piano, more portraits.

"This," says Laimi, "this is a very Finnish scene, very typical for my grandmother's generation. Here's her portrait of Alexander II, the czar who freed the serfs. There's a statue of him in the Senate square on Aleksanterinkatu. No? You don't know? In the street named after him, in Helsinki. My grandmother and her friends were in love with him. When they were young and beautiful they chased his carriage through the snow in their ballroom shoes and ruined them and didn't care. I don't know what they might have done if they'd caught him. You must have seen the statue sometime."

"But I believed . . ." says Sunny. Laimi waits. "I'm sorry, I'm ignorant. I believe you said there was a lot of bad feeling toward Russia." Laimi's voice never rises, not even for questions, and Sunny works to keep hers level as well; her own natural rising inflection sounds forced, chatty, very American in her own ears.

"Toward the government, of course. I share those bad feelings, and a lot of other people don't like Russians for personal reasons that go back a long way. But some people from the older generation still had a friendly feeling for the czar, because he did recognize Finland as a distinct nation. He liked it here. He used to come to Finland on hunting holidays. My grandparents took it rather personally. They felt they had a treaty with the czar, but not with Russians, if you follow. When there was no more czar there was no more agreement, as far as they were concerned. The Russians felt differently."

To the right of Alexander hangs a much smaller portrait on a wide ribbon.

"Do you know something about Finnish politics?"

"Only a little."

"That's Prince Friedrich Karl of Hesse. For two months he was the first king of Finland after independence, and my grandmother was more delighted than I can tell you. But she never got a chance to chase his carriage."

"Because he was assassinated?"

"No, it just wasn't a good time for monarchy after all. The German empire fell and my grandmother was so disappointed. That's why she keeps the portrait."

Laimi skirts the third portrait in the photo. "This one presumably you recognize: Our Lord Jesus Christ." A lack of inflection, impossible to interpret. Sunny adjusts her hands in her lap, holds her posture as she leans forward to look.

"It's a beautiful room," she says, her voice still too high, still too bright. "It's not what I expected, though."

"No, it's not modern, I know. It's not my kind of style. I actually don't like the furniture very much. Never tell my grandmother I said that. I just thought it might be somewhat interesting, if you haven't been in any Finnish homes before."

"This is your father's mother, or your mother's mother?"

"My father's."

"So it's your Grandmother Lehti."

"Well," says Laimi, and there's a hesitation. "It was Löf. We Finnicized our names after independence. We're Finnish, of course. We were always Finnish. But a lot of the Swedish-speaking Finns around here made the same decision."

I shouldn't be prying, thinks Sunny. And she wants to know, but certainly doesn't ask now, whether this means Laimi had grown up speaking Swedish. And did that mean Laimi had a Swedish name originally, a Swedish first name? And what was it?

Laimi shows her other photos, of trees, of lakes. Sunny finds them mostly indistinguishable from one another, blurs of leaves and water, except those with people in them. There is a picnic table with a white tablecloth, a plate of sausage and another of cakes, a pile of glinting bottles. The women wearing sun hats and full-shouldered sleeves. The men with careful mustaches. Formal, but informal too. Maybe a party, maybe they'd all dressed up for this photo. It appeared as though a lot of work had gone into the picnic: packing the heavy china, carrying the bottles, setting up the chairs.

"At the summerhouse," says Laimi. "Going to the summerhouse is real life for us. If you're still in Finland next year, I'll bring you out to ours, if you'd like. My uncle has a car, and he'll take us."

"I would love that."

"I'll be done here, I hope," says Laimi, "but we'll come back for you."

This is an old photograph, and Laimi lies in the grass before the table of seated adults, propped on her elbow, a young teenager, her lips curving, pale, arrogant. The sun is obvious, and so is her irritation with the full sleeves of her cotton dress; but there is also, almost, the heady drone of summer captured and the prickling of the grass through the fabric. And then Sunny's eyes are drowsy, a little bit. Not from boredom, but only from relaxation, as if the power of nostalgia is strong enough to be contagious.

It feels like a rebuff, then, when Laimi stops coming to the Radiant Room. She sleeps at night now, longer and longer hours, until in time she sleeps too much, waking in the morning to drink a cup of coffee and then going back to sleep, waking again for a late lunch and then going back to sleep, accruing days that end in early evenings, a dreaming, monotonous existence with an inscrutable focus.

Sunny surely knows it is nothing to do with herself; she knows this. It's only the sad feeling of having nobody to talk to now in the night that makes her think so. That, and her own self-consciousness.

It is something of a surprise then to see Laimi there again at half past three in the morning, dozing on the couch as before. Sunny hesitates in the doorway. Laimi scarcely turns her head when Sunny sits in the usual place.

"How are you feeling?" says Sunny.

"Not good," says Laimi.

She's leaning back against the cushions and her eyes are nearly closed, hands folded neatly on her belly. "Coming downstairs seemed like a good idea from upstairs."

"If you'd rather be alone, I'd understand that," Sunny says.

There's no expression on Laimi's face, and they sit without speaking. But then she says, "I think you'd better help me up."

And so, it seems to Sunny, Laimi would rather leave than sit to-gether? *What did I do wrong?* Consider that Sunny has still not had a complete night's sleep in weeks, maybe in months, that she still sees sparks in the corners, that her dexterity is dulled and she sometimes bumps against the walls, that at dinner that night she bit her tongue, hard, from lack of coordination. In this moment she takes Laimi's fore-arm and pulls her up with more force than is strictly necessary. But Laimi hesitates.

"Get up," says Sunny. "You asked for help." She pulls both arms and the blanket falls away. For a moment nothing is wrong, but by the time she gets Laimi upright there is sudden blood, red and fresh and shock-ing, pouring down through her nightgown, so much blood that it falls weightily onto the floor before the fire, into the rabbit fur slippers, and onto Sunny's shoes.

Sunny sets her back down gently, very gently but quickly and runs to reception to bring an orderly and summon the doctor on call. Only on the way back does she see that she has tracked footprints down the hall, in Laimi's blood.

"I'm sorry," she says, returning with pads and slipping them quickly under the nightgown. "Laimi, I'm so sorry," she says again, but Laimi still doesn't answer, because she has, uncharacteristically, fainted.

It was Dr. Ruotsalainen—Dr. Peter, of course, hadn't yet arrived—who removed the worst of the fibroid tumors for which Laimi had been re-ceiving radiation, tumors that had seemed benign enough, except for their presence, until they'd begun to hemorrhage. These were tumors that tended to return after being removed, and he'd been trying, and would keep trying, to get rid of them in a more permanent way. Sunny sat with Laimi while she was clammy and cold, before she fully re-gained consciousness, and stayed as she drifted up through the layers of anesthesia into sleep, remaining asleep even while making use of the vomit pan held by Sunny. Every fifteen minutes Sunny checked on her, and sometimes more often, until finally Laimi was fully awake the next day, chilled even under the heavy fur blanket.

"Good morning," Sunny says, from the chair beside the bed. There is a cool touch in the air from the window, but Laimi always wanted it left open. She must be in pain, Sunny knows. But she also knows that Laimi would just as soon not take pain medicine if she can avoid it. Her skin is the suffering color of half-risen bread, her lips and gums pale and anemic, from the loss of blood.

"I'm going to check your dressings now," she says. Laimi submits to this with her head deep in the pillow, indifferent. She is still bleeding and Sunny changes the dressings, gentle over the stitches. She pulls the bedding back up.

"You ought to have a different blanket," she says. "Fur's not sanitary."

A nod, an acknowledgment that Sunny has spoken, rather than an agreement.

The injection is ready, in case she asks for it. Sunny sees the signs she should not have missed the night before, even in her own distraction, signs she'd assumed were part of Laimi's nature, part of her Finnish reserve. In retrospect she saw physical pain in the quietness, the fading energy, the heavy sleep, the increasingly inward focus. The paleness of her face, and her dilated pupils. Her molars pressed together. Very clearly on that day Sunny recognized the solitude Laimi had created by the effort of guarding herself, holding her body rigid when she should have been at ease. Her habit of retracting one leg, a little, when sleeping or sitting, in an unconscious effort to minimize abdominal pain. And her motionlessness in the bed and elsewhere; such stillness is a sign of constant vigilance. *Sisu* is the word Sister Tutor taught her to describe something like this, a Finnish form of endurance, but more than that, fuller than that; *sisu* is facing adversity squarely, using inner reserves of strength, without complaining, and so *sisu* is something like a foundation of inner bedrock.

Sunny is sorry, she is very sorry now for her impatience in the Radiant Room. She would like to apologize again. But she knows that she can't draw attention to herself with this apology, not now when Laimi has retreated into the distance. Apologizing now would be putting her own wishes first. And that would be selfish.

Sunny goes outside, and for the first time she trusts the ice. She steps over the contorted and cracked shore onto the smooth surface and walks, quickly, away from Suvanto. She has never tested the ice before but now, ashamed of herself, wanting to scratch out her own eyes with frustration, she walks quickly over other footprints already made. And in her pale blue and white uniform, under her gray coat, she begins to run, and in a few minutes she disappears against the frozen landscape.

This is why, this year, she now recognizes the signs of insomnia in Dr. Peter. She sees the effects of weeks without good sleep slowly building. His face looks as if he's wiped it on one of the deep blue tissue papers folded between the nurses' aprons to keep them sharply white, and the thin skin around his eyes has begun to darken like the shadow of his beard. She recognizes it too in his written orders, increasingly vague, and in his handwriting, which has become, at times, almost unreadable.

"Dr. Peter?" she asks, wanting to venture a suggestion or two, from experience.

But when he looks up, preoccupied, impersonal, waiting, irritated, she says nothing to him. Feels nothing for him.

She goes, alone, finally, into town for the *joulumarkt*. She walks and looks at the city's market square, the Kauppatori, decorated for the season with thick piles of evergreen branches and filled with stalls full of handmade goods for sale. Boots on the slick ice, how do they do it? She steps carefully, slowly, and buys a few things at the stalls with *markka* from her pockets, counted out painfully and slowly as she deciphers the numbers spoken to her in Finnish. Numbers are hard. Numbers are always spoken in shorthand, *kakstoi,* but then they realize, and repeat for her, slowly: *kaksi-toista.* That means twenty, doesn't it? A pair of thick, wheat-colored knitted socks with scalloped cuffs, maybe for Laimi, and a deck of playing cards illustrated with the different fishes of the Baltic, to take to Mrs. Anderson and Sister Tutor. And a pair of ice skates, tan and stiff above the silver blades, as a necessary present for herself.

She moves along with the other people, toward the bridge and over

the frozen Aura River, past the heavy cathedral and into the square of
the Christmas Peace. In one of the buildings along the square she finds,
by accident, the old man in his chair, in his fur cap, using a small sharp
knife to make birds out of slips of pine that wait soaking in a pail of
water by his feet. He cuts, carves, fans the wood. A peacock, perhaps.
A Christmas bird to be suspended on a red thread. He doesn't look up
from his work. She drifts away to buy a cup of hot spiced punch. The
hall is full, but no one jostles the cup in her hand, and no one speaks
to her.

At one stall she finds a collection of little dolls in red wool cloaks,
with smooth waxed faces that might or might not be smiling, and small
dark eyes under peaky red caps. She feels a sudden peculiar stab of
wanting one, and can't resist touching the ambiguous little face with
her finger.

The woman at the stall speaks to her in Finnish, but *Anteeksi,
puhutko Englantia*, do you speak English? *Ei,* no; the woman realizes
she doesn't understand, and speaks more slowly, but still, Sunny doesn't
understand.

"*Joulupukki,*" says the woman, wrapping the doll. She points to it.
"*Joulupukki,*" she says again.

Back at Suvanto Sunny should of course just go and ask someone,
ask Sister Tutor, ask Laimi, that would be the natural thing. But she is
embarrassed. She looks in her dictionary. For *joulupukki*, the dictionary
says Santa Claus. But the doll isn't a Santa Claus, not even allowing for
some big difference in the costume. She looks up *pukki*. The dictionary
says *goat*. Or Santa Claus. Or, alternately, a dirty old man.

It's an overreaction and she knows it, but she feels humiliated, frustrated. It is such a small, stupid thing. She takes the doll to Sister Tutor
to ask, *What is this?*

"Ah, *joulupukki*!" says Sister Tutor, and claps her hands.

"It's for you," says Sunny, "take it." And Sister Tutor squeezes the doll
in delight with both hands, so firmly that Sunny thinks the little waxed
face will be crushed. But it isn't, and the *joulupukki* sits on the table in
the sitting room of the little house in the trees for the rest of Christmas.

Whenever she stops for tea with Sister Tutor and Mrs. Anderson, Sunny sees the little face and remembers how very much she'd wanted it, and feels warm and impatient with embarrassment again. She goes often, because Sister Tutor is still teaching her Finnish. Sunny brings a notebook and they work through the simple things. The months of the year. The colors: *punainen* is red. *Siinainen* is blue. *Valkoinen* is white. And *pinki*? Surely you can guess *pinki*!

And what then really is *joulupukki*?

"Well, we can say it's like a spirit," says Sister Tutor.

Sunny thanks her after each lesson, and Sister Tutor says, "*Kiitos!*" Maybe she thinks Sunny is asking how to say thank you, though they have of course been over this . . .

"I mean thank you, I'm thanking you very much."

"*Kiitos kiitos paljon!*"

"All right then," says Sunny, embarrassed. "*Kiitos paljon.*"

"All good," says Sister Tutor.

They walk together, Sister Tutor, Mrs. Anderson, and Sunny under a bright black sky, and she sits with them for the Christmas Eve staff dinner: there is ham of course, glazed with mustard and marinated in honey, and herring salad, and casseroles of sweet fermented turnip and rutabaga. Gingerbread, clotted cream, and cloudberry jam. And *joulutorttu*: the nicest plum tart possible, baked brown and shining in the shape of a five-pointed star. Later tonight, a long while after dinner, Sunny plans to go to the staff sauna, heated on this as on other holidays. In the morning, the others will wake early to meet for a Christmas service in the chapel. Sunny, having precious little interest, will imply, without actually perjuring herself, that she doesn't feel very well, and she'll stay in her room, reading and napping instead. And then later, on Christmas afternoon, she'll slip out for a ride, passing through the little graveyard where the long-burning candles will still be visible among the snowy graves, each in a melted hollow made wet and smooth and solid by these flickers of heat, persisting in the dark.

Twelve

In some years January, *tammikuu*—so named for the heartwood of oak and the center of winter—is the bleakest month for foreigners. In other years it is February, the grim and pearly month of *helmikuu,* that brings the threat of depression after the novelty and cheer of the holidays have passed. This is the grayest season, in which a thaw may open fissures and rough places in the world, in which loneliness grows stronger, in which rumors are carried in the air as a whiff of damp, at first unnoticed, but persistent. Wet, shifting sounds are heard and then the world outside the building noticeably drips from countless sources; it is dispiriting, this false spring in the sound of water moving in what had been a reliably muffled world.

This year a shallow thaw comes during the night. Water falls from the roof and glazes the ice of the driveway, sheeting into storm drains, water falling underfoot away into hidden water. There is no satisfaction in this release, there cannot be satisfaction until March, April, May. So the novelty of an unexpectedly different day might be nice in the morning, but by afternoon the sound is a thin trick that makes some kind of movement necessary. There is even desire to go outside, to see confirmation of the changes.

You can walk slowly and safely over dry ice but you must always be careful on wet ice, very careful not to slip and fall. Kusti as usual puts down gravel but it does not help much when the ice melts and refreezes as the temperature drops and rises and drops as it will this week. You must keep your eyes on the path, learning again how to walk and balance, always paying attention to how you place your feet. Sunny has fallen every year during a thaw and has been angry every time; she has seen the same large greenish bruises from hard falls flowering on the hips of other nurses in the sauna. Now she is careful, but the care seems to hurt her lower back, straining the muscles with constant rebalancing, constant attention to the ground. Looking up is a disappointment anyway; the tips of the branches have lost their silver fur. In such times there are outbreaks of petty ailments: pinkeye, petulance. Listlessness, lack of appetite. Fever blisters and other more intimate upsets from too many nuts and chocolates squirreled away after Christmas.

Pearl is still absent, and that drives attention toward quieter pastimes. But Laimi has come back already. Books are read and traded and taken from the communal shelves. The classics prevail. Something in the quiet and the climate encourages a return to mythologies and epics, expansive old stories that you never had time for before: the *Kalevala,* the *Odyssey,* the Icelandic sagas, *Beowulf.* Maybe the Bible. There is some talk of archaeology, the classical world, the hunt for the ancient city of Troy. With sugar spooned in coffee cups, with cookies waiting on the saucer.

For the meat: bacon joint. To drink: fresh milk. For the vegetable: turnip.

For the meat: ham. To drink: buttermilk. For the vegetable: potato and butter.

For the meat: chops. To drink: fresh milk. For the vegetable: rutabaga.

Julia asks for less food in the dining room. Just the meat is all she wants, only meat, and only a little bit of that. The diet nurse looks at the card and says, "You have to eat. You're too thin. I've been told to put more weight on you, to get your strength up."

"I need a smaller portion," Julia says. "A smaller portion."

"You need more high calorics."

"I can't," she says. "I can't eat it, I can't finish it, I can't stand this heavy food. Look at the fat on it, for god's sake, why won't you just bring me a piece of fish?"

The others at her table continue to eat without complaining.

"All right," says Anneli. "We will give you a little dinner then."

It's slightly insulting, as if they are giving Julia a child's meal. But when the little dinner arrives it is closer to what she wants, three wedges of potato, two small carrots, one pale pink slice of meat. It takes her forty minutes to clean her plate.

"I remember when I used to eat steak," she says. "And pancakes. That feels like a long time ago. I don't have the appetite anymore."

"I have the opposite problem," says Mary Minder, sympathetic now that Julia is feeling low. "Especially since I gave up smoking. I know I eat more than I should."

"It shows."

Mrs. Minder frowns, but she wants someone to sit with in the best places, Pearl's old favorite places, as she continues to string more beads even though Christmas has come and gone in a fuss of anticlimax. She won't say so, but she strings these little necklaces as belated gifts for Pearl, for whom Julia, in her opinion, makes a very sorry substitute. Nonetheless she falls into habit and sits near Julia, trailing her from room to room. They even take sauna together in the evenings, sometimes, after which she always forgives Julia for the insults of the day, because it is too hard to be angry with someone while sitting together in the sauna, in the warmth, in the shadows, while breathing, while perspiring, without clothing. And so they come to a truce, more or less. As far as Mrs. Minder is concerned, bad company is better than none at all.

The social plan was meant to be an important part of life at Suvanto, meant as a reinforcement back to health. At many comparable institutions you might not find this kind of group feeling, and you'd see the difference in the private balconies, each containing a single reclining chair, whereas here there is a long promenade upstairs that everyone must use together. Winter and summer, it's filled with recliners set out side by side. And you'll see it in the sauna, of course. And in the placement of sofas in the Radiant Room, so many opportunities to sit closely together.

In some ways, the original idea of avoiding visible hierarchy and separation has turned out to be unpracticable. Certain doors, as has been shown, must stay locked, and certain authorities must be respected for the sake of common sense. But even so, the push toward interaction is good for the patients. The mild group exercises in the Solarium, the craft tables, the games, the time together in the sauna are all beneficial.

It is irritating, almost painful, when Dr. Peter makes statements to the contrary. The exercise is all right. But what about these games? What about these art tables? It's not that he is heartless. It is only, he explains, that such pastimes create an atmosphere too similar to a holiday resort, or a summer camp taking place in winter. He doesn't want to see the patients getting too comfortable. They shouldn't *enjoy* their time here.

If anyone wants to know why Dr. Peter wants to change the Suvanto social plan, just look to examples such as the case of Pearl. Dr. Peter asks how Pearl can leave for the trip with William, and yet still keep her room. Is she somehow simultaneously well enough to travel all that way, to stuff herself with goose liver and chocolate-covered prunes, yet unwell enough to justify keeping a *hospital room* in which to sleep off those indulgences? Is that fair? When others need the bed?

He'll never understand that it's not that simple, because facts are only part of the truth. The other part of the truth is that Pearl both is and is not unwell, both is and is not a social creature. She likes to move from place to place, most especially when the place exists without her, and can be returned to with no explanations, no responsibilities. With frequent departures she conceals the fact that she cannot form friendships. *How unkind to say aloud.* Nonetheless, though it is difficult for her to be at ease with others, it is also difficult for her to be at ease alone, and this is most obvious when she is separated from the group. Being out, being away is an uncomfortable reminder that she is only comfortable at Suvanto. And if she'd known of Dr. Peter's plans, beginning to fall into place in her absence, she never would have agreed to go away with William. If only she'd known what Dr. Peter intended to do . . .

Oh, she hates him, she already hates him, he probably doesn't hate her, but that doesn't matter because don't forget what he said to her regarding the *old problem,* the problem so intensely repellent and unfair that she has rarely spoken of it, still never even to William. The memory of Dr. Peter's voice makes her bile move, sending her literally to the toilet. If that's his idea of how medicine should be done, of how she and the other patients should be spoken to . . . surely they're not going to let him stay?

"You might have some old gonorrhea in there," Dr. Peter had said, touching her knee gently with his fingers. "You need to see a bone specialist, Pearl, and have that taken care of, pretty quick."

Pearl's mouth had contracted, puckering like a speechless pink drawstring pouch. This was supposed to be a light, informal conversation! And it was only happening because she'd fallen; this was bound to happen, on the ice, at some point. It could happen to anybody. She might have been able to avoid the examination altogether, except that she'd been helped up and helped into the building and there'd been nothing she could do, beyond what she had done, which was to refuse to allow any of the doctors to look. And this, of course, cannot be. An English-speaking doctor had been requested. It had been Peter. And that was the first time he'd been called to the top floor.

"Don't misunderstand," Peter had said. "You don't have sexually transmissable gonorrhea. We won't assume you've spread this to William. This looks like an old problem."

Horrible, horrible, horrible man. A gonorrhea? Horrible man.

"Don't tell him," she'd said. "It isn't that."

"I don't know exactly what you've got here, but I'd say your choices are gonorrhea, an old tuberculosis of the joint, or maybe a really bad rheumatism."

"A long time ago . . . my family doctor said . . ."

Dr. Peter was already frowning, slightly.

"I was told it was a tuberculosis problem," she'd said, her eyes smarting under the rims. "And now it's resolved," she'd said. "I fell on the ice, that's all, there's nothing wrong so please don't tell him."

"I'm not sure that's fair, Pearl," he'd said.

"But it's an old problem! And he would worry about me, you know he would, and he doesn't have to, because it's an old problem, so why, Peter, why would you make him worry, when it's nothing?"

"He's your husband," said Dr. Peter, "and he likes to worry about you. But all right." In hindsight he'd said this more to end the awkwardness of Pearl's approaching tears than in an agreement or a promise. She could never be entirely sure he hadn't told, and wouldn't tell, but William had never said anything, and that was best. She would deny it, if William ever asked. She would call Peter a liar. She would say she'd fallen, had been hurt, had broken her knee, that's all. But she knew that Peter had taken notes, and this is also why she loves Julia for destroying her confidential file.

Even so, once she leaves Suvanto with William she does not think of writing to Julia, not a holiday greeting, not even a picture postcard from the Finnish hotel where they spend Christmas, one of the diversions on their trip to Russia. For the holiday itself William insists on hearing concerts of choral music in not one but two chilled Lutheran churches, where they perch on hard wooden pews that make her leg ache and stiffen as she sits among the silent locals. She'd been silly; she did not suspect until too late that he was trying to force her back into life, a life outside Suvanto.

Much has been said colloquially about the danger of good intentions, but only really in retrospect, and only when the results go bad. It is also true that good intentions often have good results. Good results are what Dr. Peter wants when he says illness ought to be a temporary state, that convalescence ought to be as brief as possible. He has said this and more to Sunny, who agrees. He has said many similiar things to Julia, to convince her of the wisdom of the hysterectomy.

Given her previous concerns, she is surprisingly ready to submit to the scalpel, an acceptance that does not, strictly speaking, make sense. Maybe it's because she is delighted by the cure of the old demon. Maybe it's because she feels a lot better than she has for a long time, and wouldn't mind closing the pessary away into one of her silver-papered hatboxes with other previously useful props. Because then, when all of her issues have been resolved, she can go home.

And then she could, in theory, have sex with her husband again for the first time in years?

Sunny, taken off guard, assures her, yes, of course.

"Painlessly?" says Julia.

"That's the idea," says Sunny.

And Julia, at the writing table, sinks to rest her forehead on her folded hands.

Whenever possible, the doctors who have been at Suvanto and who know the climate delay surgeries in a thaw, because of the lowering mood. There are fewer bad results, fewer complications, and quicker healing if they can wait, if the situation allows. But a doctor would not know this firsthand during a first season at Suvanto, and the thaw is unpredictable. And Dr. Peter, well, Dr. Peter sees no reason to hold off. *Don't be superstitious.* Julia's surgery is therefore scheduled, and she will lie upstairs in her recovery bed during the worst of it, and Sunny's own misgivings will linger like a mineral taste, low in the throat.

Julia has agreed, and therefore it will happen, and it is not Sunny's place to give any advice to the contrary.

Julia is forbidden to eat any breakfast that morning, strictly nothing to eat or drink after dinner the night before. And, perversely, on this day she is hungry.

"Not even coffee?" she says unhappily.

"Not even water." And Sunny watches at the sink as Julia brushes her teeth, to see that she rinses and spits without swallowing.

"You're sure you ate nothing last night?"

Julia bends over the sink, nodding.

Sunny orders a poultice of warm green soap, to soak Julia's abdomen, before she'll see to the rest of the preparations. She does want to do this herself, even though aggression seems the flip side of concern. Sunny doesn't bother anymore to try to understand the moments of anger that make the hairs on her arms stand up. She just holds herself far away, because that feels more normal than being present and furious. It matches with the effort of ignoring something dark in the sky, bruising it, something felt when she takes a moment on the promenade to find some air because today is Julia's surgery, and she's worried about the thaw. Clouds are hanging wetly, in and above the trees. What will happen? She can't intervene. Her muscles feel stiff and the bones of her back and shoulders seem to click together when she turns. She wishes she could pull out her new ice skates in the afternoon and shake off all of this but she won't step out, even if the ice looks solid and unchanged. Perhaps the clouds will part in the evening and she can go out and look for the comet the others are talking about, a distant spark hissing in the heavens. The whistling is very annoying; it is Julia letting off pressure, her lips pressed together, making noises in her room, opening and closing drawers, pausing now and then, almost furtively.

Of course it is anxiety, building. Sunny comes back into 527 and puts away any thoughts about herself; she comes in with cold compresses for the fingers of both of Julia's hands and sees that they must hold the hands above her heart if the rings are ever to come off. She takes one hand and rests it on her own shoulder. The other she holds in the cold cloths, and she soaps the loose, thin skin of Julia's slim fingers, but still the ruby rings will not come off.

"Can't you just leave them?" says Julia, but without pulling her hand away. Possibly she enjoys even this cool contact. "What harm is there in leaving them?"

"It's better for your circulation," says Sunny, whose hands are strong, perhaps too strong today, twisting and twisting the rings. Julia smiles in discomfort.

"Don't worry, I'll keep your jewelry safe until you can put it all back on."

It is two lengths of red thread that do the trick eventually, slid under the band of the loosest ring first, tugging on either side of the knuckle, pulling downward with an even, gentle pressure on both sides. An old trick, and it works. But when Julia sees the final ring lying on a white handkerchief on the table, she reaches for it.

"No," says Sunny loudly, surprising herself when she brings her own hand down on top of Julia's. She cannot be soft, or Julia might push to find the limits. "Sit still. We have to get ready. Please cooperate."

"Okay," Julia says. "But don't touch me in anger."

"Well now," says Sunny. "I could never be angry with you." Which is, if not true, nonetheless necessary to say in the moment. "Lie back," she says, closing the door. She opens the safety pins on the poultice, wiping away the soap with a towel and using a square of gauze to clean, minutely, Julia's umbilicus. Then she drapes a sheet so that only her belly, rounded but firm as a wrinkled plum, is uncovered.

"Show me again where the scar will be," says Julia.

"It will go by quickly, goose, and you'll be back in bed before you know it."

Julia watches the safety razor; Sunny is thorough and impersonal. She wipes the area afterward with alcohol that stings, and they sit for a minute while her skin dries completely.

Julia twitches her feet against the bedding. "Am I done?"

"Not yet. Nearly." Sunny pours iodine, lifts a sponge stick, and paints an outline around Julia's belly and groin. She methodically fills in this area with long, careful strokes in one direction. Again they wait, Julia with her knees apart under the sheet. When the iodine dries Sunny repaints the area in the opposite direction. Julia gazes down at the dark markings with a look of bland surprise.

"Very primitive looking," she says finally. And she thinks of the books in the Green Room, the encyclopedia filled with photos of tribal people elsewhere in the world.

"You mustn't touch it," says Sunny. "Otherwise we'll have to do it all over again." As soon as she says this she regrets it, regrets pointing out a point where trouble can be made. But something has shifted. Julia lies well on the bed and Sunny sits down beside her for a moment while the iodine again dries completely. Julia's hands are limp and bare on the sheet, so light now that they almost rise involuntarily against the weight of the absent rings. She watches while Sunny opens a surgical package and covers her belly with a sterile towel, and lifts an abdominal binder to hold it in place.

"Is this a diaper?" Julia says suddenly in horror.

"No, I'm just wrapping you to hold the towel," says Sunny, prompting her to lift her hips so that she can slide fabric into place and pin it around her.

"It feels like a diaper," she says.

"How would you know what a diaper feels like?"

"I have a very good memory."

"Don't move too much," says Sunny. "You're going to have to ride over in a chair to keep it all in place."

She combs Julia's hair into two braids, as is always done before surgery.

"I look dreadful," says Julia. She is different without makeup, without jewelry, without her hair in a twist. She looks, though Sunny would not say this, like an ancient creature wrapped in a little girl's nightgown, forlorn, like something from a ghost story.

"Nobody will see," Sunny promises. The orderly arrives and Julia is shifted quickly, lightly into the chair and wheeled down the hall to the elevator. Sunny walks with her the whole way to the anesthesia room in the clinical wing. It is lunchtime, and as she promised, there is nobody in the halls to see them go.

Sunny is not a surgical nurse, and she will not be present in the operating room. But she will be waiting, she says. She promises.

Back in Julia's room she smoothes out the black kimono and hangs it on the hook behind the door. The belt has been taken away for good, but Sunny assumes Julia will want to wear it later, when she is finally awake again, and feeling better.

Thirteen

One bird follows another, small and dark against the pale, indifferent clouds. The black canopies of the bare birches move in the air, shifting with the weight of more small birds inside, the birds that twitch, twitch, twitch their tails. Pines and other trees behind the main building are emerging in the thaw, needles and a network of black veins, wet and gleaming.

If you go out, you now walk without any rhythm at all, putting your feet wherever you can. You see this shuffling among the younger nurses who step out to the bus on their day off in their prettiest winter clothes, in pastel caps of blue and pink and yellow, like birds' eggs. Later, coming home, the bus wheels spin in the darkened snow of the road up the incline, listing slightly to one side and then ominously to the other, and the driver then indicates, as he has before, that they are stuck. And the nurses get off, silently except for the sounds of boots. On foot they disappear over the paths through the trees toward the lit windows of the nurses' pavilion, and the driver does something, slips into or out of gear, that allows the bus to roll away backward, slowly and with great attention, down the hill and out of sight.

All evening chunks of snow fall from the roof past the windows, falling slowly, heavily, so that their whiteness fills the dark windows momentarily. No matter how many times, it startles again and again. Some, in the instant, think they see a face impossibly appearing at the window. Each time, no matter how many times, Sunny expects a body, someone falling from the promenade.

It will get easier later, if the thaw continues, when more of the ice shrinks away and the dark paths rise up out of the snow; it is reassuring to see the ground again. Though this also means that the gritty roofs and roads begin to be exposed, and the snow in retreating becomes dirty, rotting away at the feet of pruned-down bushes and hedges, revealing the wet brown stumps of what hides in hibernation.

Sunny worries. She knows that everything ebbs during thaw— energy, life force, spirits. The ugliness outside is a signal of something deeper making itself felt. She goes out but she can't take her bicycle, and cannot walk to the orchard or the cemetery without wading through disintegrating snow hiding cold water and freezing mud beneath. She stays on the rough center of the path to protect her back. She follows the lines marked out by Kusti, still deciding one's route with his box of gravel. At the edges of the path she sees old footprints, the tracks of invisible dogs, pheasants, rabbits, and farther out there are the tracks of hunters stopping and momentarily leaning on their guns as they are passing through. Though hunting on the grounds is forbidden, for the obvious reasons. The longer the thaw, the more old footprints appear from under the snow, and these melt to gray, then black, disfiguring the yard into a welter of bruises. As they grow and lose their shape they expose still more of the naked ground, the mud, and the dying yellow grass. And then the residents will no longer want to look out of their windows.

There is a register of death in mind, less a morbid fascination than a fact, a list that can only be expected to grow in one direction. And while some have surely been good deaths, and anyway unavoidable, there have been those less good, less timely, and many of these have come on days like this.

Julia is wheeled back to her room from the recovery area that night, lifted lightly back into her bed, and seemingly, surely, all will be well now? Her skin and her breath smell cool, metallic. She's still unconscious. Sunny touches Julia's chin, turns her head to the side to keep her airway clear. Hot water bottles are safely wrapped in flannel and tucked gently, comfortably around her arms and legs, and the sheet is tented to keep even the lightest weight from touching her belly; she still does not awaken. Her surgical wound is dressed and her door is left open. She will be looked after regularly. Every fifteen minutes someone will come to check. For the first several hours it is Sunny, and then she smoothes the blanket and goes back to her sitting room.

Book in hand, she drifts, curtains closed tonight against the darkness. But knocking, knocking, knocking wakes her. What time is it? *Come to Julia's room!*—it's the night nurse, she's only a young one and she's not calm. Something is blocking Julia's breathing, Julia is not breathing.

"I can't see anything in her mouth—"

"Did you call the doctor?"

"I did of course—"

Sunny is at the bedside, Julia is quiet, she's motionless, it's unnatural, there is no vaporous mark of breath when Sunny holds the mirror and this is bad, and when Sunny feels for the pulse in her throat and wrist she can't find it anywhere. Sunny moves the sheet aside, pulls up the nightgown, and presses, presses, looking for the artery, below bandages that are unexpectedly white and unstained. She pulls the pillow away and opens Julia's mouth in the minute before Dr. Peter comes, and she does these things without calling out for anything, without alarming the other residents asleep in the other rooms. She moves aside for Dr. Peter but stays close as he puts his palm over Julia's brow and tips her head back, slips his fingers far and deep into Julia's mouth, very far and very deep. Finding nothing he takes up the ventilator mask, presses it down hard over her nose and mouth, airtight, squeezes the bag himself—the air won't penetrate, her airway is blocked. Quickly, quickly. Look at Julia's face, gradually darkening, going a congested ashy blue, like pewter, it's terrible and he is working, looking again, probing, quickly and insistently, but the damage, the damage has been done. Bring the reading lamp, hold it. He tries again with the mask, squeezing the bag. Nothing. How long has she been like this? When did this happen?

She should gag, but doesn't, her chest should inflate, but doesn't, and she has been there too long already. He listens for her heart, places his fingers firmly for the pulse. Finds neither. His fingers rest lightly on her throat. His mind is fumbling, blunt and tired in the face of a decision. Do they rush to the other wing, rushing her on a trolley? Do they go? Go now? He steps back. Then he steps forward again, picks up a length of the red thread from the bedside table, the same spool Sunny had used to pull the rings from Julia's swollen fingers. He touches Julia's face, gently holds her eyelid open with thumb and fore-finger, and draws the thread lightly across the surface of one open eye, then the other. She doesn't flinch. Well. That's it. That's proof, you see, she didn't flinch. *This should not have happened.*

The stillness seems like a trick of Julia's, a game, and they hold the mirror to her lips again, her nostrils, even though the thread is proof. Sunny is sure, though. She can see that quality emerging now already in Julia's face, the sharpening nostrils, the absence of the tension that normally or-ganizes the features of a human face. Dr. Peter would not be fooled in any case, even though he scuffs his feet when walking, exhausted. He sets down the mirror. There are red welts on his knuckles; he's cut himself on Julia's teeth. He looks up at Sunny. *What is this? How did this happen?*

It happens as part of a pattern. The lowest time of night in the low-est season, deep in the darkest moments of winter.

Later, a good while later, Sunny steps out of Julia's room, closing the door softly behind her, and walks down the hall to the supply room.

Everything feels muted to her, and the nurses' station appears distant when she turns her head. The night lighting as indirect and shadowless as ever. The silence of her steps as she passes the doors of the other patients, still asleep. Her keys, though, when she takes them from her pocket, seem loud, thin and jangling. She unlocks the supply room and passes the shelves of neat bleached aprons, the sheets and pillowcases, the patients' gowns, and from the last linen shelf she lifts down one of the packages set aside for patient deaths.

Back in the room she closes the door behind her, a ritual beginning, because this is what you should be doing now, this is policy and practice. She draws a silent basin of warm water for a final bed bath, and then methodically slides her hands under the bedding to collect the hot water bottles banked around Julia's legs. She gathers the bedspread and the blankets, folds them, and leaves them on the chair, feeling the warmth left in the fabric. She turns Julia, heavy now, unresisting, onto her side to spread a bath blanket under her. *My god.* She removes Julia's gown and arranges her in a resting position under a top sheet, but doesn't cover her face, not yet, although she would like to cover her face, and soon, because Julia, already dusky, is now settling into a softer shade of heliotrope, excepting her lips, and the beds of her fingernails, and her toes, much more deeply and reluctantly blue than even the duvet crumpled around her. But Sunny has done this before, many times, and she brings the basin closer and gently washes Julia's face, her neck, her chest, her arms, her hands, and each finger, and then turns her again to wash her back. Someone must inevitably do this, and Sunny had said, *I will.* She dries her carefully with a soft towel, blotting the water from her eyebrows and eyelashes, before drawing the sheet back over her shoulders. She straightens Julia's limbs and leaves one pillow beneath her head. She folds back the top sheet and bathes the legs, one at a time, the feet, the dark toes. And then everything, her abdomen, and even her incision, after removing the bandages.

Afterward she replaces the surgical dressings with clean ones. She has forgotten to bring nonsterile bandages; sterile ones aren't needed now, but Sunny does not want to leave the room until she has done everything, and so she opens the package already there and uses them. And pins on a diaper, as well; it is normal to do so. *I'm sorry.*

She combs Julia's hair with a comb from the bureau and leaves it loose. She has dressed her in the unbleached linen gown they keep for the dead, and drawn the particular cotton stockings up over her legs as well. She turns away as she writes the information required for the tag: Julia's name, the date, the time. Her eyes and nose hurt, and she has a squeezing pain in the top of her throat, but that doesn't matter. She pins the tag to the shoulder of Julia's gown with a safety pin. And then she unfolds the unbleached sheet in which Julia will be wrapped to be taken away, slips it under, and smoothes the gown again before wrapping the folds and pinning them securely in place. She writes another tag, and pins this to the outside.

Now that these tasks have been completed she waits, there in the closed room, as if there is more to do, or as if someone more should come now. She stands waiting at the foot of the bed. After a minute she opens the jewelry box, removes Julia's rings, and seals them into an envelope. She signs her name across the seal and notes the date again, beginning a list of possessions for the office, for when they call the husband to notify him, for the time when he will, presumably, claim them.

Then it seems there really is nothing more to be done. Sunny stands for another minute, but doesn't feel anything, nothing like the change in air pressure around her waist that she might have felt, in other rooms, in other situations. She opens the door. It is not yet time for the day shift, and she makes a signal to the pale night nurse to send the orderlies who will take the body away now. And this, Sunny believes as they glide toward her, will be the last that she will see of Julia.

She places her hands on Julia's body, through the layers of fabric, gently repositioning her head more comfortably against the pillow. And then they take her.

When she has tried to sleep, and failed, she will rise and she will walk as far and as fast as she can in the morning darkness, coming to the bridge over the river. After the preceding days of thaw the frozen water looks like the surface of a bad tooth, concentric rings of gray turning brown, and then a rotten dark hole and a current pulsing in the center. She stops, holding the handrails, soaking her woolen gloves. She looks behind her; in the dripping, moving trees it is as if someone is stepping audibly and constantly just beyond her field of vision.

There are more animal tracks opening up on the banks, compacted into ice when the snow was fresh, and now emerging in the thaw. On the bridge the snow has melted around the hard bits, in this case, the prints of booted human feet. Impossible not to know that some of these are Julia's. They would have passed unnoticed in other life. And that is what we call the time before we came here: other life.

Sunny feels ill and steps past the bridge, leaning forward into a buzzing blankness. She can hear the sound of the river. The air is suddenly wet and cold against her cheeks and forehead. The ground is slippery and she isn't sure of her footing, sliding down a few feet, closer to the water, but she catches herself. And with great practicality, as is her way, she is sick there under the bridge, vomiting where no one can see, or come to help.

Fourteen

What you need after a shock is repetition of detail, the telling and re-telling, so that a manageable story emerges with clear, easy outlines. It's the normal way of understanding an unexpected death. After a shock we reassure ourselves in low voices, while others continue passing quietly all around. Routine continues, and we take encouragement from all the comforts that give peace, without now disguising the fact that we are being looked after, and looked at, constantly. That is how it felt; we hoped the routine would explain. We hoped we could pass our days unwinding in the seclusion of our rooms, or in the Green Room among the plants, or on a sofa in the Radiant Room, among others or not, and it could be easy to wait, but we never thought being sick might actually end our lives. Now Julia reminds us that we're also going to die, some-time. And it doesn't seem to matter that much, because everything and nothing is important in the newly serious world.

But even in the days before the thaw, even when one could still see

Julia moving in her room, whistling perversely, even when one could still feel the pressure of her cane, wasn't there a persistent feeling in retrospect that something might happen? And now of course something has. *And we'll grieve, whether we liked her or not.*

Drinking too much coffee, her eyeballs singing in her skull, Sunny nonetheless pours out another measure, thick and dark. There is a layer of something floating, something sliding off onto the rim of the cup. Add milk and it will run ahead like oil before soap, climbing the sides. A residue from the pot, she suspects, though it has been scalded and scoured many times. She can't sleep again. It's best to keep moving. Of course the staff are human. Of course she is affected. Not in the same way as the others, because she sees such happenings more often and is better able to step back. This is what the residents want, even as they fall into weeping; they want Sunny there with them to maintain order in the face of precisely this. And so she will fall into routine, into role.

But later, awake in her bed, she feels the demands of other lives on the floor beyond the privacy doors. All the moments of that day come through the walls to pierce her where she lies, connecting her to those women lying in the other beds. It is not so fine or so strong a connection that one of them suddenly awakening might twitch Sunny's muscles; it is more like an imprint of Sunny's own movements during that day, from the early preparations in Julia's room to the later ones, tugging her in memory, tugging her up and down the hall, in and out of Julia's room, past all of the other doors, and finally leading back here to her quarters. She is aware of Julia's empty bed. She is aware of Mrs. Minder in her own bed, morosely rubbing petroleum jelly into her cuticles, into her nails, with hands as plump as starfish. She's been crying, and wants to sleep in white cotton gloves, to seal the comforting softness in. Well, the gloves were white at one time. Now they are suspiciously yellowed, and if only Sunny could tune such images out, she'd be able to fall asleep.

But no one sleeps well. The up-patients are perhaps a little infatuated with Julia's death, seeing her now only in that certain light of posthumous forgiveness of any human vexatiousness. Those who were not fond of her feel guilty now. As if it can't be true that they really did dis-like her. As if, in the true light of mortality, one doesn't really dislike anyone, as though dislike is only ever on the surface, only an illusion obscuring the bright dark center of each of us. Differences and dis-likes will grow weaker from now on, eventually fading away in mem-ory. Isn't that right?

That's the pattern. And how much easier it is to turn to a pattern. And thus: She had been so beautiful, in her time, you can see it in the photos, she had been so talented, though none knew *precisely* in what way . . . some suspected that she only liked to pose for photo-graphs taken by Mr. Dey, with costumes and with props such as musi-cal instruments, possibly never used at all. No, stupid, she was a dancer, she was a teacher, she taught tango in the ballrooms and the cafés in Helsinki, in Turku, in Tampere, years ago. Now because she is dead her behavior is understandable, forgivable, and even brings a tearful smile. Because in any case, talent or beauty or whatever, it had all been taken away, though none knew when or how . . . the misfortune of the illness . . . which illness, exactly? Perhaps (some cannot control them-selves and so it is said) perhaps it is better like this, quickly, and now she will not suffer? *Please, my dears, no; is that how you'd like to go?*

Sunny does not exactly despise the residents for making such easy statements or for falling so predictably toward the pattern, because she recognizes nature's way of protecting them. And she knows that to fall toward the pattern does not mean that they are insincere. It only means that they need a rope in the hand, a way to describe the person who has died so that others can grasp in a moment the reasons that Julia was, or now seems to have been, special. Privately, it is not the death (in any case inevitable, one could argue, for all of us eventually) that is diffi-cult for Sunny. It is the small array of humiliations before death, that Julia was hungry and not allowed to eat, that she wanted to wear her rings and was told that she could not, that she was barefaced and em-barrassed . . . but memory is merciful and eventually Sunny will think of the final day only as an echo, the smallest part of having known her, of looking after her in as as kindly a way as possible.

And isn't that a consolation? Absolutely, to have certainty of past kindness is the only consolation in such times. She's glad now for having kept her temper, for having almost always been level and good. Of course in any normal circumstance you couldn't live like that, not all the time, how could you, how could anyone? The up-patients, having responded to Julia more naturally, now feel ashamed; they use the endless repetitions to explain themselves, to assuage guilt about moments of unflattering candor. But it's not their fault. They know that what happened to Julia isn't their fault. Eventually it becomes a welcome diversion, to begin to speculate about whose fault it is. To speculate about Dr. Peter: what he'd done to her, and why he hadn't done it better.

It would be rather cruel, had this not been a hospital, to fill Julia's bed again so soon with another patient. But it is, after all, a hospital. The ward maids do their work and everything is made ready for the woman who has slept overnight screened away in a semiprivate room downstairs with plugs in her ears and a shade over her eyes to protect her from any sudden stimuli, any light or sound that could provoke the convulsions to be feared in a dangerous pregnancy, when the blood pressure is so alarmingly high. The arrangement has been unsatisfactory and worrying to Dr. Peter, but there was no private room available except that of Pearl, which he had already, of course, decided to take, and had accordingly scheduled to be cleared out the following day. But now Julia's is available. Even this is not ideal, because the new woman will be so far away from the clinical wing, from Dr. Peter and Nurse Frida. But here she is; the woman is very pregnant, and those caring for her are concerned by her slight, persistent headache and especially by the way her tissues have begun flooding with brine, swelling her feet, her legs, her vulva, and her pretty, twitching face. This woman needs the quiet and the suspension of life on the upper floor; she must drowse in the bed with the lights dimmed down as low as possible.

The woman must be watched, and because she now occupies Room 527 it will be Sunny who becomes temporarily responsible. It will be Sunny who must regularly watch her blood pressure, and who must double-check her meals to see that only unsalted chicken and vegetables are brought. Who must monitor her scanty urine for smokiness, for albumin, for any sign of kidney distress, who must pay close attention and send for help immediately if anything, anything at all changes during the day, in the hours while she is there, or during the night, because she is still the head nurse of her floor.

It is after midnight on the day after Julia's death that Sunny is summoned from her rooms. She takes a moment to get into her uniform and reaches the hall in time to see the orderlies moving to the elevator with the woman on a trolley, but unlike the departure of Julia, this is not quiet: Nurse Frida's voice is loud, Nurse Frida doesn't care about protecting the sensibilities of the up-patients or about letting them sleep, and doors are beginning to open along the corridor. The pregnant woman's eyes are fixed and her teeth are outlined in blood—she has bitten her tongue. Even the wheels of the trolley are jittery under her trembling body.

"Come with me now, Dr. Peter's on the way," says Nurse Frida. Her nursing cap is different, fancy, tied on quickly with two wide ribbons under the chin.

"I have no obstetrics training," says Sunny. "I'm no good to you." And what she means is, *I can't, I won't, don't force me, please.*

"Shush," says Frida; she is Dr. Peter's own nurse from town and doesn't answer to Sunny. "I might need you." she says. "You're better than nothing."

This is how it happens that Sunny is there in the operating room, an unfamiliar place very much out of her territory, where she knows that she is a useless witness to the rubber flesh of the woman's hips and outer thighs as the nightgown is lifted.

"*Voi Jumalauta,*" says Nurse Frida, "she's in labor, the seizure brought on labor."

Sunny looks away. Some effort has already been made to convert the room. She sees a suction cup and three pairs of forceps, at least one of which Dr. Peter will almost certainly use. He'll slide them in and fasten them around the baby's fragile skull, and he'll squeeze as gently as he can and he'll pull and he'll draw the weight of the baby right out through the area of her mother's injury, through dark soft flesh the bruisy color of rotten fruit, and Sunny knows that she's about to be sick again, and this time she can't hide it. The insides of her ears feel hot and wet with the warning of imminent nausea. She is trying to slip out of the room when Dr. Peter comes in through the swinging door and hands her something as he passes.

Dr. Peter is calm, gentle. Frida moves the cart and hands over a speculum.

"Don't worry, we have time," says Dr. Peter, looking up to the woman, who may not hear him at all. "You'll be fine, the baby will be fine," he says, patting her knee with one gloved hand. Still, Frida translates. "Don't worry. You're going to have a normal birth, right now, don't worry, everything is fine." Frida looks at Dr. Peter, with a question on her face. A normal birth?

"Baby's on the way," he says. "No section here tonight."

Frida holds a catheter. Dr. Peter draws off amniotic fluid, but Sunny can't see what he's doing, how he does this, and she fears that he'll hurt the woman; she presses her fingers over her mouth but the feel of anything near her face makes her instantly sicker. Suddenly there is a new smell, sweet and powdery, coming from the woman, and it is like the smell of babies. Frida takes the woman's bare foot in her hand and leans toward her, bending the knee gently outward with the weight of her own body. She holds the woman's foot firmly and warmly, like holding her hand, comforting. And Dr. Peter holds the other foot, pressing in the same slow way. And then you don't see the woman's legs anymore, not as part of her body anymore; she is only round then, only round, strange and not strange, all the contours have shifted and her body is not the same, and maybe this is normal, but how can this be normal? That the woman's flesh folds when they reposition her, that her legs are boneless and heavy and have to be moved for her? Her hips, thinks Sunny, her hips are going to be popped from their sockets.

"I see hair," says Frida. "I can see hair . . ."

Nothing looks like it is supposed to look, all the angles are wrong.

Sunny looks away, looks down at what she's been clutching tightly against her chest; it's Dr. Peter's overcoat. He'd been at his house, and had evidently run the length of the covered walkway and into the building without stopping long enough to drop it at the door. Sunny moves again, incrementally, and then there is the dark hair, crowning, the little skull—little and frighteningly large at the same time, and completely the wrong color—the head, one shoulder, Dr. Peter gently turning him, rotating. Face compacted and blue. Suddenly the baby is coming. They pull him out so quickly. And then there's the high cry of air moving for the first time in the baby's tender, tiny lungs.

It will be said after that the birth came quickly.

"She only had the one fit," says Frida. "Dr. Peter says she'll be fine if her blood pressure drops." Her voice is normal again; she's young, without the shell that anyone will develop in time. She takes the baby, wants to keep him warm, bathes him under warm water in the large echoing sink, and she is infinitely gentle. At first to Sunny the baby does not look human, facing downward in the beginning of independent life, blinking and jerking in small spasms. He looks like he's been buttered, and fresh red blood smears glancingly over the wax. Frida rubs water over the baby's body, holding him from beneath with one hand and lightly, affectionately scratching the grease out of his hair with her fingertips. It is her matter-of-factness that shocks Sunny, her natural handling of the heavy bluish body. And the baby's face, the black and limpid eyes, the life all internal, a moment of extremity disappearing even as it is happening, disappearing without memory . . . his eyes, his privacy. In Frida's hands he has the visible weight and the significance already of another human being. Sunny feels a rushing, a weakness because of his life, because of his luck, because he would be taken home and this moment of redness, of exposure, would seal up behind him like a scar, abjection covered, folded in. His eyes, as Frida turns him, do not register Sunny or anything else, not yet. He jerks, throwing his arm over his face without intention. There is a small red scratch on his head, curving like a crescent moon. Sunny cannot look away from him, though the floor and the walls are shining, shining unbearably. *Keep him down here,* Sunny wants to say. *Don't take him upstairs.*

She will see this baby again. His mother will be returned to 527 with a drip bag in her arm and the heating panels in the ceiling will be turned up to the level they call Tropicana. The baby will next appear in a lace cap, a vest, swaddled tightly to hold his shoulders down from his head, his arms to his sides. And this sight makes the blood move painfully in Sunny's head, to see him lying there, corseted, pinned; it seems to her that he is barely able to draw breath. Frida is the one who wraps him, smiling down at him, touching his nose with her fingertip, kissing his flaky temples, swaddling him like the folding of a paper angel, and then on the first day of the family visit adding a broad blue ribbon tied in a bow and lifting him to his father. Who says *thank you,* as if Frida has helped to make the baby.

Sunny watches as the father carefully receives the warm solid weight of the baby. His wife is sitting up in bed—Julia's bed—with the blankets tucked neatly all around and a small pitcher of warm cocoa waiting on her nightstand. She's smiling. This is, of course, a good outcome, something to be glad about, and Sunny folds her arms as she turns away. *They'll do it again. They'll have another, in no time. Even with the blood pressure. Even if it kills her.*

Sunny's experience with infants is limited, it's been too long, she does not want to be involved with the baby, either. She only knows that she feels the impulse to slip scissors under the wrappings and clip the baby free.

"No, no," says Frida. "Babies love to be swaddled. It's more comfortable for them. It reminds them of being inside, squeezed and safe, like he was before."

The soundproofing cannot muffle the normal crying, the piercing vibrato of a newborn. The doors to the other rooms remain closed. Some of the women love babies, of course, many women love babies, but the situation is strange. The mother is a stranger who has suddenly, too soon, replaced a companion. Nonetheless a few pairs of booties are given by the knitters, perennially knitting for such surprises, and the shawl from the case downstairs is removed, shaken, and presented as a gift for the first baby born in the hospital; shortsighted, restless-fingered, the knitters are often surprisingly ready to seize the moment.

Mrs. Minder is packing and preparing to leave. A question of migraines, mostly, she says, but her tiny muddy teeth have been chattering from shock for days, and her fingers tremble as she strikes long sulfurous matches, furtively smoking on the promenade for peace and quiet. Even when the baby is asleep one stops to listen for the sound of crying, especially during the night. It is too much, too much at once. Julia is dead, that would be enough. But Pearl is gone, and Frida's shouting and the woman's condition scared them and reminded them again of sudden danger, and now there is a baby crying, and the husband of the woman is there, visiting, it's understandable, but he's a stranger as well and it's uncomfortable. It's messy and it's too much. Unfamiliar people move too quickly, between the room and the elevator, and Mrs. Minder no longer wants to run in the hall in her nightgown. There is a rumor that Pearl's room is going to be given to another maternity case. *Please don't go, Mrs. Minder, we know what will happen to your room . . .*

The new mother's room is filled with flowers and a box of imported oranges wrapped in stiff scarlet tissue paper. And when Pearl returns, unannounced and unexpected, and stops in the doorway with a silk scarf wrapped around her hair, she sees the woman wanly propped in the bed in an open pink dressing gown, nursing the baby at her large, soft, green-veined breast.

She stands and looks and sees that the safe existence of the upper floor is over, and her smile appears as natural to her face as the lipstick patted over her lips.

"Where is Julia?" she says.

Nurse Todd steps forward to explain.

Fifteen

Every day there are moments in which strange feelings color the walls and floors and we find ourselves standing at windows, at junctures, standing at the doors and looking out. Because we don't know how much time has passed, or indeed whether any time has passed. Luckily the schedule pushes on in the background, and then all at once events begin to happen quickly.

Pearl is shocked. The others have already had their few days to make peace with Julia's death, and to reassess their true feelings, and now they are a little more contained as they sit with her in the Radiant Room, huddling toward her as scalding tears track through her powder and rouge. Some cry along, but not with the same intensity as before, so that to Pearl it all seems even more dreamlike, more the rehearsal of a play than anything real.

Those who live together know things without realizing them, for example, that questions would be painful. No one has asked Pearl why she's returned so suddenly from the sudden trip. In the storm of grief there is no good moment to ask about that, or the now-absent fox fur hat. Bareheaded, Pearl's hair is messy, her face is crumpled, uncomposed, and even the most general inquiry would seem wrong. And also, context being all, innocent questions might imply deeper and more wounding questions: *Why are you back so soon?* would become *What's really wrong? Were you and William ever happy? Why did he marry you in the first place?*

Pearl weeps, and wishes she could talk to Julia, who once said that she knew the secret of weathering an intractable husband. That Julia had been rude and overly persistent in that moment, harassing her, a little, Pearl has chosen to forget.

When Pearl tries to think of Julia she wants grief to obliterate everything else, but even after she swallows her sleep aid she feels fury against William, fury against his chipped hairbrush, his chipped razor handle, his shaving mirror ever in danger of being broken, none of which matters to him. She is angry, repeating in her mind that he has never been careful with anything, always hot-handed and clumsy. Bighearted, yes, but correspondingly overbearing. Unbearable.

I should think of Julia, she thinks. But he's a beast and he can't control himself. For him the dropping of the hairbrush near the toilet, a quick clattering on the tiles of the bathroom floor in their hotel, becomes a kind of virtue. *You don't need to be so careful,* he'd said to her, *you don't have to be so self-protective all the time! You're stronger than you think.* His movement is always forward, always forward. He doesn't care about making mistakes, about ruining things in the rush forward.

"Don't touch anything else until you've washed," she'd said, as he reaches to the floor, groping for the hairbrush.

They have had, not a fight, but drawn-out moments of unpleasantness on the trip. He has heard her complaints, her sudden concern for her sinuses, frequent threats of nausea and train sickness, attacks of pins and needles in the feet, and the fear of blood clots from sitting still for too long while zigzagging overland to the east, to the north, a little south, then east again. She complains about each of the stopping points where he has meetings, endless meetings during which she is free to sip coffee, to look at cathedrals, and to shop, if there are shops, and ordinarily there are not. He has heard her tapping her forehead with her finger to check her sinuses for tenderness, a tapping that seems to echo in the hotel rooms, in the sleeping compartments. He searched for a dropped pellet of wax judged too dirty now to be inserted into Pearl's ear as protection against not only William's snoring, but also the relentless noise of the train's progress and the hissing hotel radiators, and, against her tapping and sniffling, her rustling in her cosmetic case, he has, for the first time ever, stuck the pellet into his own ear.

She languidly drops the fox fur hat from her berth, enjoying the extravagance of tossing it down so that he steps on it with his bare foot and is startled in the night. With the motion of the train her piled belongings shift on the floor of the small compartment. Her toiletry bag overflows. There are different soaps, one for hair, one for the body, one for the face, and another, a strong one, lemon-scented, for the feet. There is a bottle of imported soap for sensitive areas with a picture of sweetness on the front: a pool of milk with honey pouring in, and almonds falling, though one or two look rather unfortunately like something else found floating.

It prompts him to say the words again. He has been married before. He says them in his own defense, by which he means that he is not overly bothered by the explosion of soaps and perfumes and cosmetics and hairpins. But the phrase will always go over badly. She will always take it as his basis for judging her too self-indulgent.

In the night the hat is trod upon again, the toiletry bag is upset again. Pearl sleeps on with new plugs in her ears and does not find until morning that the liquid soap has been spilled over the hat. She rinses it in the sink. The bleached pink hairs are greasy and come loose, black-tipped and sticking horribly to her fingers. She is inconsolable and cries, and then abruptly demands to get off the train and be taken back to Suvanto.

"You can't go back," says William. "You don't belong there, Pearl."

"I do belong," she says.

He is sitting on the lower bunk, feet crossed at the ankles, and although he is too large a person, framewise, to be really comfortable contained in any such small place, he makes it work; her bunk is not yet folded sensibly away because washing her hat is more important than making room for him. She'd have to stop fussing and collect her pillows, robe, footies, earplugs, and whatever else she may have left lying under the blanket. "I don't want anything to happen to you," he says. "Honest to god, Pearl, but you're making it hard to keep trying."

"What are you talking about?" she says.

"I want to see you happy, Pearl," he says.

"Then let me go back, I'll be happier if I go back."

"It's too early for you," he says. "What if . . . what if there's still time to have a family?" He realizes that he has made her suspicious. "I don't want to argue," he says.

"Wait," says Pearl. "You don't think—William, you can't possibly think—at this point?"

"It's not the most ridiculous idea in the world," he says. "Is it?"

She wants to get away from him, immediately. Getting off the train had been a half-idle threat, but once spoken her threat of returning to Suvanto gathers gravity, and then becomes inevitable. She looks out the window at the flashing white fields.

"What aren't you telling me?" she says.

"When I took you there it was only meant to be temporary," he says.

"What's happening?"

"Operations," he says, "and a maternity ward. It's not the right place for you, either way." He's no longer looking at her.

"Then what is the right place for me, William?" she asks, still looking out of the window.

It comes over William now, the realization—not that she is disagreeable, not even that she is difficult to live with—but that it's true: she's not well. He might do everything in his power to help her—Christ, hadn't he already tried?—and it wouldn't make any difference, because she has actively chosen to make herself ill. She is, as she has always tried to convince him, *not like other women*. He has tried to lift her out of this sad state, has honestly tried to stop the course of her voluntary decrepitude, but she won't be lifted. And this is revolting. He is sorry, but he's done his best, and he won't change his mind. The decision comes over him not entirely without anger. *I've tried, I've failed.*

"Go on, then," he says. "Go ahead and pack."

He strides to the ticket agent. Another train will arrive, going back in the other direction, in just twenty minutes. An old man in a dark porter's suit takes charge of Pearl's bags, reluctantly accepts a tip to look after her, and slowly wheels the baggage down the platform.

A look at the watch. A brief look between them. A bell. A quick unemotional kiss on the cheek from him, a surprise; his nose is so cold against her skin. He's sorry that this is what she wanted. The train chugs.

Then, on the platform, only cold and quiet, trees, rocks, and snow all around. The sound of her own heart. The sound of nothing.

Is it sudden? To her it feels very sudden. But then the tapping and tapping of her sinuses is proof of something like a sounding in water that surrounds her, evidence that she is isolated; she does not know what she does not know about other people.

Her room at Suvanto has not yet been given away and her possessions all remain, her clothing hanging in the wardrobe, which has taken on the smell already of old stems in a vase of water, a very specific smell of neglect after even just a few days. Her nightstand is already cluttered with lotions and moisturizers, acrid-smelling earplugs and the wisps of cotton they arrive in, water glasses, tissues. She shakes three of her ornamental pillows—they are extravagant, down-filled and covered with imported cotton—and lies on her back, sinking into them, making wrinkles that will need starch later. She cannot believe that Julia is gone. She cannot believe that William has released her, didn't even accompany her back but sent her off alone, even though she has in some sense expected it, anticipated it forever, and she cannot believe that the quiet of the only place she feels comfortable is now ruined, and she cannot imagine that Julia agreed to surgery, and she knows that Dr. Peter is responsible for everything that now forces her to chew the lacy edge of her pillowcase, leaving a rough wet line of lipstick and saliva, leaving the cotton browning from the night creams, the neck creams, the hand creams too generously applied in a fury of fury, then rinsed off in furious tears.

She is angry. But outright anger is not familiar to her. Too much has been unconfronted in long years of habit. She pushes her pillows to the floor and lays her head flat against the mattress. Despite her earplugs she can feel the echoes of something faint; even through the deadening insulation of the stuffing there is some sound of the building, a pulsation, perhaps imagined. And in the echo a new, still realization enters her, and it is as if a curtain made of her own concerns has slowly parted to reveal the ugliness of her self-preoccupation, at such a time as this. At such a time, when Julia is dead, lying in another room somewhere, dead, dead, can it really be true that she is dead?

How does she know which door is Sunny's? Of course she would figure it out, this only seems strange because she has never before been through the muffling door to the Buttermilk stair, has never crossed the lines demarcating the patients' territory from that strictly reserved for staff.

She is not at all who Sunny expected to open her door to at a quarter to nine at night. Frankly, she very nearly did not answer. Of course Sunny could not really ignore a summons serious enough to bring a knock to the door, but it had occurred to her that it might be Frida. She'd rather avoid speaking to Frida, ever again. She is on her way out, invited to Sister Tutor and Mrs. Anderson's for a glass of sherry and a radio broadcast to begin at five past the hour, a program about Sibelius, mostly with music, and Sister Tutor will translate the other parts for her if needed.

But here is Pearl. She has cried off her makeup, all but the shocking coral lipstick, which brings out the pallor of distress. Tonight with her hair undone, without rouge, her features seem to fill only the middle two-thirds of her face, as if a giant finger and thumb have gently pushed her eyes and mouth together, leaving an expanse of forehead and a corresponding expanse of chin, both softened by a fine blond down normally only visible in sunlight, now oddly obvious and shining like sweat.

"I want to see Julia," says Pearl.

Sunny thinks, *Good lord, nobody told her . . .*

"Take me to the clinical wing," says Pearl. "Unlock the doors for me, please."

"I'm sorry," says Sunny. "I know it's a shock, but I can't do that."

Pearl is tall, and taller still when she is inclining toward Sunny too closely like this. She hasn't heard, obviously; she's waiting for a different answer. *Yes. I have the keys, right here. We'll go together, later.*

"Pearl," says Sunny firmly, "go back to bed." She raises her left hand and points toward the stairway doors in a habitual gesture of easy authority. She understands Pearl's feelings, of course she does. But she has to leave now. Arriving late is not the right response to an evening invitation, not here.

"I went to Peter," says Pearl, falling back half a step. "He said it was better not to see the body—that's what he said. The body." Pearl's gaze is unnatural, her pupils big and dark, motionless even when she blinks. She's been given a sleep aid, a real one, Sunny realizes, or some other sedative.

"I understand why you're upset," Sunny says. "You and Julia were friends."

"That's right," says Pearl, focusing on Sunny's face. "We were friends."

Sunny takes Pearl by the shoulders, lightly but expertly, and walks her to the door with a touch that appears more kind than coercive.

"There's no way to avoid the grief," Sunny says, gently. "Everyone here feels it." She opens the door to the Orvokki corridor and gives Pearl a benevolent push. "Good night," she says. "Sleep well."

"I'll only sleep for an hour," says Pearl. "Then we'll go see Julia."

"Good night, Pearl," says Sunny, turning away.

Pearl suddenly catches Sunny's wrist with cold, perfumed hands. "Thank you, Sunny," she says. "I knew you'd listen."

Near eleven Sunny puts on her boots in the front hall of the small house while Mrs. Anderson collects her gloves from the heating panel. She and Sister Tutor both offer to walk her back to the main building.

"No, but thanks. It isn't far," she says, knowing it isn't really the distance that makes them offer. "I have my bike," she says. "It will be quicker if I ride, now that the paths are clear." And she thanks them again, moving away before they can put their boots on and insist, though Sister Tutor manages to press a few small salted licorice candies into her pockets at the door.

It is very quiet, and very dark now that so much of the snow has melted. Sunny avoids the ruts in the center of the half-frozen path, thinly separated from the lane by a line of trees and slushy, low-lying water. She knows that Sister Tutor and Mrs. Anderson have been especially kind to her and will continue being kind from now on. She becomes aware, over the sound of her own ticking bicycle spokes, of the sound of other bicycle spokes ticking along somewhere nearby, a bit more quickly—there is another rider in the dark, on another path running alongside the lane, not entirely visible except as movement, now outpacing her. The other path is one that anyone getting back on the late bus might take toward the nurses' pavilion, but her pulse is leaping at the base of her throat and her fingers twitch on the hand brake in deciding whether to stop there in the dark and in doing so let the other rider pass. Who would it be, riding here? Except herself? And why not just stop and let the other cross without seeing her? For some reason the thought of standing in the darkness after the other rider crosses her path is too ominous to allow. She wants to be away, closer to home, and then she realizes that she doesn't want to have to see the other rider; she would rather let the rider pass behind her, unseen.

She pedals hard, pushes with her knees, standing on the pedals to push and push through distance and protective trees, and whoever is there must surely be someone regular and safe in any case, would have to be, right, so what would it matter, to see the rider or not? She realizes that the paths will converge just ahead and then, despite her stern self-assurances, she panics and the electricity in her joints causes her front tire to slip in the deep wet rut, and she skids, and nearly falls, catching herself in the slush on one foot, roughly. The other rider pulls ahead. She rights her bicycle and stands flat-footed, her boots on the remnants of ice to either side, believing she now recognizes the whine of the other bicycle. It's only Evelyn, right, only Evelyn Todd? And she's probably heard Sunny, but what would it matter, another person on the grounds besides herself, as she goes pedaling along the path? Evelyn Todd flashes between the trees, disappearing forward with a sharply upright posture, and then she's gone again. Sunny shifts her footing. The cold is suddenly brutal underfoot, icy water rising around her boots from the still-frozen ground. She's breathing quickly, deep breaths of harsh air that taste of blood and saliva.

When Evelyn Todd's tires are out of earshot Sunny hears nothing but an occasional creaking, high in the heavy air. It's not necessarily unusual to pass another so closely at night in the woods in Finland and not look up. But it does seem peculiar for Evelyn Todd to appear and disappear so quickly, when up close the trees have always seemed comfortably sparse and penetrable. Suddenly they feel like a dense, concealing front in the darkness, and Sunny stands, stricken by the potential for anonymity, for losing oneself in the silence, in the cold, in the trees that had earlier seemed tame, that had until now seemed an extension of the hospital itself.

Back in the hospital yard, Sunny dismounts to wheel her bike into the shed, as usual, without using her pocket flashlight. But once inside she hears something out of place, and then someone touches her, uncertainly, from the shadows.

"Sunny," says Pearl in a whisper, and Sunny flinches away even as she realizes who it is. "Please," says Pearl, and her voice is thick, halting.

"I keep thinking there might have been a mistake, and maybe it isn't true, and now she's lying someplace in the dark, and maybe it's not too late to do something. I know it's silly. But I can't help it."

"Mrs. Weber," says Sunny. "I was with Julia, and you can believe me. She had problems after the anesthesia and there was nothing more Dr. Peter could do."

"Peter was there when she died," says Pearl.

"At the bedside," says Sunny. "He did everything he could."

"I'm sure he did," says Pearl.

Sunny leans her bike in its usual place and moves to step back out into the yard.

"Julia was my friend," says Pearl, touching Sunny's arm. "Everybody says it's true, but I can't believe she's dead. I just don't believe it. There's nobody else I can ask for help, Sunny. Only you."

Pearl stands close enough—again, too close—that Sunny is enveloped in her odors of cold fox fur and roses. Her eyes have adjusted to the dimness in the shed, and though she can't make out Pearl's face she sees a faint gray nimbus around her in the light from the yard, in the haze of Pearl's breath, and her own, condensing and rising between them. Sunny remembers the feeling in Julia's room that night, a nagging feeling that someone else should have come into the room, and thinks, not logically, that maybe Pearl had been meant to be there then. It does not strictly make sense. But it seems to. And once this has occurred to her, this memory of that feeling, it becomes a foregone conclusion that she will take Pearl inside, briefly. No more than a few minutes. Sunny is uncomfortable with the mood of a secret favor given, but she can understand too well Pearl's bewildered disconnection from what the others around her are feeling.

They leave their shoes at the sill and pass in stockinged feet through parts of the wing familiar to patients, past the treatment rooms, darkish, coldish, though some attempt has been made to soften this by making them a combination of examination rooms and, perhaps, consulting rooms, with normal wooden chairs and furniture other than white enamel. They turn into a more private area. They pass the door to the pathology lab, with its window protected by wire mesh in case of misguided mischief in search of drugs, but open slightly at the bottom to receive the specimens collected overnight. Through this slit in the mesh, just visible, are the cages for those rabbits newly taken from the hutches, huddled softly together and waiting for their turn in diagnosing someone's problem.

Through a small anteroom beyond this, to the north, is the mortuary. It is a small, cold room, with tile walls and metal shelves; there is only one form waiting there, wrapped in the sheet that Sunny herself prepared and pinned shut. Now Sunny unpins the sheet, repeating her own actions in reverse, hesitating. She has never opened, only closed. Now she finds that Julia is not the same. Julia is smaller, flatter, denser, and her flesh is preternaturally cold, as the dead are always spoken of. But she is also as they are never politely spoken of: sexless, squared, yellow, her chin sunken toward her chest.

Pearl does not cry. She bows her head to look at Julia's face, perhaps too closely.

"It's enough," says Sunny, touching her arm; Pearl was not wearing a coat outside, and she still shivers. She must have been watching from the windows, waiting, and had slipped out to the shed unprepared.

"Why can't I believe it?"

"That's normal," says Sunny. "It's the shock."

"Can I have just a little bit of time alone with her?" Pearl's hand, firm, glinting with rings, pinches Sunny's arm, beseeching. Sunny steps aside, as far as the anteroom, leaves the door open. There is no sound on this corridor, neither of machinery nor of people. She intends to give Pearl a moment of privacy but a movement makes her look back. Pearl has brought a kohl crayon and is quickly sketching Julia's customary heavy eyebrows, darkening her eyelids. Sunny comes to stop this and Pearl avoids her, bending down and trying to smear her own lips over Julia's, trying to smudge and transfer the lipstick; it is the shock of the dead lips that breaks Pearl's artificial calm.

There is not time to do everything, to clean Julia's face and rewrap her properly and take hold of Pearl in the same moment. Sunny tucks the sheet back in place with one hand and takes Pearl with the other. Pearl is silently weeping now, scrubbing at her lips with her fingers, not having understood that the odor of the kiss will linger. Sunny can see panic rising in Pearl's chest, and knows that if Pearl's hysteria spills over she will have a long hard job getting her back to her room, and an explanation will be required—why on earth would she take Pearl into the morgue? Sunny herself has no explanation, not at the moment.

"Calm down, Pearl, or I'll call Dr. Peter," she says, sorry now to have let such a situation happen. She pushes Pearl's hands away and lifts her chin slightly with two fingers, to make serious eye contact, but also so that if Pearl needs a slap there will be ample room. But Dr. Peter, it seems, is enough of a threat to enforce quiet, all during the shambling, tearful walk along the hall, up the stairs, and back to the residential floor, where Sunny wrathfully gives Pearl a pill, a big one, watching as she swallows it, the barrier firmly in place once more. *I should have known better than to trust Pearl . . .*

After which Sunny will be obliged to return alone through the quiet, empty corridors, retracing their steps to retrieve their outdoor shoes. And worse, she knows she must return alone down the hall to the mortuary, to wipe Julia's lips and brow with a damp tissue—quickly, quickly—and to pin the winding sheet closed over her face once again before going, quickly as she can, back to the populated floors.

Sixteen

Usually a memorial, if taking place at Suvanto, would occur in the chapel on a Sunday morning, with a few words spoken by a visiting clergyman from town, followed by coffee, and then in due course by lunch. But even that much is unusual, since most of those who might die have only been here a short time, and they are taken home again right after. But for Julia? It is Saturday night, and something more impromptu should happen in her honor, everyone would say so. Unresolved feelings have kept the up-patients awake in the Radiant Room. Some are playing cards quietly as usual, but Pearl sits with her feet tucked up under her skirt, staring at the flames, fingering the beads on the hem of her dark dress. Mrs. Minder would like to play Ladies, but even she knows better than to suggest any of the old games now, and instead she sits on the hearth morosely, poking the cards, one by one, uppers and lowers still separated, into the embers under the grate with a pair of tongs.

Pearl stands and goes to the bookshelves and pulls out a tango record she had earlier hidden behind the set of encyclopedias. She is sorry now for having hidden it from Julia. She puts it on, balances the needle, which goes awry and must be weighted with a coin on the arm. Some look up, remembering an evening when Julia had played this same song and danced a little by herself, barefooted, a limping performance in which she clutched her fur coat dramatically around herself like a partner.

I'll teach you, she'd said. But they had all been too embarrassed. Even Pearl had refused then, but now she makes the same unsmiling motion of invitation to the others. Some of them self-consciously stand, ankles and knee joints cracking. They are still embarrassed, and they certainly don't know how to dance the way Julia did, but they'll stand in observation. This is the scene when Sunny glances in, taking a last look around before going upstairs to her book. The stillness and the standing surprise her, and she hesitates, at the edge of the draft curtain, watching. Perhaps the wistfulness, the loneliness that she feels is clear on her face when she meets the eyes of Laimi, still seated on the couch; they are the only two not making an effort to join in. Then Laimi smiles, and Sunny is surprised, and disconcerted, to see amusement in her face.

The others stand like figures posed in a frieze, in a tableau, a moment caught and fixed just before some change will enter and disrupt, scattering the group, extinguishing the flames, sending the needle roughly skidding across the record's surface. Sunny moves, fractionally, about to step out, and the women turn to look at her, heads clicking into place in series, a communal gaze like something handed down the line, and this is so quickly and so neatly executed that Sunny, too, freezes, until the song ends.

There should be a movement toward the stairs and bed. But wait, wait a moment: nobody is tired, and don't they all wordlessly agree that some fresh air and moonlight would clear the head? Shoes and coats are collected and some drift to the front door. The porter watches, sees Sunny, says nothing. It is a very clear, very cold night, with stars so sharp and plentiful that it is painful to look up. The group takes the dark path toward the beach, arms linked, hands clutching one another's sleeves as they move over the wet ground. Some were already in their dressing gowns, but in the moment have put their coats on over.

There is a collar of clouds waiting on the horizon. Two of the ladies bring out binoculars from coat pockets, and these are passed from hand to hand so that all can look at the comet above, visible now and moving so slowly that it seems motionless in the dark sky. As motionless as the persuasively scarred face of the bright, nearly full moon.

"It's a shame Julia didn't get to see that," someone says, too sentimental, too conventional. *Stop! Julia wouldn't give a damn. Now is the time for some genuine feeling.* But the sound of her name hangs in the cold air like suspended vapor.

"Poor Julia," says Pearl.

Once the name has been said they all want to repeat it, a compulsion there in the darkness, near the darkening and weakening ice. Someone repeats the name, *Poor Julia,* someone else repeats it again, and then someone else as well, not together but each separately so that Julia's name is heard like the crying of a flock of geese overhead in the darkness, with their peeping cries distinct and overlapping.

Sunny has come outside to watch their progress on the dark path and is standing just behind them. She looks at the women, but then away: it is not right to examine their faces in this moment, when they forget themselves. She looks up instead. The exposed sky is hard and empty behind the stars. She feels something shifting, seemingly underfoot, like water under the ice on other days, and something welling inside. She thinks she'd also like to say Julia's name, quietly, into the sky, just because. Why not. Because, poor Julia.

Some of the women reach for each other, pairing off, joining hands or linking arms in the darkness. Mary Minder slips in to stand close with Pearl. Sunny watches them, feels a small movement at her elbow, and then Laimi touches her arm.

"Sunny," she says. "Take me back to the room."

Laimi's voice makes Sunny instantly, absurdly angry, and she wants to swat Laimi's hand, because for once she'd felt at ease. For once she'd felt a shared need to acknowledge whatever was being acknowledged within a group. For god's sake, was Laimi so completely devoid of feeling? Could she be that petty? Why else call Sunny back, away from something, why remind her of the divide that marked her place in life—paradoxically above and yet in service to the other women—instead of waiting just a few more minutes? But in the same instant Sunny feels ashamed at this near-eruption of inner ugliness, a feeling of shame compounded by the memory of the times when she had momentarily allowed her impatience to rear up, wrongly, unfairly, at Laimi. At Laimi, who had been genuinely ill. Sunny can't undo those errors in judgment, but she can at least avoid making another, and she will conceal, completely, her resentment at being called away from a moment in which she might have disappeared among the others.

Laimi says, "Now, please, at once."

Sunny takes Laimi's arm. Laimi hadn't particularly liked Julia, but had it been that bad, to want to leave now? Because it seems that even obscured in the darkness, there was no sign of pain on Laimi's face or in her manner. But Laimi lets her arm be taken, which must mean something, and in a few minutes these two have disappeared into the trees together, along the path, through the doors, past the porter and into the twilight of Suvanto.

Laimi stops, goes back, and initials the book with the time of their return.

None of the women on the beach have noticed. They do not look down, nor at each other, but only upward at the sky, their world now drained of color, except the gray and silver of the moon, and the white fire of the comet, very tiny in the vastness; even Mary Minder for once is not looking around nervously, not weighing the situation, but merely looking upward with her mouth slightly open and her teeth glinting darkly.

Laimi releases Sunny's arm. The curtains in her room are open, the window is black, and she is looking at the glass. Sunny will go now. But then Laimi makes a sudden movement and pulls the curtains rapidly along the waxed track, a faint zipping sound, and she closes the door as well.

When the curtain and the door are closed, she and Sunny are separated from the events taking place outside at the edge of the water. That moment, for Sunny, has been broken; she cannot imagine going back downstairs, seeking her shoes again, and taking the path back to the others, who must in any case be returning soon from the cold and the dark. Anyway, the magic was not to be found in insistently joining them, but in feeling a spontaneous tug on the common string at a time when nothing was needed of her and yet her presence still seemed entirely natural. Nobody would have expected anything of her, and, more importantly, nobody would have wondered why she was there.

"Please," says Laimi. "Sit with me for a while."

As once before Sunny takes the second chair at the small table, and they look across the table at one another.

"Saturday night," says Laimi.

"Yes," says Sunny.

"What would you be doing now, in your other life, if you weren't here?"

"I don't know," says Sunny. "I may have gone to a movie. Or I might be visiting a friend." They are awkward, and the conversation must be pushed. "That's not true. I would have been home with my mother, up until she died. Reading to her, probably, she liked that. Long books, novels." And Sunny thinks, remembers. But then she says belatedly, courteously, "And what would you be doing?"

"Saturday night, I might be with friends. Maybe to sauna."

"And did you go, tonight?"

"No, not here. I don't like to go here. It's not the same, the heat isn't really the same at all." Laimi turns in her chair and touches the switch of an electric teakettle.

"Don't let me keep you awake," says Sunny.

"Stay," says Laimi. "I'll feel better if you stay here, with me, for a while."

Sunny resists the urge to glance at her watch, not for her own sake necessarily but from the wish not to keep Laimi from her bed.

"Okay," says Sunny. "Of course I'll stay."

"And could you maybe bring me something from down the hall?"

"What's the matter?" It is rare enough for Laimi to take a painkiller of any kind that Sunny is concerned now.

"Only a headache. But I wouldn't mind an aspirin."

Sunny goes to get one, tips it into a white cup. She stops at the desk where the night nurse has taken off her glasses and is cleaning them with a tissue. Sunny makes a quick note, the usual for any medications given, even this.

"What's that?" says the night nurse, putting her glasses back on and discreetly covering her magazine with a stack of paperwork.

"Laimi has a headache," says Sunny. "I'm going to sit up with her."

"If you want to go to bed I'll see to it."

"It's all right, I don't mind." Sunny notes the time by her watch, scrawls her initials next to medications given. Back in the room, Laimi has made two cups of coffee and is waiting.

"I don't want to keep you up," says Sunny, for the second time.

"I'm not tired." Laimi accepts the aspirin, sets it aside instead of swallowing it.

"Let me know if you change your mind, and I'll go," says Sunny.

"All right," says Laimi. "I'll let you know."

Sunny does not want the coffee but again she will not refuse something offered, not here. She stirs in sugar with a small spoon. Thinks of Julia hoarding flatware.

"Well, it's sad," says Laimi, also stirring sugar. "But you must be pretty used to people dying by now."

"Still, it's always a shock."

"Is it really a shock? You didn't expect it?"

"No," says Sunny. "Why would I? She wasn't that sick."

"I know," says Laimi. "It's just that sometimes in retrospect these things start to appear inevitable. The first person I knew who died was my grandfather. It was shocking for me, but the adults weren't surprised, and when I look back I'm not surprised either. Do you remember the photos of the summerhouse?"

"I do."

"Those were taken not long before. He's in the photos. Every year we packed up the house at the end of June and moved to the cottage until the end of August and my mother's parents came with us. My grandfather was dying, all summer, and I didn't realize. So I didn't take advantage of that time with him. I don't have any particular last memories. Only composite memories from other summers."

"You didn't know," says Sunny.

"Everyone knows everything, all the time," says Laimi. "I went out picking berries the day he died. He was in bed when I left, and I knew something was strange. I wish I'd stayed in the house. I wish they hadn't let me lose myself in the meadows. For years after that I couldn't tolerate the odor of fresh berries without feeling sick."

"Maybe they didn't want to upset you, in case he didn't die."

"He was always going to die there, that summer. He wanted to die at the cottage instead of being moved back to town in the fall."

"It happens that way," says Sunny. "A lot of older people choose the timing of the end, at least when it comes naturally."

"It was inevitable." Laimi folds her hands around her coffee cup.

"How is your head?"

"It's fine. I'll only take the aspirin if I really have to. He was the same, actually, with doctors. But there was a healer, and he asked for her. Some people appreciate the really old familiar ways when they know they're dying."

"It happens with religion. I've seen it with patients here."

"That day after I was gone he asked to be taken to the bathhouse that he'd helped my father build on the property a long time before. He wanted to die in the sauna. He didn't want to be carried, he wanted to walk, but it took all the last of his strength. My father helped, but only a little. He had to let him do it himself. And when my grandfather got to the bathhouse he made himself comfortable on the bench. They brought him some blankets and a pillow. And it happened just the way he wanted."

"In the sauna?" Sunny's thoughts are filled with heat, the dampness of the steam.

"The sauna wasn't heated, I don't mean that. It used to be more common. Sometimes you hear about the older people, when they were very weak, getting up out of bed at the end and making it back to the sauna. It's amazing, really."

"I guess it's not a pull I understand," says Sunny.

"I think it's where they could remember most of the good things about being alive. I know it doesn't feel the same for you. But for him, there would have been decades of familiar shadows, and the smell of the wood and the smoke and the birch leaves that we were using in the sauna at the summerhouse, the sound of the benches creaking under him. I can understand it. He used to sleep there sometimes anyway, on the bench when all the bedrooms in the house were full of company. Such as if we were expecting summer guests, for example. I'm happy to think it was a lot like that, just one more time, him falling asleep in the peace of the place."

Laimi's eyes, grayish blue, are small and bright, highly placed over high cheekbones. She tucks her hair behind her ear. This is the most she has ever spoken to Sunny at a time. Her voice is low, and compelling, and Sunny doesn't know what to say.

"Are you bored yet?" Laimi says.

"No," says Sunny. "No, of course not."

"Are you wondering why I'm talking about the summerhouse so much?"

"No," says Sunny. "Not really."

"You might like the other kind of sauna," she says. "The proper Finnish sauna has a wood-burning stove, so the carbon in the smoke is a purifier, and the sauna was always the cleanest part of the old houses. That's where the sick were taken care of and that's where the babies were born. Those old habits are a little less well thought of now. You can imagine how opinions change."

"Were you born there?"

"I was."

"In the same sauna where your grandfather passed away?"

"Yes, the same one. It's still there. We still use it, in the summer. Nobody's had a baby in it for quite a while, though."

Any residual thoughts of the others outside vanish from Sunny's mind as she imagines the creaking, the warmth. She thinks of her own mother, the painful memory pushed habitually away.

"What if there were complications?"

"Babies were born for thousands of years before anybody had hospitals."

Sunny hesitates, but says nothing of her family, her mother's injury. Instead she says, "And do you think it was your grandfather's time to die, and that deciding not to see the doctors was the right decision?"

"Of course. My mother wanted to bring another doctor to see him, but it was the old man's decision and she accepted that. Though she wasn't happy when the healer came. She had trouble accepting that, though I'm sure it reassured him." Laimi makes a motion in the air. "The healer made a cut on his back and pulled blood out with a suction horn. The old women used to do that. No, my mother didn't like that. Later on, she went over to the Evangelicals."

"A cut on the back?"

"Yes. I had it too." She touches the back of her neck, above the scar that Sunny has seen in the past, like a small bolt of lightning across the flesh, and they lapse into a long period of quiet, there in the closed room, motionless at the table. When Sunny next glances at her watch she is surprised to see how much time has passed. On any other day she would already have slept and would soon be sitting upright in her bed, in expectation of putting on her uniform to begin the day. But it is Sunday. She can go along to her bed and sleep as late as she wants.

"I think it's important," says Laimi, but she stops. Sunny waits. "It's important," says Laimi again, "not to take their identity from the dead. We ought to just let them be who they were. Don't you think?"

"I'm not sure I know what you mean."

"I don't want to be cruel. But Julia was not a particularly nice woman. I'm sure it can be explained but that doesn't change her. Maybe she wasn't happy. She didn't like to live in Finland, obviously, so she was lonely, probably, and maybe she deserves some sympathy for that. But it's unfair to make her a different person now."

And although Sunny does agree, it is hard not to defend the dead. "Maybe it was her husband's fault. Maybe he made her live in Finland."

"I don't know. They stuck with the Danes. She didn't speak Finnish at all, you know, she never tried. I know it's hard, but after years she could have made the effort to learn something. You speak quite a lot more than she did, just in the time you've been here."

"But she spoke Swedish, that's something," says Sunny, slightly ashamed.

"She did not. She spoke Danish and expected everyone to work out what she meant. You didn't speak enough Swedish to hear the difference. She wasn't nice. She ought to be remembered that way."

"Well," concedes Sunny, "maybe. But she was unhappy here. She didn't want to come to Suvanto in the first place. She wanted to go back to Turku."

"I don't want to be here," says Laimi. "I'd rather be in Turku, too, believe me."

"It's not that bad, surely," says Sunny, wondering how she's come to be defending not just Julia, but all of them, despite her own misgivings.

"I don't know where you've been spending your time," says Laimi. "But on this floor, the atmosphere isn't good. Maybe you're getting too comfortable here. Maybe you don't notice."

And Sunny wants to answer that no, she doesn't like it here, not all that much, but she finds herself caught between defending and de-crying the place, and says nothing, because both answers feel true.

Laimi stretches slightly, and reaches to draw the curtains open.

"Sunny," she says, and Sunny waits for the question she both ex-pects and dreads. "Why didn't you come at midsummer?"

And here it is, the terrible thing. Laimi had invited her to come to the summerhouse, to come for the entire summer holiday, if she wanted.

And she did want to. She would have been welcomed there. She would have met Laimi's extended family, and this would be the way to see all of the things that Laimi had described for her. There would have been the wood-burning sauna, and the boat, and she could even, if she'd wanted, have learned to fish. They'd have tucked their pant legs into borrowed rubber boots and gone into the meadows after mushrooms. They'd have picked berries, companionably silent as they worked. And by the time she returned to Suvanto, her Finnish would have been so much better, so much more natural. She would have started to think in Finnish, sometimes. She would have had dreams in Finnish, in which she could say anything she wanted, and understand anything said to her. It had been planned ahead of time. Laimi and her uncle would fetch Sunny at the train station in Turku, and they would all continue on in his car to meet the others. And it would have been lovely.

But once Laimi had gone on ahead to meet her uncle, Sunny had known that she couldn't go. She'd written a letter to Laimi at her grandmother's, which must have arrived just in time. *I can't come, but thanks so much for inviting me. See you in September.*

"I'm sorry," she says now. "I was afraid I would be in the way."

"But you were invited."

"I know."

"But you were invited. I invited you, and you accepted."

She can see that she has not given enough of an answer. This will be her only chance to explain, and to apologize, and she knows this.

"Laimi," she says. "I don't know how to behave around people who don't need me, and you didn't need me there. I was afraid that if I went to the summerhouse I would do everything wrong and I wouldn't be able to communicate very well with anyone, and I was sure you would realize that you didn't like having me there. And I know you would have been too polite to let me know. I didn't want it to be like that."

"And so you felt more comfortable staying *here*."

Sunny nods.

"It's snowing," Laimi says, looking to the outer world. From the tone of her voice, it is clear that what she means is, *And now you should go.*

Eighteen

One danger of constant observation is that all the world, even tragedy, comes to seem anecdotal. There are too many people floating in and floating out of the rooms and corridors. A reluctance to say what has happened. Except that Dr. Peter has met with an accident. A fatal one. Unfortunately.

A story quickly develops that it was Julia who had broken Dr. Peter's neck and left him there behind the clinical building, in revenge for having persuaded her to have the surgery. It is not surprising that some of the patients want to believe in a ghost story rather than in a fatal accident, or in murder. In time, though, accident is accepted as an answer. Most agree that a brown bear must have come out of the woods and that Dr. Peter had unluckily crossed its path, Frida probably too. Because Frida, by the way, is missing. Did this accord with the actual habits of bears in the area, at that time of the winter? Does it accord with Dr. Peter and Frida taking different routes away from the building? Does it matter that Frida's coat still hangs on a hook in the clinical wing? Someone decided that this was what had happened, or at least decided to put this version of events into circulation. And memories from earlier that year of a bear attack less than a hundred miles away seemed to give weight to the story.

The police were notified. The examination of Dr. Peter's body was performed in town; this seemed logical. Inevitably the mythology of his life began to form, and some said he had devoted his life to taking care of others, that he was a good doctor, a compassionate man, an attentive and thorough surgeon—yes, he was, even given recent circumstances. That he was a sound husband, no doubt, and the beloved father of two young children. How must they be feeling? Years earlier he had expressed a wish to be cremated. Pamela and the two children left on the day that his body was removed to a crematorium far, far away, following the mortuary truck in a car owned by the hospital, and without making any good-byes.

Sunny does not, of course, accept the explanation that a ghost killed Dr. Peter, and anyway, the ghost of Julia? Nonsense. (And equally nonsense to think of Frida having any hand in this. Where is she, though?) Sunny does, however, accept that some natural force probably contributed to whatever happened; the comet, the moon, the thaw. It is not surprising that some temporary madness could creep over the minds of people who are not part of the land, who have hidden themselves in the cold black pines without true thought for this life. It is not surprising if some become unsettled by physical forces much bigger than themselves. And by the sudden death of one of their number? Would you say that, really? And imply what that implies? Yes, because although there *was* torn flesh, that small deep laceration on the back of his right hand did not appear accidental. It was elliptical, and regular, with a serrated-looking interstitial border; it was just the sort of wound a fingertip might fit into, or a few fingertips in turn, pressing and scratching to touch the small clearing of barely exposed bone.

But come now: most of the up-patients did not even like Julia. If the truth is stated, if ill must be spoken of the dead, then admit it: probably only Pearl really cared for her. And of course Mary Minder will claim to have cared. But does that matter?

Questions are asked, a repetition of details is requested. Sunny should be able to, but cannot, remember every single detail about the evening, because habitual routine makes all evenings into the same evening. There was music played in the Radiant Room. And then a group went outside to look for the comet. The porter at reception remembers a nurse among them, was it Sunny coming in with Laimi, it probably was though he says he is not positive he'd previously seen either of the two of them go out with the group, but must have, he's almost sure, there was a nurse among them. The book is there and everyone knows they must sign in and out, it's not the porter's job to enforce a rule that everyone knows is for their own well-being. Laimi signed herself in, anyway. Others straggled in a short time later. Everyone? It's impossible to say.

Does Sunny wear her indoor shoes outdoors? Her outdoor shoes inside? Not usually. But at times, once in a while, if there isn't time to stop, and someone needs her, but no, she wore her indoor shoes upstairs with Laimi. They stopped together to change their shoes. Did she go back outside at any point? Of course not. She was with Laimi. The night nurse will say the same. She gave an aspirin. She signed for it.

Can Sunny account for her keys? Her keys stay on her belt, or in the key pocket of her blue cardigan.

All night?

Every night.

But did anyone ask the right questions? Did anyone think of how many traces of how many actions are removed, destroyed, laundered away every day in such an environment? Good routines, of course, do not depend on any one person but continue unto themselves, every cog moving in turn.

Dry laundry, foul laundry, shoe porch, beauty.

There are more rumors. The boy in the shoe porch says the outside door was found unbolted and standing open after that night, that a drift of new snow came in and covered half the shoes, covering the rubber grating on the floor where the patients stomp off dirt and sand, stomp off ice and snow; that he had turned up the heat, accelerating the smell of feet from the damp walking shoes, had dried and brushed and polished them as quickly as he could, and had swept out slush and many pine needles, all before lunch, all before it was quite realized that anything was wrong.

The girls from the Beauty Room say that they have given a couple of manicures, some with dirty nails, broken nails. They don't really remember who among so many patients had the broken fingernails. Who even wondered anything, at the time?

The foul laundry was discharged as usual, and of course no one there looked too closely at any stained or bloody fabrics going under the boiling water.

And anyway no one would have noticed something like Pearl's earrings lying on the nightstand in a small spot of water, as from melted snow. The same if there was grit, if there were grains of sand in the sheets, on the floors. These ward maids do their jobs thoroughly, but hardly need to pay attention, they've done it all so many times before. Well, actually, the ward maids may have spoken to one another, but they had nothing public to say, no questions to ask. They don't board with the nurses; they are shifted away to one side after doing the worst of the work, and wouldn't necessarily think of coming forward.

Memory returns as slowly as need be, a pool of water and a reluctance notwithstanding. Because it cannot be explained away, the eye cannot be explained away. Especially not considering the many bedjackets and cardigan sweaters whose pockets contain small sewing wallets holding carded rows of large needles, large enough for those with less than perfect eyesight. Rows of needles standing neatly, already threaded and waiting.

Afterward, William Weber says, "This is my fault. If I hadn't sent her back this might not have happened." But he wouldn't really have made that statement: to say such a thing would mean a recognition of a possibility previously unsaid . . . only in retrospect, then, does it seem like something he should have said. Let us say that in retrospect, it occurred to him that by sending Pearl back, he started a chain of events leading to Dr. Peter's accident (and Frida's), a chain of events opening out of the moral flaw that he had seen, and that had troubled him about the up-patients earlier.

He believes now that there is an evolutionary, biological caution at work, that when a person—a woman, he means—gives off the constant signal of need, requiring so much attention and so much care, with so much talk of pain and private things, that red flags should be triggered in the nervous systems of normal people. And that the impulse to get away is very strong and incidentally very normal, and that an environment in which so many of such women live together is an affront to normalcy. It could probably be explained in scientific ways, and perhaps he could have asked Peter about this. Maybe the simplest explanation is that such women will suck and suck away at anyone else's energies. That not only will they give a weak, unfair exchange in return for the attention they need, but they will create even more pain as a comfort to themselves.

In the daily life of Pearl, as proof, the biggest change after the finding of Dr. Peter's body is—not grief for Peter, not sorrow for William—but the aching of her own knee, a reminder of the childhood problem, persistent and growing progressively harder to ignore. A pain that throbs and pushes her deeper, deeper with each heartbeat, like a nail into the wood of her private world.

Pearl sleeps fitfully, troubled with fretful dreams, wakened by the throbbing of her knee under the painful pressure of the blankets. It's clear now, again, that she wasn't serious earlier when she said she liked to take walks outside . . . any little exertion, any physical activity sets off the old pain. Here is the root of the real illness of her life. The truth is that as a child, she suffered a serious case of bone mischief, a deep, ugly infection of bone tuberculosis. She had not lied to Peter about this.

Honestly? Why not just say so from the beginning! You might

think it easier to confide a problem of the knee and hip before hinting
at a private female problem. But for Pearl, understand, the details had
taken on such an ugly feeling, such an animal feeling, that she couldn't
accept it, wasn't reconciled to being infected with that bacillus, a cow
disease that caused the joint of her left knee to swell and swell, striking
up toward the hip ball and socket, becoming hard, stiff with cold ab-
scesses, and immensely painful.

It had been nothing at first, only a sprain or a twist, her mother felt
sure. Pearl had been put into bed with her knee wrapped like a treasure in cotton wool and for a week she had waited there, without much
distraction from the pain of that knee, red as refrigerated meat under
the blankets. Not much to do besides following the workings of her
own brain backward in a pattern as curved as horns, backward and
down and in again, to the animal brain where pain lives; she had curled
up inside the knee, had been drawn down into the knee, into the leg
and hip, beyond the surface, to the recesses, all connected, all thrown
permanently off balance. Unfortunately it's common enough, or so the
doctor had said when he was called eventually. Had her mother done
her duty? This was how the doctor phrased it: "Have you done your
duty?"

Pearl's mother had tried to do her duty as long as possible, that is to
say that Pearl had of course been breast-fed for as long as possible. But
she's a big girl now! The doctor gives a level look and presumes, now,
that she's drinking cow's milk? She is.

What kind?

Cow's milk. Top milk. Full fat.

What kind of cow? Where are you getting it?

The milk is delivered, and Pearl's mother names the company, but
that's a distributor, not a dairy, how can she not know where the milk
originates? You need to know, have the cows been fed in stalls or outside? In fresh air and sunlight? Most importantly, are you buying from
a tuberculin-tested herd? If not, you have not done your duty. Because
it is a mother's most sacred duty to see that the milk her children drink
comes from the purest sources only.

She didn't know she was supposed to ask! Where is she from? North, near the border, Whatcom County. Lots of farms up there, says the doctor, lots of dairies up there, it's surprising you didn't know. But now you know. Too bad it's too late.

If there was an oversight regarding the milk then this is probably the channel through which the bacilli had entered her blood and found her knee hospitable, through her open gasping mouth, her sucking pink lips, her red and purple tongue seeking and swallowing the festering infection. Or, as the doctor called it, the dirty milk.

The knee, the disfigurement, it is a hardship, but it can be treated. Pearl's leg was extended with weights and leather straps buckled to pull, to pull the leg and mercifully keep the bone heads from touching. To prevent pain. To allow sleep. To allow Pearl to drift away into sleep without waking in a scream as her spasmed leg muscles relaxed enough to let the warped bones come painfully back together.

Still, it was a horror to contemplate the good news of a surgery ordered to take place not once but several times. A painful curetting of the bone. Why, why had no one in the house thought to boil every mouthful of milk? An oversight with consequences. And a photograph was taken as proof, Pearl's fair hair in two braided ponytails . . . it would hurt now to see the care with which those braids were fastened with two small white ribbons. Pearl in a white vest and a pair of white cotton underpants, seated in profile with her left leg retracted to show the extent of the bony protrusion. Not a photograph of a child, but a photograph of a tubercular joint. She did not ever see the photo, and doesn't know whether her face appeared, or whether she would be recognizable, or whether instead the knee would have expanded to demand the full attention of anyone looking, hard, massive, out of proportion, a fossil. But she knows that the photo must exist somewhere, with a caption indicating that she is lucky to have received a rapid treatment.

She lies in her bed now upstairs at Suvanto. *I hate everything, everyone,* she thinks, and means it. Beyond this, there is no thought of anything or anyone else.

Nineteen

For the month of February: paperwhites and daffodils, imported bulbs brought earlier, during happier times, in suitcases to be grown by the Mrs. Doctors indoors. Near the grate, away from the windows and any tiny flickering possibility of draft, the bulbs are stirring and will bloom there soon. What's for the snack? *Keksi* in fancy shapes—a star, a crescent moon, a fish. Cheerful shapes. Because after the death of Dr. Peter, and the unfathomable disappearance of Nurse Frida, a silent confusion has descended.

Mrs. Minder has not left after all, she roams and carries a small hankie in the collar of her blouse. Touches it to her red nose, touches it to her eyes, then slips it under her collar next to her skin, secures it under a brassiere strap so that the limp damp thing rides on her shoulder, a crumpled little ghost appearing throughout the day. Takes a cookie. Takes a bite. Puts it back down on the communal dish.

Sunny's English-speaking staff are watchful. They are careful to count the up-patients, tracking them as they stroll toward the trees, reluctant to escort them out of sight except in staff pairs. An evening curfew is set. This doesn't stop the Finnish nurses, though, who are tough and sensible, and who go out as much as before, maybe more than before, walking the paths or skiing to the meadows, leaving their foreign counterparts indoors. They go out together into the landscape to find peace in the trees. To shake off the miasma and fill their lungs with the clear outside air.

And maybe they are right, maybe fresh air is an answer. And so there is a final ice picnic. Coffee from a thermos is served on the swimming platform and someone takes a photograph or two with hollow enthusiasm. These photographs are less nostalgic than the others in the Radiant Room album. It's partly knowing the date that makes them all seem strained, tired, distorted. Pearl, for example, is smiling, but there are vertical dark creases in the wrong places—forehead, chin—that pucker and reveal her age, newly. And all the lipids available in jars cannot penetrate beyond a lifetime of drawing the face together in this direction in a secret frown like the closing of pages together. And she limps. She uses Julia's cane, with its little brass pinecone handle. She says it is because her belly aches. She holds the cane behind her skirt when the camera comes out.

But mostly no, thank you, no one cared for souvenirs anymore. Too much charm and patience have been exhausted. A look caught over the shoulder is an unwelcome look. Eyes and buttons reflect too much snowlight, and gleaming overexposures wipe out the contours of the surfaces, making the backgrounds less substantial, revealing them as sets, lunar and stark.

You would think that everything must change, suddenly and cataclysmically, after such events. But only some things change, and most of those can be made to look normal. The night nurse gives her notice, she says that she is leaving because she is getting married. When she is pressed about the wedding plans, pressed about why the hurry, she blushes. *I'm not pregnant!* Finally she will admit that she does not plan to marry until spring. But still, she wants to go away soon, back to her family.

For the snack: little open-faced sandwiches of *katkarapu*.

Some cold comfort—though that is hardly the proper word for it—comes from resolving Julia's death, anyway: there are the results from the postmortem. You wouldn't say it out loud, but you could say that Julia brought the end on herself. She'd eaten, obviously, and she had lied about it. When and where? A nocturnal visit to the kitchen? Something hidden in a drawer? There hadn't been any way to catch it, to stop it, not without knowing. You don't want to hear this, of course, but this is what happened while she was still unconscious: a solid strip of ham two inches long, thrown up from her irritated stomach into the esophagus and then quickly inhaled back down. The two ends plugging each of the trachea's two deep branching airways as neatly, as firmly, as fatally as if they had been carefully tamped in on purpose.

The fool . . . it had all been explained to her, first by the doctor and then again by Sunny. Had the warning been in English? It must have been, Sunny would only have given it in English. Julia must have understood at least once when she was told not to eat, she had to have understood.

Dr. Peter should have known this, yes? He ought to have known, because it was his responsibility to know everything. To make sure that all was well.

It doesn't matter. It's senseless. He couldn't possibly have known. But it's over, and Sunny adds the report to her files.

William Weber walks the perimeter without stepping inside the building. He never stays long. He doesn't go to the doctor villas, and he doesn't ask to speak with his wife. They have not spoken since the parting on the train platform. He walks the paths in a sealskin coat and good boots and speaks to no one, seemingly, except for quiet Kusti, maybe to avoid acknowledging a public sympathy. He is seen in the trees, his car is noted. Where does he go, after this? William will go to Pamela, of course. In what capacity? In the capacity of uncle to the children. Shame on you for asking. Of course he goes, and when he goes and does not return it seems that the population of Suvanto exists apart from the outside world once more, until the day in March, in *maaliskuu,* when, out on the ice in the lengthening afternoon, a sharp and compact ship is seen moving slowly between Suvanto and the far distant other shore. It moves with a cruising determination, unhurried and unconcerned, and it takes a moment for the incongruity to register; there have been no vessels on the water here since autumn and the ice has seemed, as it does whenever it is present, permanent and indefatigable.

Sunny stands in the center of two tracks made by an anonymous skier crossing the frozen bay. The ice is solid under her feet, but there will be increasingly limited opportunities now for trusting it, now that spring is tilting closer, and there is, at no very great distance, the icebreaker crumpling the surface and leaving thick bluish slabs piled on either side of its trajectory. For half an hour she stands as the ship passes effortlessly but no doubt with a calculated back and forward fall, borrowing from gravity to cut the way. She cannot see the open water left behind, cannot see beyond the piles of ice thrown up but it must be there, the water, and it must be dark and cold. And though there may be time yet for it to scab over and be sound again, the break has been made. The icebreaker, gray and brown but seemingly much darker and so finely detailed against the whiteness, passes out of sight.

At her back, the windows of Suvanto catch the sun in places. She is too far out to see if anyone stands at the windows, watching the ice and watching her. The possibility seems monstrous, deliberately concealing. And this, as much as anything, is the sudden end of her resolve. She gives the Head of Nursing the shortest notice acceptable under her contract, and will not be dissuaded.

Twenty

Maaliskuu is the month when bare earth returns but April, *huhtikuu,* is the time to step off the path and disappear into the woods with your ax in hand; *huhtikuu* is the month of felling and of burning. Sunny moves through these final days quickly, easily, buoyed by routine even though change is afoot in all directions. The grounds are warming under longer hours of daylight and there is a gathering, growing throb rising from below. She has already disengaged herself from the future of the place and all the people she knows there. It is easily done. There is pressure to go, a force gathering at her back, propelling her away now as strongly as it had held her in place before. And her head, her head is aching again. The sun is making her head ache.

It would seem so obvious, and yet the realization has taken so long: these people are not, cannot be connected to her. She looks at Sister Tutor and Mrs. Anderson and cannot understand why they stay, why they will stay on indefinitely, but she can't spend much effort on such questions: step aside, and step away. She likes them very much, but she knows she won't ever see them again after she goes.

She does the best she can with the expansion of her duties for the moment, with her changing role as one of the single, celibate women tending to the new mothers. She is the one they turn to now with certain quiet questions that they won't ask the doctors. Sunny sets her jaw and gives the advice—in the kind yet clinical approach—and does what she can to answer. She doesn't know about babies, someone else will have to speak about the babies. But she does field the questions about how to make intimacy more comfortable. *Can you tell me how to do that?* they ask. *What should I do?* If they go as far as asking, then she can go as far as telling. And she explains, she uses the words, and then suggests a cone of lubricating cocoa butter inserted ten minutes beforehand . . . a pad, perhaps, to save the linens . . .

Pale-faced, but secure in the role: did she ever expect to be giving such advice? No, and it never really gets easier. But the women are happy with her answers, and will listen to her and remember all that she says, and that is something bigger than embarrassment. But still there should be some better way of communicating such things, a better way of hearing because hearing the answers like this, from Sunny, in her apron and emblem, makes the answers into a suggestion that something is wrong. There is nothing wrong with you, she says, trust me, these are normal situations in your married life, there is nothing wrong with you, nothing at all.

Are you married? they ask, shyly.

"No," says Sunny. "I'm not. But I know you're normal."

And this celibacy is seemingly always the case, no matter who else they might find to ask, because those are the rules, that in many situations nurses aren't permitted to keep their jobs if they marry—that would complicate everything. Married nurses wouldn't live in a dormitory, would they? And here, they couldn't guarantee a commute in the snow, could they, nor being called in on short notice if needed? It isn't fair, but it isn't uncommon.

Mrs. Anderson shakes her head. "Ought to let everyone just get married," she says, "if they want to. Do you know how many kitchen maids I've lost to elopements, or trouble? Every spring, it happens."

"Well," says Sunny. "People are human, aren't they."

Sunny writes letters, receives letters; there is a university hospital far, far away in New York, where she will be hired, a hospital with a training program for nurses where she will in time slide into teaching. Where she will live in an apartment of her own. She turns her aprons in to the laundry and will not claim them before she leaves. She packs her civilian clothes and a few books into the red suitcase, given to her many years before as another graduation gift from her family. And then she waits.

Julia's husband has been sought by means of a telephone call and a message left at what seems to be a residential hotel—using the number provided by Julia on the forms Sunny filled out with her so many months ago—asking that Mr. Dey please get in touch, if he would be so good. A second attempt is made by telegram—deemed undeliverable—and then a letter is posted without expectation of reply. Sunny is waiting for a final glimpse of Julia's other life, through him, but as time passes, too much time, this fades into quiet disgust. She does not want to feel sorry for Julia. After a decent interval standard arrangements are made for interment in the little local cemetery, and Julia is buried wearing the ruby rings and the full contents of her jewelry box; Sunny pins a rather splendid array of brooches and hat pins across the front of Julia's nicest black dress before handing it over to the trusted local undertaker. If the husband ever does come forward, looking for the bits of gold, well, too late.

She tidies her office and makes notes to explain the filing system, though her successor will be Evelyn Todd and there has been time to explain the details. The boundaries have blurred, their hands meeting among the brown files. Nurse Todd nodding, nodding, her hands already proprietary. Possibly not listening. Possibly looking to Sunny's desk chair and feeling it take her weight already. Eyes on Sunny's key ring. *Take them,* Sunny will say. And this will be the triumph of Evelyn Todd, who will look away from Sunny then with hardly another thought of her, ever. Because this was what she had wanted, already, every day of their time together.

There is one last thing to be done when Nurse Todd steps away. Sunny opens the bottom desk drawer and takes the little file of personal items collected over her years at Suvanto. She has always intended to do something proper with them.

She will leave her bicycle in the shed for other nurses to use, if they want. The day before her departure she rides along the paths one last time, out to the cemetery. The snow is gone now and spring is palpably coming up through the softening ground. The green plants will soon be full and mobile in the air like feathers, but this is still the transitional time, and no grass has grown yet on Julia's grave; all will be better soon, in May, in *toukokuu,* the month of sowing. For now the grave has been covered with pine boughs so that it does not look as forlorn as it might.

Sunny has thought to leave a button from Julia's nightgown, found in the sheets, pressed lightly into the soil here, and to leave the other small things in some pretty corner. It is an austere little cemetery, and difficult to guess at the personalities of the people under the compact black or gray headstones, apart from the Finnish names engraved and then illuminated in gradually fading gold. Sunny has been coming once or twice a week lately. Now that the ground has thawed she sees signs that other visitors have been there to wash the markers and sweep away dead leaves, and to turn over patches of soil for planting flowers. In some places bulbs are already putting up small white fingers into the shade, waiting to turn green in the sun. She wishes she had thought to bring some bulbs to plant. But the caretakers will turn over the soil and sow grass anyway. Sunny crouches down and parts the pine boughs to reveal the dirt. She pushes the button down among the moss and roots, among fragments like bits of bone, porous, as dark as the soil, and damp. She knows it isn't bone, that Julia was buried, not cremated. She'd seen the grave being prepared. She had seen an opaque column of what she thought was smoke rising from among the headstones. She'd come toward it and found a long rectangle cleared in the snow, a sheet of dull metal resting on the ground, with thick steam rising out from under it; someone, maybe Kusti, thawing the ground before digging Julia's grave.

For the other items Sunny decides on a place just inside the low stone wall surrounding the cemetery, near some budding bushes inside the gate, a place not yet populated. For most of the small items—a hairpin, a stub of a pencil—she easily remembers the woman who had left it. But there is something unfamiliar in the file, a metal ornament, small and round and cool, white enamel with a deep blue cross in the center: it is Frida's nursing emblem.

It had happened as a step into the irrational, a simple step through a door opening into chaos. But in that chaos there was a hierarchy, revealed in the moment among the up-patients—revealed and remembered only in the flash of that moment coming clear in memory—and some in that remembered moment are angry, purely angry. And others are not angry with Dr. Peter himself, only angry at the change he represents. They recognize that life is unpredictable, like everyone always says, and full of sad misfortunes, as everyone already knows, and these, not coincidentally, are the knitters, who may be slightly older and who may have worked meditatively through bad times before, through other instances of personal grief and outrage.

But even the knitters are not immune to the pull of something pulling from under the granite ground, and although they are slower, they do follow. There is a sulfurous smell of eggs rustling from the cotton skirts of nightgowns, a scratching sound from the wool of flapping coats.

Some who were angry wanted to tear him apart with their fingernails, but others wanted more than that to bind him tight and keep him close—to hush, to fold, to stitch and tie, to snap thread between their sharp new teeth—and how ghastly on the quiet path there, those crouched movements of the women on their knees, movements that could almost have been mistaken for ministrations, the touching, the arranging. He may already be dead, and they are closing his eyes, with firm fingers that are too firm, with too much attention: with two tiny embroidery stitches, tiny bites with the needle into the flesh of his eye-lid, flesh that is so thin, but so resistant. Two tiny stitches for the right eye. So easy to miss. And then they are crossing his arms, folding his fingers together . . . if there is disagreement between those who have hated him and those who want to stitch because he helped them with their pain and problems earlier, there is also, in that quiet place beyond the electric lights, an equilibrium between destruction and care, and those who moved together to punish him step aside and let the older ones choose a needle with the incongruous aid of a pocket flashlight.

Aside from the caring horror of the eye stitched shut, there is the bone-deep abrasion on his hand to contemplate, the suggestive oval with stippled margins; this wound began with a set of teeth fastening onto his flesh. Alongside this any other detail goes practically unnoticed, but there was also a needle left in the palm of his other hand, as a needle would be jabbed into a spool of thread in a workbasket. And that puncture, small and vicious, was done surreptitiously, by Mary Minder, all on her own initiative.

Remember: a constellation of images rather than any one symbol. The moon with a shadow like a dark comma, indicating change to come. Other shadows like two empty suns in the sky. The comet seen through binoculars, frightening when you adjusted the focus forward, backward; impossible to see any two points of the comet clearly at the same time, that horned head of cold ice shining in a halo of vapor, hanging without moving. Though it *was* moving, too fast to see and too vast to imagine, a speeding trajectory that came into the eyes in two white tunnels boring through every head, making it easy to understand the effects of the active sky on the ancients: in that remembered moment the bodies in the heavens were exerting an influence that you now, in the cities and under electric lights, believe you scarcely feel.

Was he retreating? Imagine that he was, and because of the thaw imagine that the ground is difficult to navigate, even and especially on the paths where the compaction of the doctors' footsteps created an uneven layer of hard, slippery ice. And because sometime during that night the snow returns, imagine that this light layer of snow, if already fallen then, does not help him keep his footing. That he thinks it will and trusts it but falls anyway, and that he is momentarily disoriented by snow in the eyes, a quick powder melting but still blinding. And that while he is rising they are on him, and that their combined weight simply conspires to snap his neck with an audible, regretful sound. Imagine that he would have soon been on his way back to the villas, back to the warmth and light, but that after they confronted him and pursued him and smothered him, he was purposefully slipped over the side of the path into the ravine. Because this is where he is found, later, by one of Kusti's men.

But where is the trail of events just before these events? What happened in the time after Laimi asked Sunny to accompany her back to the room? On the shore, where the hum occurred, a spark of something ran through those assembled like the spark of ignition in incense that precedes smoke. In returning to the building, a detour: from the pocket of a coat, a key ring is extracted. The side entrance near the juncture with the clinical building is opened.

These are the recurring traces that come to Sunny repeatedly, dreams or disturbances that imply that she is responsible . . . Rest assured, though, she knows she ought to rest assured, because she remembers being in Laimi's room, there is no doubt. That's where she was, without a doubt.

And yet there is the pull, the memory of the hallway, the passage past the door to the pathology laboratory, the slit in the mesh, the red eyes of the startled rabbits inside through the darkness. The workroom adjoining the refrigerated room that she had unwisely shown to Pearl; the autopsy kit open and displayed on a table. There is Frida with a damp towel stained with the last of the makeup from Julia's compacted, flattened face, settled now like an ancient mask. They will open Julia's chest. Dr. Peter holds a blade with two points. Is that accurate? It may not be, but in the confines of this story someone must be split, disarticulated, and Julia lies waiting. See the sheet pulled aside, see the softness of her hair tucked away from her face. Realize that the first cut was made days before, a curving smile stitched across her belly hidden in the sheets and not yet exposed.

A small group of the up-patients is there, in their fur coats, with hats pulled down, with hoods pulled up, quietly moving in the hall, uncomfortable, clutching one another's arms, unsure of themselves but not retreating. Most likely they just wanted to see her, as Pearl had. They would have wanted to say good-bye. Very clear is the memory of the texture of the spool on the table, the twine that would be used to close Julia's chest afterward.

Dr. Peter and Frida look up from under the spotlight they have trained down on Julia, expecting what? A cleaning crew? Someone else working there in the evening? Is it evening? Turn on the radio; in such darkness, they give the date with the hour, it's normal to be confused about the passage of time. There is a click as the switch for the overhead light is touched by a gloved hand. Dr. Peter coming forward in the dimness, palms out, guiding the up-patients backward—the slow, precise steps of the group in their outdoor shoes—Frida's voice, shrill on the last syllable—the spotlight still trained on Julia, left behind. Julia, forgotten. This is not about Julia anymore.

Then the moment when they first touch him, instead of the other way around. Hands reach to take him by both arms. Someone puts a gloved finger into his mouth. He shakes them off but they are insistent. He has no choice then but to bite that finger as he shakes his arms against their furry bodies. This bite is like the spark. Someone cries out. Frida slaps at them, hard, but they do not notice, they are pulling him with shockingly firm grips and now they are near the back door of the clinical building and the door is pushed open. There is the quiet boom of his feet on the wooden platform. For a moment he is separate and turns to face them, clouds of breath rising all around. He will face them because they have ejected him from the rooms that are rightfully his own territory and not theirs at all.

He stands in his thin white coat in the shadows of the covered walkway, the cold instantly embracing him. As a group they press toward him and he thinks he can speak to them. But he steps backward to increase the distance, to gain perspective, and mistakenly he slightly slips and they slip and they rise and as he is rising they let themselves fall down upon him with a sound of breathing, the flapping nightgowns, and this is how his neck is broken.

And don't forget Frida, who would never stand motionless during such dangerous nonsense, and who would already be lifting the handset to call the desk for orderlies to come and stop this and remove them all. And so, someone must stand behind and someone must stop her. Is this the role meant for Sunny, the role she would have been expected to slip into even though it was not planned, not rehearsed? Even though it was not altogether spontaneous, either?

Another light clicks off. There are two strong hands in the dark hall reaching for Frida with restraint in mind. Is there a moment during which she misunderstands, believes that this person is coming back toward her to help? If so, it might explain her hesitation, her disorientation. If it is someone she might have thought to depend on—someone in uniform, for example—then this moment in the hall, in the night lighting, would be one of confusion and then of horror as intent loomed clear, a moment of madness in what had been only the same neat hallway, newly familiar, but seemingly ordinary, stable. The side external door, then—if others on the staff cannot be relied upon then Frida will go someplace else as quickly as possible—the dormitories must be full of sleeping normal staff—the pavilion—it seems to her in the moment that she must get help from someone from beyond this building where there is some contagious violence. Nothing is clear, it is a snap decision made in a moment. The side door then, the handle depressed and pushed with the force of flight and she is running—

But where does Frida run? It is dark. She is new here. She must choose a path clear enough of wet ice, or she will fall, she knows this, and someone has now come out behind her through the side door, and the sound of the door undoes her. She takes one of the paths, and now, here, is the beach. And here, now, is someone healthy, someone quick, almost catching up—

What options, what options? She runs over the broken lip of the shore and onto the ice because there will be no trees to disguise the pursuer, because there are lights from houses on the shore, and though these are clearly too far away to be of help they are reassuring and she thinks she will cut across the ice to another path a little farther along the curving shore, quicker than following the curving beach, and she'll take that path, which must lead to the dormitories where a hundred people will wake and help her.

But Frida is new here, and in her fright she forgets that the ice, tonight, is rotting away into nothing more than cold water. In places the current has pushed it, piled it softly back on itself like several tons of crumpled tissue paper.

A wet shushing, her heels lowering, and then freezing water fills her shoes, covers her ankles; a hesitant sound of something damp splitting, and the surface separates, slides, and sinks apart beneath her. The shock is immediate.

Frida!

She doesn't suffer.

One can't know both, not firsthand, one cannot remember and therefore have seen both the death of Dr. Peter and the drowning of Nurse Frida, if in fact this is what happened to her; never having found her makes it even harder to know. One can't have seen both. And one can't have seen either and yet at the same time have been in Laimi's room. Sunny had been in Laimi's room, because Laimi had invited her there, to ask for an explanation, an accounting. So those other memories aren't memories, only a bad dream, only speculation. This is what Sunny believes. And she pushes the emblem down with everything else, into the cool damp dirt.

Epilogue

We love games and music and a firm routine, and we promise to stay quiet in our rooms at night. In the mornings we'll ask for breakfast, a bath, some bowel salts, and a little assistance at the end of the process; give us these, and we'll agree to anything. We don't expect changes or improvements. We'll cooperate with anyone who puts us safely to bed when the pines start creaking, heavy with old snow and the silent white foxes that watch our bedroom windows at night. Bring our sleep aids. Pull the blackout shades. Lock us in. We'll never be tempted out of the building again. We belong in these reliably muffled rooms, and we are happy.

We love repetition. It deadens pain and lifts the responsibilities of other life. And even if Sunny supposedly gets no pleasure from returning she'll still come back, a repeat of the long voyage upward, backward, and north. Her elevator doors open over a corridor gritty with sand and salt. She hesitates. She can hear the frogs now. She can smell the standing water where mosquito larvae hang, waiting. She doesn't want to step over, doesn't want to foul her shoes or slip in the muck. This floor has not been waxed in years and we understand the hesitation, because we bruise easily too, we've seen our flesh turn indigo, verdigris, canary. Step carefully. The fires are lit. She surprises us at dinner hour.

We're happy to see her. We've missed her. And we feel at liberty to admit that sometimes, in the beginning, we felt neglected, especially since we did everything we were told: *Enjoy your dinner. Go to bed. Put on your dressing gown! Show your vagina. Take your pill. Shake your garments. File your fingernails. Share your candy. Curl up inside, like you were before. Sign your initials. Follow the Finns; they'll know where it's safe.*

We want to know: will she take better care of us now?

Sunny's hand goes to the pocket of her apron: a letter came, there was a letter . . .

Julia gets up to show that everything is practically painless now, even her feet, still swollen, and look: she'll circle the table, barefoot, warm and quick in her familiar fur. Creating a distraction, yes? Everything the same, yet slightly different than it was.

But Sunny knows there was a letter, she wrote to Mr. Dey and a letter came back from the landlord, she couldn't read it but the letter said something like *kuollut,* dead, Mr. Dey is dead. It said something like *kesakuu,* June, your husband had been dead since June. You must have known that, Julia, didn't you, before you came to Suvanto?

Don't press us, Sunny, you have to understand that this is fun, it's only fun. None of this is *serious.* Julia is only pretending to be dead. Pearl has thrown her outdoor shoes into the fire; Mrs. Minder touches a teaspoon to the candles, lifting wax like honey. It's only fun! This is the life you trained for, Sunny, as long as you continue to avoid the other side of the building, a very unpleasant place where men in coats and hats regularly stand outside in the snow, calling up to the windows: some of them say, *Come home!* Some of them say, *Hold up the baby, show me the baby!* And then strangers, new women we've never known, come to the windows and shift their dressing gowns to reveal the fullness of their breasts, newly voluptuous and pulsing warmly against the glass. But don't worry, Sunny, as long as you keep everything familiar, as long as you stay safe with us, you won't have to touch them, any of them. Remember, you came back with the understanding that you'd never have to.

But Sunny says she won't be staying.

No, we say, you're wrong, you want to resume your responsibilities, and through them the illusion of control. We'll allow you to take care of us, and you can feel good about choosing to do so.

But Sunny says it again: she won't stay. She only came to rectify a regret, a bad feeling. She can't undo past errors in judgment. But she can at least avoid making another. She's looking for Laimi.

We're incredulous: Laimi doesn't need you! Laimi went over the ice on her skis. Stay, Sunny, stay here, where your life has meaning because you care more about caring for others—even unworthy others—than you do about your own happiness. We'll confirm this every day. Because it's true, Sunny. We're the proof you wanted.

Sunny hears the grating of the elevator and Nurse Todd is suddenly behind her, looming in the doorway. But this is not Nurse Todd. This is Matron now. We all agree she's Matron now, and she wears Matron's antiquated cap: starched, complicated, beautiful, and terrifying in its implication of institutional order now reinstated. She wears it with black ribbons, the loose ends hanging low, past Matron's round, powerful shoulders. Under her uniform are the lineaments of a strict and unyielding corset, lacing her into an upright, all-directional fury of sublimated discomfort. There are blood spots on her fresh white apron, remnants of our blood, her blood, everybody's old blood mingled through mosquitoes, needles, flea-infested feathers, and many broken brooches. At her collar is a plain white emblem, and beside it a blue cameo, of a classical face in profile, a confiscated, compulsory gift.

Sunny moves quietly aside. We pull out Matron's chair, because Matron always sits at the head of the table, with Pearl now always at the foot. Another chair is brought for Sunny and we all make room to install her at Matron's right hand. It's time for dinner; we already feel some anxiety about the bread being slow to arrive. Matron points at Sunny, and her fingernails are the pink of living bone.

You, says Matron. *Sit down now.*

Surely it had never been Sunny, on that night?

Canopy of empty birch, creaking pine, ice in the air, falling, a prism, a quick cold sparkling in the throat, inhaling. The rutted path, extending, extending, roads blinking open on both sides, new roads where snow drops soundlessly from branches. And the bay is frozen to the bottom, perfectly safe. Her skates are waiting, and the blades are sharp, but the boots are perfectly broken in. She ties new laces. There are ski tracks on the ice, easy to follow. And gladly, very gladly, Sunny goes.

Acknowledgments

I owe a debt of deep gratitude to the Finnish Fulbright-ASLA Program, and would like to thank Leila Mustanoja, executive director emerita, and Terhi Mölsä, then deputy director and now executive director, as well as Tuula Laurila, Terhi Topi, Leena Matilainen, Anni Lemiläinen, Katariina Keskinen, Johanna Lahti, and the entire staff of the Fulbright Center for their help and warm hospitality. Thanks also to Monica Nylund, international officer at Åbo Akademi University in the city of Turku, Firefighter #47 at the Old Fire Station in Tampere, Mikä at Lastenlinna (the Children's Castle Hospital) in Meilahti, the Lois Roth Endowment, Nichole Heron, Cyril Sabra, Sam Wall, Arielle Greenberg, and Elina Brotherus, for the use of her photograph. Sincere thanks to Helena Kaartinen, the local history and tourism officer in Paimio, for extensive tours of Paimio Sanatorium and for taking me to meet head nurse Leena Järvi; they both graciously provided details

I could not have found elsewhere. (Many people helped me in Finland; any inaccuracies or infeasibilities in this book are, of course, entirely my own.) Heartfelt thanks to Darren Byrne for everything, including his steadfast belief in the book from Helsinki onward, and for sharing his deep knowledge of European history and confoundingly astute travel know-how; thanks also to everyone at Hopefield. Thanks to George Saunders, Chris Kennedy, Junot Díaz, Mary Caponegro, Mike Simpson, Rebecca Curtis, Erin Lambert, Diane Williams, Arthur Flowers, Malena Mörling, Cheryl Strayed, and the English department at Syracuse University. Thank you, Doug Unger, for bringing me to Las Vegas to finish this novel, and thanks also to the English department at the University of Nevada, Las Vegas, Glenn Schaeffer, Dr. Carol Harter, and the Black Mountain Institute. Richard Wiley, thank you for all that you've done, from big to little, including being the first to read this novel in its entirety and then emboldening me to show it to others. Thanks, Tom Bissell, for all your priceless help and all your sincere encouragement. To Dave Hickey: thank you for the moral support, the reality checks, the good advice, and the unbounded intellectual generosity. Alissa Nutting, you're a fabulous reader; many thanks. Juan Martinez, I have enjoyed the help of your appreciation for all that is morbidly bad, and hence good. I'd also like to thank Jim and Sue Baird, Embry Clark, Jessica Lucero, Dr. Vu Tran, Beverly and Mark Baumgartner, Bliss Esposito, Jaq Greenspon, Amber Withycombe, Leah Bailly, Maritza White, and everybody in Las Vegas who helped ease my culture shock; Dr. Lee Hickock, in Seattle, for being a matchlessly good doctor and excellent surgeon when I needed him; the late Gordon Beck, professor of classics at Evergreen; and the late Professor Don Finkel, also at Evergreen, for asking me a question about *The Bacchae* in 1988 that I couldn't answer. Endless thanks to Ethan Nosowsky for being so generous with his time, insight, and editorial attention, and for the countless ways in which he's made this a much better book, and to Fiona McCrae and everyone at Graywolf for their support. Super essential thanks, Jim Rutman, for kind friendship, keen good humor, and finding the perfect home for this novel; I cannot thank you enough, really and truly, for all of it. Overdue thanks to my sister, Danielle, for lots of logistical, emotional, psychological, and financial support, to Dad and Libby for being my ideal readers, to Mom for handling inordinate amounts of paperwork, and to my aunt Diane for literally scores of airmail letters. Thanks to all the rest of my family; I wish that Wesley, Anne, Irene, Oscar, Jean, Barb, Virginia, Ron, and Shawn could have seen this book in print.